DARTH BANE

DYNASTY OF EVIL

STAR WARS

DARTH BANE
DYNASTY OF EVIL

A NOVEL OF THE OLD REPUBLIC

Drew Karpyshyn

DEL REY BALLANTINE BOOKS
NEW YORK

Copyright © 2009 by Lucasfilm Ltd. & ® or ™ where indicated.

All Rights Reserved. Used Under Authorization.

Published in the United States by Del Rey, an imprint of The Random House Publishing Group, a division of Random House, Inc., New York.

DEL REY is a registered trademark and the Del Rey colophon is a trademark of Random House, Inc.

ISBN 978-0-345-51156-0

Printed in the United States of America on acid-free paper

www.starwars.com
www.delreybooks.com

2 4 6 8 9 7 5 3

To my wife, Jennifer.
As we start a new chapter in our life,
there is no one I would rather share it with.

ACKNOWLEDGMENTS

I want to thank Shelly Shapiro for all her comments and feedback on the early drafts. This wasn't an easy novel to write, but she helped me create a worthy finale to this trilogy.

I also want to thank all the fans who have taken the time to follow Des on his journey from a simple miner to the Dark Lord of the Sith. Embrace the dark side.

5000 YEARS BEFORE
STAR WARS: A New Hope

Lost Tribe of the Sith:
  Precipice
  Skyborn
  Paragon

1020 *YEARS BEFORE STAR WARS: A New Hope*

Darth Bane: Path of Destruction
Darth Bane: Rule of Two
Darth Bane: Dynasty of Evil

33 YEARS BEFORE
STAR WARS: A New Hope

Darth Maul: Saboteur*

32.5 *YEARS BEFORE STAR WARS: A New Hope*

Cloak of Deception
Darth Maul: Shadow Hunter

32 *YEARS BEFORE STAR WARS: A New Hope*

> **STAR WARS: EPISODE I**
> **THE PHANTOM MENACE**

29 *YEARS BEFORE STAR WARS: A New Hope*

Rogue Planet

27 *YEARS BEFORE STAR WARS: A New Hope*

Outbound Flight

22.5 *YEARS BEFORE STAR WARS: A New Hope*

The Approaching Storm

22-19 *YEARS BEFORE STAR WARS: A New Hope*

> **STAR WARS: EPISODE II**
> **ATTACK OF THE CLONES**

The Clone Wars
The Clone Wars: Wild Space
The Clone Wars: No Prisoners
The Clone Wars Gambit: Stealth
The Clone Wars Gambit: Siege

Republic Commando:
  Hard Contact
  Triple Zero
  True Colors
  Order 66

Imperial Commando:
  501st

Shatterpoint
The Cestus Deception
The Hive*
MedStar I: Battle Surgeons
MedStar II: Jedi Healer
Jedi Trial
Yoda: Dark Rendezvous
Labyrinth of Evil

> **STAR WARS: EPISODE III**
> **REVENGE OF THE SITH**

Dark Lord: The Rise of Darth Vader
Coruscant Nights:
  Jedi Twilight
  Street of Shadows
  Patterns of Force

10-0 *YEARS BEFORE STAR WARS: A New Hope*

The Han Solo Trilogy:
  The Paradise Snare
  The Hutt Gambit
  Rebel Dawn

5-1 *YEARS BEFORE STAR WARS: A New Hope*

The Adventures of Lando
  Calrissian
The Han Solo Adventures
The Force Unleashed
Death Troopers

STAR WARS: A New Hope
YEAR 0

Death Star

> **STAR WARS: EPISODE IV**
> **A NEW HOPE**

0-3 *YEARS AFTER STAR WARS: A New Hope*

Tales from the Mos Eisley
  Cantina
Allegiance
Galaxies: The Ruins of
  Dantooine

Splinter of the Mind's Eye

3 *YEARS AFTER STAR WARS: A New Hope*

> **STAR WARS: EPISODE V**
> **THE EMPIRE STRIKES BACK**

Tales of the Bounty Hunters

3.5 *YEARS AFTER STAR WARS: A New Hope*

Shadows of the Empire

4 *YEARS AFTER STAR WARS: A New Hope*

> **STAR WARS: EPISODE VI**
> **RETURN OF THE JEDI**

Tales from Jabba's Palace
Tales from the Empire
Tales from the New Republic

The Bounty Hunter Wars:
  The Mandalorian Armor
  Slave Ship
  Hard Merchandise

The Truce at Bakura

5 *YEARS AFTER STAR WARS: A New Hope*

Luke Skywalker and the Shadows of
  Mindor

6.5-7.5 YEARS AFTER
STAR WARS: A New Hope

X-Wing:
Rogue Squadron
Wedge's Gamble
The Krytos Trap
The Bacta War
Wraith Squadron
Iron Fist
Solo Command

8 YEARS AFTER STAR WARS: A New Hope
The Courtship of Princess Leia
A Forest Apart*
Tatooine Ghost

9 YEARS AFTER STAR WARS: A New Hope
The Thrawn Trilogy:
Heir to the Empire
Dark Force Rising
The Last Command

X-Wing: Isard's Revenge

11 YEARS AFTER STAR WARS: A New Hope
The Jedi Academy Trilogy:
Jedi Search
Dark Apprentice
Champions of the Force

I, Jedi

12-13 YEARS AFTER STAR WARS: A New Hope
Children of the Jedi
Darksaber
Planet of Twilight
X-Wing: Starfighters of Adumar

14 YEARS AFTER STAR WARS: A New Hope
The Crystal Star

16-17 YEARS AFTER STAR WARS: A New Hope
The Black Fleet Crisis Trilogy:
Before the Storm
Shield of Lies
Tyrant's Test

17 YEARS AFTER STAR WARS: A New Hope
The New Rebellion

18 YEARS AFTER STAR WARS: A New Hope
The Corellian Trilogy:
Ambush at Corellia
Assault at Selonia
Showdown at Centerpoint

19 YEARS AFTER STAR WARS: A New Hope
The Hand of Thrawn Duology:
Specter of the Past
Vision of the Future

22 YEARS AFTER STAR WARS: A New Hope
Fool's Bargain*
Survivor's Quest

25 YEARS AFTER
STAR WARS: A New Hope

Boba Fett: A Practical Man*

The New Jedi Order:
Vector Prime
Dark Tide I: Onslaught
Dark Tide II: Ruin
Agents of Chaos I: Hero's Trial
Agents of Chaos II: Jedi Eclipse
Balance Point
Recovery*
Edge of Victory I: Conquest
Edge of Victory II: Rebirth
Star by Star
Dark Journey
Enemy Lines I: Rebel Dream
Enemy Lines II: Rebel Stand
Traitor
Destiny's Way
Ylesia*
Force Heretic I: Remnant
Force Heretic II: Refugee
Force Heretic III: Reunion
The Final Prophecy
The Unifying Force

35 YEARS AFTER STAR WARS: A New Hope
The Dark Nest Trilogy:
The Joiner King
The Unseen Queen
The Swarm War

40 YEARS AFTER
STAR WARS: A New Hope

Legacy of the Force:
Betrayal
Bloodlines
Tempest
Exile
Sacrifice
Inferno
Fury
Revelation
Invincible

Crosscurrent

Millennium Falcon

Fate of the Jedi:
Outcast
Omen
Abyss
Backlash
Allies

*An ebook novella

Darth Bane; Dark Lord of the Sith (human male)

Darth Zannah; Sith apprentice (human female)

The Huntress; assassin (Iktotchi female)

Lucia; bodyguard (human female)

Serra; princess (human female)

Set Harth; Dark Jedi (human male)

A long time ago in a galaxy far, far away . . .

DARTH BANE
DYNASTY OF EVIL

Darth Bane, the reigning Dark Lord of the Sith, kicked the covers from his bed and swung his feet over the edge, resting them on the cold marble floor. He tilted his head from side to side, straining to work out the knots in his heavily muscled neck and shoulders.

He finally rose with an audible grunt. Taking a deep breath, he exhaled slowly, reaching his arms up high above his head as he stretched to his full two-meter height. He could feel the sharp *pop-pop-pop* of each individual vertebra along his spine loosening as he extended himself until his fingertips brushed against the ceiling.

Satisfied, he lowered his arms and scooped up his lightsaber from the ornate nightstand at the side of the bed. The curved handle felt reassuring in his grip. Familiar. Solid. Yet holding it couldn't stop his free hand from trembling ever so slightly. Scowling, he clenched his left hand into a fist, the fingers digging into the flesh of his palm—a crude but effective way to tame the tremor.

Moving silently, he slipped from the bedchamber out into the hallways of the mansion he now called home. Luminous tapestries covered the walls and colorful, handwoven rugs lined the corridors as he made his way past room after room, each decorated with custom-made furniture, rare objets d'art, and other unmistakable signs of wealth. It took him almost a full minute to traverse the length of the building and reach the back door that led out to the open-air grounds surrounding his estate.

Barefoot and naked from the waist up, he shivered and glanced down at the abstract mosaic of the stone courtyard illuminated in the light of Ciutric IV's twin moons. Goose bumps crawled across his flesh, but he ignored the night's chill as he ignited his lightsaber and began to practice the aggressive forms of Djem So.

His muscles groaned in protest, his joints clicking and grinding as he moved carefully through a variety of sequences. *Slash. Feint. Thrust.* The soles of his feet slapped softly against the surface of the courtyard stones, a sporadic rhythm marking the progress of every advance and retreat against his imaginary opponent.

The last vestiges of sleep and fatigue clung stubbornly to his body, spurring the tiny voice inside that urged him to abandon his training and return to the comfort of his bed. Bane drowned it out by silently reciting the opening line of the Sith Code: *Peace is a lie; there is only passion.*

Ten standard years had passed since he had lost his orbalisk armor. Ten years since his body had been burned almost beyond recognition by the devastating power of Force lightning unleashed from his own hand. Ten years since the healer Caleb had brought him back from the brink of death and Zannah, his apprentice, had slaughtered Caleb and the Jedi who had come to find them.

Thanks to Zannah's manipulations, the Jedi now believed the Sith to be extinct. Bane and his apprentice had spent the decade since those events perpetuating that myth: living in the shadows, gathering resources, and harboring their strength for the day they would strike back against the Jedi. On that glorious day the Sith would reveal themselves, even as they wiped their enemies from existence.

Bane knew he might never live to see that day. He was in his midforties now, and the first faint scars of time and age had begun to leave their marks on his body. Yet he had dedicated himself to the idea that one day, even if it took centuries, the Sith—*his* Sith—would rule the galaxy.

As he continued to ignore the aches and pains that inevitably accompanied the first half of his nightly regime, Bane's movements began to pick up speed. The air hissed and crackled as it was split time and time again by the crimson blade that had become an extension of his indomitable will.

He still cut an imposing figure. The powerful muscles built up during a youth spent working the mines on Apatros rippled beneath his skin, flexing with each slash and strike of his lightsaber. But a tiny sliver of the brute strength he once possessed had been whittled away.

He leapt high in the air, his lightsaber arcing above his head before chopping straight down in a blow powerful enough to cleave an enemy in two. His feet hit the hard surface of the courtyard stones with a sharp, sudden smack as he landed. Bane still moved with fierce grace and terrifying intensity. His lightsaber still flickered with blinding speed as he performed his martial drills, yet it was the merest fraction slower than it had once been.

The aging process was subtle, but inescapable. Bane accepted this; what he lost in strength and speed he could easily compensate for with wisdom, knowledge, and experience. But it was not age that was to blame for the involuntary tremor that sometimes afflicted his left hand.

A shadow passed over one of the twin moons; a dark cloud heavy with the threat of a fierce storm. Bane paused, briefly considering cutting his ritual short to avoid the impending downpour. But his muscles were warm now, and the blood was pumping furiously through his veins. The minor aches and pains were gone, banished by the adrenaline rush of intense physical training. Now was no time to quit.

Feeling a blast of cold wind blow in, he crouched low and opened himself up to the Force, letting it flow through him. Drawing on it to extend his awareness out to encompass each individual bead of rain as it fell from the sky, he resolved not to let a single drop touch his exposed flesh.

He could sense the power of the dark side building inside him. It began, as it always did, with a faint spark, a tiny flicker of light and heat. Muscles tense and coiled in anticipation, he fed the spark, fueling it with his own passion, letting his anger and fury transform the flame into an inferno waiting to be unleashed.

As the first fat drops splattered onto the patio stones around him, Bane exploded into action. Abandoning the overpowering style of Djem So, he shifted to the quicker sequences of Soresu, his lightsaber tracing tight circles above his head in a series of movements designed to intercept enemy blaster bolts.

The wind rose to a howling gale, and the scattered drops quickly became a downpour. His body and mind united as one, he channeled the infinite power of the Force against the driving rain. Tiny clouds of hissing steam formed as his blade picked off the descending drops while Bane twisted, twirled, and contorted his body to evade those few that managed to slip through his defenses.

For the next ten minutes he battled the pelting storm, reveling in the power of the dark side. And then, as suddenly as it had begun, the tempest was gone, the dark cloud scurrying away on the breeze. Breathing hard, Bane extinguished his lightsaber. His skin was sheened in sweat, but not a single drop of rain had touched his bare flesh.

Sudden storms were an almost nightly occurrence on Ciutric, particularly here in the lush forest on the outskirts of the capital city of Daplona. Yet this minor inconvenience was easily tolerated when set against all the advantages the planet had to offer.

Located on the Outer Rim, far from the seat of galactic power and far from the prying eyes of the Jedi Council, Ciutric had the good fortune to exist at the nexus of several hyperspace trading routes. Vessels stopped at the planet frequently, giving rise to a small but highly profitable industrial society centered on trade and shipping.

More importantly to Bane, the constant flow of visitors from regions scattered across the galaxy gave him easy access to contacts and information, allowing him to build up a network of informants and agents that he could personally oversee.

This would have been impossible had his body still been covered with the orbalisks—a host of chitinous parasites that fed upon his flesh in exchange for the strength and protection they afforded. His living armor had made him nearly invincible in one-on-one combat, yet its monstrous appearance had forced him to remain hidden from the eyes of the galaxy.

Back then, his plans to build up wealth, influence, and political power had been crippled by his physical deformity. Forced into a life of isolation lest the Jedi become aware of his existence, he had worked only through emissaries and go-betweens. He had relied on Zannah to be his eyes and ears. All the information he received was funneled through her; every goal and task was accomplished by her hand. As a result, Bane had been forced to act more cautiously, slowing his efforts and delaying his plans.

Things were different now. He was still a fearsome figure to behold, but no more so than any mercenary, bounty hunter, or retired soldier. Clad in the typical garb of their adopted homeworld, he was remarkable more for his height than anything else—noticeable, but hardly unique. He was able to mingle with the crowds, interact with those who possessed information, and forge relationships with valuable political allies.

He no longer had to remain hidden, for now he was able to conceal his true self behind an assumed identity. To this end, Bane had purchased a small estate a few minutes outside Daplona. Adopting the guise of siblings Sepp and Allia Omek, wealthy import–export merchants, he and Zannah had carefully cultivated their new identities in the planet's influential social, political, and economic circles.

Their estate was close enough to the city to give them easy access to everything Ciutric had to offer, yet isolated enough to allow Zannah to continue her lessons in the ways of the Sith. Stagnation and complacency were the seeds that would lead to the ultimate destruction of the Jedi; as the Dark Lord, Bane had to be vigilant against allowing his own Order to fall into the same trap. It was necessary not just to train his apprentice, but also to continue to increase his own skills and knowledge.

A cool zephyr wafted across the courtyard, chilling Bane's sweat-soaked body. His physical training was done for the evening; now it was time for the truly important work to begin.

A few dozen strides brought him to the small annex at the rear of the estate. The door was locked, sealed by a coded security system. Punching in the digits, he gently pushed the door open and stepped into the building that served as his private library.

The interior consisted of a single square room, five meters on each side, lit only by a single soft light hanging from the ceiling. The walls were lined by shelves overflowing with the scrolls, tomes, and manuscripts he had assembled over the years: the teachings of the ancient Sith. In the center of the room stood a large podium and a small pedestal. On the pedestal rested the Dark Lord's greatest treasure: his Holocron.

A four-sided crystal pyramid small enough to be held in the palm, the Holocron contained the sum of all Bane's knowledge and understanding. Everything he had learned about the ways of the dark side—all his teachings, all his philosophies—had been transferred into the Holocron, recorded for all eternity. It was his legacy, a way to share an entire lifetime of wisdom with those who would follow him in the line of Sith Masters.

The Holocron would pass to Zannah on his death, providing she could one day prove herself strong enough to wrest the mantle of Dark Lord away from him. Bane was no longer certain that day would come.

The Sith had existed in one form or another for thousands of years. Throughout their existence they had waged an endless war against the Jedi . . . and one another. Time and time again the followers of the dark side had been thwarted by their own rivalries and internal power struggles.

A common theme resonated across the long history of the Sith Order. Any great leader would inevitably be overthrown by an alliance of his or her followers. Lacking a strong leader the lesser Sith would quickly turn against one another, further weakening the Order.

Of all the Sith Masters, only Bane had understood the inescapable futility of this cycle. And only he had been strong enough to break it. Under his leadership the Sith had been reborn. Now they numbered only two—one Master and one apprentice; one to embody the power of the dark side, the other to crave it.

Thus would the Sith line always flow from the strongest, the one most worthy. Bane's Rule of Two ensured that the power of both Master and apprentice would grow from generation to generation until the Sith were finally able to exterminate the Jedi and usher in a new galactic age.

That was why Bane had chosen Zannah as his apprentice: she had the potential to one day surpass even his own abilities. On that day she would usurp him as the Dark Lord of the Sith and choose an apprentice of her own. Bane would die, but the Sith would live on.

Or so he had once believed. Yet now there was doubt in his mind.

Two decades had passed since he had plucked the ten-year-old girl from the battlefields of Ruusan, yet Zannah still seemed content merely to serve. She had embraced his lessons and had shown an incredible affinity for the Force. Over the years Bane had tracked her progress carefully, and he could no longer say with certainty which one of them would survive a confrontation between them. But her reluctance to challenge him had left her Master wondering if Zannah lacked the fierce ambition necessary to become the Dark Lord of the Sith.

Stepping into the library, he reached out with his left hand to close the door behind him. As he did so, he noticed the all-too-familiar trembling in his fingers. He snatched his hand back involuntarily, clenching it once more into a fist as he kicked the door shut.

Age was beginning to take its toll on Bane, but it was nothing compared with the toll already wrought upon his body by decades of drawing upon the dark side of the Force. He couldn't help but smile at the grim irony: through the dark side he had access to near-infinite power, but it was power that came with a terrible cost. Flesh and bone lacked the strength to withstand the unfathomable energy unleashed by the Force. The unquenchable fire of the dark side was consuming him, devouring him bit by bit. After decades of focusing and channeling its power, his body was beginning to break down.

His condition was exacerbated by the lingering effects of the orbalisk armor that had been killing him even as it gifted him with incredible strength and speed.

The parasites had pushed his body well beyond its natural limits, aging him prematurely and intensifying the degeneration wrought by the power of the dark side. The orbalisks were gone now, but their damage could not be undone.

The first outward manifestations of his failing health had been subtle: his eyes had become sunken and drawn, his skin a touch more pale and pockmarked than was normal for his age. The last year, however, had seen more pronounced deterioration, culminating with the involuntary tremor that seized his left hand with increasing frequency.

And there was nothing he could do about it. The Jedi could draw upon the light side to heal injury and disease. But the dark side was a weapon; the sick and frail did not deserve to be cured. Only the strong were worthy of survival.

He had tried to conceal the tremor from his apprentice, but Zannah was too quick, too cunning, to have missed such an obvious mark of weakness in her Master.

Bane had expected the tremor to be the catalyst Zannah needed to challenge him. Yet even now, with his body showing undeniable evidence of his growing vulnerability, she seemed content to maintain the status quo. Whether she acted out of fear, indecision, or perhaps even compassion for her Master, Bane didn't know—but none of these traits was acceptable in one chosen to carry on his legacy.

There was another potential explanation, of course—yet it was the most troubling of all. It was possible Zannah had noticed his deteriorating physical abilities and had simply decided to wait. In five years his body would be a ruined husk, and she could dispatch him with virtually no risk.

In most circumstances Bane would have admired this strategy, but in this case it flew in the face of the most fundamental tenet of the Rule of Two. An apprentice had to earn the title of Dark Lord, wresting it from the Master in a confrontation that pushed them both to the edge of their abilities. If Zannah intended to challenge him only after he was crippled by illness and infirmity, then she was unfit to be his heir. Yet Bane was not willing to initiate their confrontation himself. If he fell, the Sith would be ruled by a Master who did not accept or understand the key principle upon which the new Order had been founded. If he was victorious, he would be left without an apprentice, and his failing body would give out long before he could find and properly train another.

There was only one solution: Bane needed to find a way to extend his life. He had to find a way to restore and rejuvenate his body . . . or replace it. A year ago he would have thought such a thing to be impossible. Now he knew better.

From one of the shelves he took down a thick tome, its leather cover pockmarked, the pages yellow and cracked with age. Moving carefully, he set it down on the podium, opening it to the page he had marked the night before.

Like most of the volumes on the shelves of his library, this one had been purchased from a private collector. The galaxy might believe the Sith to be extinct, but the dark side still exerted an inexorable pull on the psyches of men and women across every species, and a black market of illegal Sith paraphernalia flourished among those with wealth and power.

The attempts of the Jedi to locate and confiscate anything that could be linked to the Sith had only succeeded in driving up the prices and forcing collectors to work through middlebeings to preserve their anonymity.

This suited Bane perfectly. He had been able to assemble and expand his library without fear of drawing attention to himself: he was just another Sith fetishist, another anonymous collector obsessed with the dark side, willing to spend a small fortune to possess banned manuscripts and artifacts.

Most of what he had acquired was of little use: amulets or other trinkets of negligible power; secondhand copies of histories he had memorized long ago during his studies on Korriban; incomplete works written in indecipherable, long-dead languages. But on occasion he had been lucky enough to come across a treasure of real value.

The worn, tattered book before him was one such treasure. One of his agents had purchased it several months earlier—an event too fortuitous to be attributed to chance. The Force worked in mysterious ways, and Bane believed the book had been meant to come into his possession—the answer to his problem.

Like most of his collection, it was a historical account of one of the ancient Sith. Most of the pages contained names, dates, and other information that had no practical use for Bane. However, there was a small section that made a brief reference to a man named Darth Andeddu. Andeddu, the account claimed, had lived for centuries, using the dark side of the Force to extend his life and maintain his body well beyond its natural span.

In the typical fashion of the Sith before Bane's reformations, Andeddu's reign came to a violent end when he was betrayed and overthrown by his own followers. Yet his Holocron, the repository of his greatest secrets—including the secret of near-eternal life—was never found.

That was all: less than two pages in total. In the brief passage there was no mention of where or when Andeddu had lived. No mention of what had become of his followers after he was overthrown. Yet the very lack of information was what made the piece so compelling.

Why were there so few details? Why had he not come across references to Darth Andeddu in all his previous years of study?

There was only one explanation that made any sense: The Jedi had managed to purge him from the galactic record. Over the centuries they had collected every datapad, holodisk, and written work that mentioned Darth Andeddu and spirited them away to the Jedi Archives, burying them forever in order to keep his secrets hidden.

But despite their efforts, this one reference in an old, forgotten, and otherwise insignificant manuscript had survived to make its way into Bane's hands. For the past two months, ever since this tome had come into his possession, the Dark Lord had ended his nightly martial training with a visit to the library to ponder the mystery of Andeddu's missing Holocron. Cross-referencing the manuscript before him with the vast wealth of knowledge scattered across a thousand other volumes in his collection, he had struggled to assemble the pieces of the puzzle, only to fail time and time again.

Yet he refused to give up his search. Everything he had worked for, everything he had built depended on it. He *would* discover the location of Andeddu's Holocron. He *would* unlock the secret of eternal life to give him time to find and train another apprentice.

Without it, he would wither away and die. Zannah would claim the title of Dark Lord through default, making a mockery of the Rule of Two and leaving the fate of the Order in the hands of an unworthy Master.

If he failed to find Andeddu's Holocron, the Sith were doomed.

1

"... adhering to the rules established through the procedures out-lined in the preceding, as well as all subsequent, articles. Our sixth demand stipulates that a body of . . ."

Medd Tandar rubbed a long-fingered hand across the pro-nounced frontal ridge of his tall, conical cranium, hoping to massage away the looming headache that had been building over the last twenty minutes.

Gelba, the being he had come to the planet of Doan to negotiate with, paused in the reading of her petition to ask, "Something wrong, Master Jedi?"

"I am not a Master," the Cerean reminded the self-appointed leader of the rebels. "I am only a Jedi Knight." With a sigh he dropped his hand. After a moment's pause he forced himself to add, "I'm fine. Please continue."

With a curt nod, Gelba resumed with her seemingly endless list of ultimatums. "Our sixth demand stipulates that a body of elected rep-resentatives from the mining caste be given absolute jurisdiction over the following eleven matters: One, the determination of wages in accordance with galactic standards. Two, the establishment of a weekly standard of hours any given employee can be ordered to work. Three, an approved list of safety apparel to be provided by . . ."

The short, muscular human woman droned on, her voice echoing strangely off the irregular walls of the underground cave. The other miners in attendance—three human men and two women crowding close to Gelba—were seemingly transfixed by her words. Medd couldn't help but think that, should their tools ever fail, the miners could simply use their leader's voice to cut through the stone.

Officially, Medd was here to try to end the violence between the rebels and the royal family. Like all Cereans, he possessed a binary brain structure, allowing him to simultaneously process both sides of a conflict. Theoretically, this made him an ideal candidate to mediate and resolve complex political situations such as the one that had developed on this small mining world. In practice, however, he was discovering that playing the part of a diplomat was far more trying than he had first imagined.

Located on the Outer Rim, Doan was an ugly, brown ball of rock. More than 80 percent of the planetary landmass had been converted into massive strip-mining operations. Even from space, the disfigurement of the world was immediately apparent. Furrows five kilometers wide and hundreds of kilometers long crisscrossed the torn landscape like indelible scars. Great quarries hewn from the bedrock descended hundreds of meters deep, irreparable pockmarks on the face of the planet.

From within the smog-filled atmosphere, the ceaseless activity of the gigantic machines was visible. Excavation equipment scurried back and forth like oversized insects, digging and churning up the dirt. Towering drilling rigs stood on mechanical legs, tunneling to previously unplumbed depths. Gigantic hovering freighters cast shadows that blotted out the pale sun as they waited patiently for their cavernous cargo holds to be filled with dirt, dust, and pulverized stone.

Scattered across the planet were a handful of five-kilometer-tall columns of irregular, dark brown stone several hundred meters in diameter. They jutted up from the ravaged landscape like fingers reaching for the sky. The flat plateaus atop these natural pillars were covered by assemblages of mansions, castles, and palaces overlooking the environmental wreckage below.

The rare mineral deposits and rampant mining on Doan had turned the small planet into a very wealthy world. That wealth, however, was concentrated almost exclusively in the hands of the nobility, who dwelled in the exclusive estates that towered above the rest of the planet. Most of the populace was made up of Doan society's lower castes, beings condemned to spend their lives engaged in constant physical labor or employed in menial service positions with no chance of advancement.

These were the beings Gelba represented. Unlike the elite, they made their homes down on the planet's surface in tiny makeshift huts surrounded by the open pits and furrows, or in small caverns tunneled down into the rocky ground. Medd had been given a small taste of their life the instant he stepped from the climate-controlled confines of his shuttle. A wall of oppressive heat thrown up from the barren, sun-scorched ground had enveloped him. He'd quickly wrapped a swatch of cloth around his head, covering his nose and mouth to guard against the swirling clouds of dust that threatened to choke the air from his lungs.

The man Gelba had sent to greet him also had his face covered, making communication all the more difficult amid the rumbling of the mining machines. Fortunately, there was no need to speak as his guide led him across the facility: the Jedi had simply gawked at the sheer scope of the environmental damage.

They had continued in silence until reaching a small, rough-hewn tunnel. Medd had to crouch to avoid scraping his head on the jagged ceiling. The tunnel went for several hundred meters, sloping gently downward until it emerged in a large natural chamber lit by glow lamps.

Tool marks scored the walls and floor. The cavern had been stripped of any valuable mineral deposits long before; all that remained were dozens of irregular rock formations rising up from the uneven floor, some less than a meter high, others stretching up to the ceiling a full ten meters above. They might have been beautiful had they not all been the exact same shade of dull brown that dominated Doan's surface.

The makeshift rebel headquarters was unfurnished, but the high ceiling allowed the Cerean to finally stand up straight. More importantly, the underground chamber offered some small refuge from the heat, dust, and noise of the surface, enabling them all to remove the muffling cloth covering their faces. Given the shrillness of Gelba's voice, Medd was debating if this was entirely a good thing.

"Our next demand is the immediate abolition of the royal family, and the surrender of all its estates to the elected representatives specified in item three of section five, subsection C. Furthermore, fines and penalties shall be levied against—"

"Please stop," Medd said, holding up a hand. Mercifully, Gelba honored his request. "As I explained to you before, the Jedi Council can do nothing to grant your demands. I am not here to eliminate the royal family. I am only here to offer my services as a mediator in the negotiations between your group and the Doan nobility."

"They refuse to negotiate with us!" one of the miners shouted.

"Can you blame them?" Medd countered. "You killed the crown prince."

"That was a mistake," Gelba said. "We didn't mean to destroy his airspeeder. We only wanted to force it into an emergency landing. We were trying to capture him alive."

"Your intentions are irrelevant now," Medd told her, keeping his voice calm and even. "By killing the heir to the throne, you brought the wrath of the royal family down on you."

"Are you defending their actions?" Gelba demanded. "They hunt my people like animals! They imprison us without trial! They torture us for information, and execute us if we resist! Now even the Jedi turn a blind eye to our suffering. You're no better than the Galactic Senate!"

Medd understood the miners' frustration. Doan had been a member of the Republic for centuries, but there had been no serious efforts by the Republic Senate or any governing body to address the injustices of their societal structure. Comprising millions of member worlds, each with its own unique traditions and systems of government, the Republic had adopted a policy of noninterference except in the most extreme cases.

Officially, idealists condemned the lack of a democratic government on Doan. But historically the population had always been granted the basic necessities of life: food, shelter, freedom from slavery, and even legal recourse in cases where a noble abused the privileges of rank. While the rich on Doan undoubtedly exploited the poor, there were many other worlds where the situation was much, much worse.

However, the reluctance of the Senate to become involved had not stopped the efforts of those who sought to change the status quo. Over the last decade, a movement demanding political and social equality had sprung up among the lower castes. Naturally, there was resistance from the nobility, and recently the tension had escalated into violence, culminating in the assassination of the Doan crown prince nearly three standard months earlier.

In response, the king had declared a state of martial law. Since then, there had been a steady stream of troubling reports supporting Gelba's accusations. Yet galactic sympathy for the rebels was slow to build. Many in the Senate saw them as terrorists, and as much as

Medd sympathized with their plight, he was unable to act without Senate authority.

The Jedi were legally bound by galactic law to remain neutral in all civil wars and internal power struggles, unless the violence threatened to spread to other Republic worlds. All the experts agreed there was little chance of that happening.

"What is being done to your people is wrong," Medd agreed, choosing his words carefully. "I will do what I can to convince the king to stop his persecution of your people. But I cannot promise anything."

"Then why are you here?" Gelba demanded.

Medd hesitated. In the end, he decided that straightforward truth was the only recourse. "A few weeks ago one of your teams dug up a small tomb."

"Doan is covered with old tombs," Gelba replied. "Centuries ago we used to bury our dead . . . back before the nobility decided they would dig up the whole planet."

"There was a small cache of artifacts inside the tomb," Medd continued. "An amulet. A ring. Some old parchment scrolls."

"Anything we dig up belongs to us!" one of the miners shouted angrily.

"It's one of our oldest laws," Gelba confirmed. "Even the royal family knows better than to try and violate it."

"My Master believes those artifacts may be touched by the dark side," Medd said. "I must bring them back to our Temple on Coruscant for safekeeping."

Gelba glared at him with narrowed eyes, but didn't speak.

"We will pay you, of course," Medd added.

"You Jedi portray yourselves as guardians," Gelba said. "Champions of the weak and downtrodden. But you care more about a handful of gold trinkets than you do about the lives of men and women who are suffering."

"I will try to help you," Medd promised. "I will speak to the king on your behalf. But first I must have those—"

He stopped abruptly, the echo of his words still hanging in the cavern. *Something's wrong.* There was a sudden sickness in the pit of his stomach, a sense of impending danger.

"What?" Gelba demanded. "What is it?"

A disturbance in the Force, Medd thought, his hand dropping to the lightsaber on his belt. "Somebody's coming."

"Impossible. The sentries at the tunnel outside would have—ungh!"

Gelba's words were cut off by the unmistakable sound of a blaster's retort. She staggered back and fell to the ground, a smoking hole in her chest. With cries of alarm the other miners scattered, scrambling for cover behind the rock formations that filled the cavern. Two of them didn't make it, felled by deadly accurate shots that took them right between the shoulder blades.

Medd held his ground, igniting his lightsaber and peering into the shadows that lined the walls of the cave. Unable to pierce the darkness with his eyes, he opened himself to the Force—and staggered back as if he had been punched in the stomach.

Normally, the Force washed over him like a warm bath of white light, strengthening him, centering him. This time, however, it struck him like a frozen fist in the gut.

Another blaster bolt whistled by his ear. Dropping to his knees, Medd crawled to cover behind the nearest rock formation, bewildered and confused. As a Jedi, he had trained his entire life to transform himself into a servant of the Force. He had learned to let the light side flow through him, empowering him, enhancing his physical senses, guiding his thoughts and actions. Now the very source of his power had seemingly betrayed him.

He could hear blaster bolts ricocheting throughout the chamber as the miners returned fire against their unseen opponent, but he shut out the sounds of battle. He didn't understand what had happened to him; he only knew he had to find some way to fight it.

Panting, the Jedi silently recited the first lines of the Jedi Code, struggling to regain his composure. *There is no emotion; there is peace.* The mantra of his Order allowed him to bring his breathing under control. A few seconds later he felt composed enough to reach out carefully to try to touch the Force once more.

Instead of peace and serenity, he felt only anger and hatred. Instinctively, his mind recoiled, and Medd realized what had happened. Somehow the power he was drawing on had been tainted by the dark side, corrupted and poisoned.

He still couldn't explain it, but now he at least knew how to try to resist the effects. Blocking out his fear, the Jedi allowed the Force to flow through him once more in the faintest, guarded trickle. As he did so, he focused his mind on cleansing it of the impurities that had overwhelmed his senses. Slowly, he felt the power of the light side washing over him . . . though it was far less than what he was used to.

Stepping out from behind the rocks, he called out in a loud voice, "Show yourself!"

A blaster bolt ripped from the darkness toward him. At the last second he deflected it with his lightsaber, sending it off harmlessly into the corner—a technique he had mastered years ago while still a Padawan.

Too close, he thought to himself. *You're slow, hesitant. Trust in the Force.*

The power of the Force enveloped him, but something about it still felt wrong. Its strength flickered and ebbed, like a static-filled transmission. Something—or someone—was disrupting his ability to focus. A dark veil had fallen across his consciousness, interfering with his ability to draw upon the Force. For a Jedi there was nothing more terrifying, but Medd had no intention of retreating.

"Leave the miners alone," he called out, his voice betraying none of the uncertainty he felt. "Show yourself and face me!"

From the far corner of the room a young Iktotchi woman stepped
forth, holding a blaster pistol in each hand. She was clad in a simple
black cloak, but she had thrown her hood back to reveal the
downward-curving horns that protruded from the sides of her head
and tapered to a sharp point just above her shoulders. Her reddish
skin was accentuated by black tattoos on her chin—four sharp, thin
lines extending like fangs from her lower lip.

"The miners are dead," she told him. There was something cruel
in her voice, as if she was taunting him with the knowledge.

Gingerly using the Force to extend his awareness, Medd realized it
was true. As if peering through an obscuring haze, he could just
manage to see the bodies of the miners strewn about the chamber,
each branded by a lethal shot to the head or chest. In the few seconds
it had taken him to collect himself, she had slain them all.

"You're an assassin," he surmised. "Sent by the royal family to kill
the rebel leaders."

She tilted her head in acknowledgment, and opened her mouth as
if she was about to speak. Then, without warning, she fired another
round of blaster bolts at him.

The ruse nearly worked. With the Force flowing through him he
should have sensed her deception long before she acted, but whatever
power was obscuring his ability to touch the light side had left him
vulnerable.

Instead of trying to deflect the bolts a second time, Medd threw
himself to the side, landing hard on the ground.

You're as clumsy as a youngling, he chided himself as he scrambled
back to his feet.

Unwilling to expose himself to another barrage, he thrust out his
free hand, palm facing out. Using the Force, he yanked the weapons
from his enemy's grasp. The effort sent a searing bolt of pain through
the entire length of his head, causing him to wince and take a half
step back. But the blasters sailed through the air and landed harmlessly on the ground beside him.

To his surprise, the assassin seemed unconcerned. Could she sense his fear and uncertainty? The Iktotchi were known to have limited precognitive abilities; it was said they could use the Force to see glimpses of the future. Some even claimed they were telepathic. Was it possible she was somehow using her abilities to disrupt his connection to the Force?

"If you surrender, I will promise you a fair trial," Medd told her, trying to project an image of absolute confidence and self-assurance.

She smiled at him, revealing sharp, pointed teeth. "There will be no trial."

The Iktotchi threw herself into a back handspring, her robe fluttering as she flipped out of view behind the cover of a thick stone outcropping. At the same instant, one of the blasters at Medd's feet beeped sharply.

The Jedi had thought he had disarmed his foe, but instead he had fallen into her well-laid trap. He had just enough time to register that the power cell had been set to overload before it detonated. With his last thought he tried to call upon the Force to shield him from the blast, but he was unable to pierce the debilitating fog that clouded his mind. He felt nothing but fear, anger, and hatred.

As the explosion ended his life, Medd finally understood the true horror of the dark side.

2

The nightmare was familiar, yet still terrifying.

She is eight years old again, a young girl huddled in the corner of the small hut she shares with her father. Outside, beyond the tattered curtain that serves as their door, her father sits by the fire, calmly stirring a boiling pot.

He's ordered her to stay inside, hidden from view, until the visitor leaves. She can see him through tiny holes worn in the curtain, looming over their camp. He's big. Taller and thicker than her father. His head is shaved; his clothes and armor are black. She knows he's one of the Sith. She can see that he's dying.

That's why he's here. Caleb is a great healer. Her father could save this man . . . but he doesn't want to.

The man doesn't speak. He can't. Poison has swollen his tongue. But what he needs is clear.

"I know what you are," her father tells the man. "I will not help you."

The big man's hand drops to the hilt of his lightsaber and he takes a half step forward.

"I am not afraid to die," Caleb tells him. "You may torture me if you want."

Without warning, her father plunges his own hand into the boiling pot over the fire. Expressionless, he lets the flesh blister and cook before withdrawing it.

"Pain means nothing to me."

She can see the Sith is confused. He is a brute, a man who uses violence and intimidation to get what he wants. These things won't work on her father.

The big man's head turns slowly toward her. Terrified, she can feel her heart pounding. She squeezes her eyes shut, trying not to breathe.

Her eyes snap open as she is swept off her feet by a terrible, unseen power. It lifts her into the air and carries her outside. Upside down, she is suspended by an invisible hand above the boiling cooking pot. Helpless, trembling, she can feel wisps of hot steam rising up to crawl across her cheeks.

"Daddy," she whimpers. "Help me."

The expression in Caleb's eyes is one she has never seen in her father before—fear.

"All right," he mutters, defeated. "You win. You will have your cure."

Serra woke with a start, wiping away the tears running down her cheeks. Even now, twenty years later, the dream still filled her with terror. But her tears weren't those of fear.

The first rays of the morning sun were streaming through the palace window. Knowing she wouldn't be able to fall back asleep, Serra kicked aside the shimmersilk sheets and got up.

The memory of the confrontation always filled her with shame and humiliation. Her father had been a strong man—a man of indomitable will and courage. It was she who was weak. If not for her, he could have defied the dark man who had come to them.

If she had been stronger, he wouldn't have had to send her away.

"The dark man will return one day," her father had warned her on

her sixteenth birthday. "*He must not find you. You must go. Leave this place. Change your name. Change your identity. Never think of me again.*"

That was impossible, of course. Caleb had been her entire world. Everything she knew about the healing arts—and about disease, illness, and poisons—she had learned at his knee.

Crossing the room to her wardrobe, she began to sift through her vast collection of clothes, trying to decide what to wear. Her entire childhood had been spent wearing simple, functional clothing; discarding it only when it became too threadbare and worn to be mended. Now she could go an entire month without wearing the same outfit twice.

She didn't dream about the dark man every night. For a while, in the first year of her marriage, she had hardly dreamed about him at all. Over the past few months, however, the dream had come more frequently . . . and with it, the ever-growing desire to learn the fate of her father.

Caleb had sent her away out of love. Serra understood that. She knew her father had only wanted what was best for her; that was why she had honored his request and never gone back to see him. But she missed him. She missed the feeling of his strong, callused hands ruffling her hair. She missed the sound of his quiet but firm voice reciting the lessons of his trade; the sweet scent of healing herbs that had always wafted up from his shirt when he hugged her.

Most of all she missed the sense of safety and security she felt whenever he was around. Now, more than ever, she needed to hear him tell her everything was going to be okay. But that could never be. Instead she had to cling to the memory of the last words he ever spoke to her.

"*It is a terrible thing, when a father cannot be there for his child. For this, I am sorry. But there is no other way. Please know that I will always love you, and whatever happens you will always be my daughter.*"

I am Caleb's daughter, she thought to herself, still idly flipping through the hangers of her wardrobe. *I am strong, just like my father.*

She finally selected a pair of dark pants and a blue top, emblazoned with the insignia of the Doan royal family . . . a gift from her husband. She missed him, too, though it was different than it was with her father. Caleb had sent her away, but Gerran had been taken from her by the rebels.

As she dressed, Serra tried not to think of her crown prince. The pain was too sharp, his assassination too recent. The miners responsible for the attack were still out there . . . but not for much longer, she hoped.

A soft knock at the door interrupted her train of thought.

"Come in," she called out, knowing only one person could be at the door of her private chambers this early in the morning.

Her personal bodyguard, Lucia, entered the room. At first glance the soldier was unremarkable: a fit, dark-skinned woman in her early forties with short, curly black hair. But beneath the fabric of her Royal Guard uniform it was possible to catch glimpses of hard, well-defined muscles, and there was an intensity in her eyes that warned she was not someone to be taken lightly.

Serra knew that Lucia had fought during the New Sith Wars twenty years ago. A sniper in the famed Gloom Walkers unit, she had actually served on the side of the Brotherhood of Darkness, the army that fought against the Republic. But as Caleb had explained to his daughter on many occasions, the soldiers who served in the conflict were far different from their Sith Masters.

The Sith and Jedi were fighting an eternal war over philosophical ideals, a war her father had wanted no part of. For the average soldiers who made up the bulk of the armies, however, the war was about something else. Those who rallied to the Sith cause—men and women like Lucia—did so out of the belief that the Republic had turned its back on them. Disenfranchised by the Galactic Senate, they had fought a war to free themselves from what they saw as the tyrannical rule of the Republic.

They were ordinary people who became victims of forces beyond their control; expendable pawns to be slaughtered in battles waged by those who believed themselves to be great and powerful.

"How did you sleep?" Lucia asked, stepping into the room and shutting the door behind her to ensure their privacy.

"Not well," Serra admitted.

There was no point in lying to the woman who had been her near-constant companion for the past seven years. Lucia would see right through it.

"The nightmares again?"

The princess nodded, but didn't say any more. She had never revealed the content of her nightmares—or her true identity—to Lucia, and the older woman respected her enough not to ask about it. They both had dark times in their past that they preferred not to talk about; it was one of the things that had drawn them together.

"The king wishes to speak with you," Lucia informed her.

For the king to send for her so early, it had to be important news.

"What does he want?"

"I think it has something to do with the terrorists who killed your husband," her bodyguard replied, picking up a delicate black veil from its stand in the corner of the room.

Serra's heart jumped, and her fingers fumbled over the last button on her top. Then she regained control of her emotions, and stood perfectly still as the older woman placed the veil atop her head. According to Doan custom, Serra was required to wear the mourning shroud for a full year following her husband's death . . . or until her beloved was avenged.

Lucia moved with practiced precision, quickly tying up Serra's long black hair and pinning it in place under the veil. The soldier was only average height—slightly shorter than her mistress—so Serra bent slightly to accommodate her.

"You're a princess," Lucia chided her. "Stand up straight."

Serra couldn't help but smile. Over the past seven years, Lucia had become like the mother she'd never had—assuming her mother had served as a sniper with the fabled Gloom Walkers during the Sith Wars.

Lucia finished adjusting the veil and stepped back to give her charge one final inspection.

"Stunning, as always," she pronounced.

Escorted by her bodyguard, Serra made her way through the palace to the throne room, where the king was waiting for them.

———

As they marched down the castle halls, Lucia fell into her customary position, one step behind and to the left of the princess. Because most people were right-handed, being on Serra's left side gave her the best chance to interpose her own body between a blade or blaster fired by a would-be assassin approaching from head-on. Not that there was much chance of anyone attempting anything here in the walls of the Royal Manse, but Lucia was always ready and willing to give her life for the sake of her charge.

With the collapse of the Brotherhood of Darkness two decades ago, Lucia—like many of her comrades who had served in the Sith armies—had become a prisoner of war. For six months she had been incarcerated on a work planet, welding and repairing ships until the Senate granted a universal pardon to all those who had served in the rank and file of the Brotherhood's armies.

Over the next thirteen years Lucia had worked as a hired body-guard, a freelance mercenary, and finally a bounty hunter. That was how she had first met Serra . . . and how she had earned the long, angry scar that ran from her navel all the way up to her rib cage.

She had been tracking down Salto Zendar, one of four Meerian brothers who had come up with the shortsighted plan to kidnap a high-ranking Muun official from the InterGalactic Banking Clan head office and hold him for ransom. The miserably ill-fated venture had resulted in two of the brothers being killed by security forces when they tried to break into the IBC offices on Muunilinst. A third was captured alive while the fourth—Salto—managed to escape despite being critically wounded by security forces.

The reward put out for his capture by the IBC was big enough to attract bounty hunters from as far away as the Mid Rim, and Lucia had been no exception. Using contacts from her days in the Gloom Walkers, she tracked Salto to a hospital on the nearby world of Bandomeer where he was being treated for his wounds.

However, when Lucia tried to take him into custody, a young human working at the hospital as a healer had stepped between her and her quarry. Despite the arsenal of weapons on Lucia's back, the tall, dark-haired woman had refused to back down, claiming she wouldn't let the patient be moved while he was still in critical condition.

The healer had shown no fear, even when Lucia had drawn her blaster and ordered her to step aside. She had simply shook her head and held her ground.

It might have ended right there; Lucia wasn't willing to shoot an innocent woman just to collect the price on Salto's head. Unfortunately, she wasn't the only bounty hunter at the hospital that day: Salto had been as bad at covering his tracks as he was at kidnapping.

While she and Serra were locked in their confrontation, a Twi'lek had burst into the room, blasters drawn. Lucia turned just in time to get shot point-blank in the stomach, her weapon falling from her hand as she slumped to the floor.

When Serra tried to stop the Twi'lek from taking Salto, he had slammed the butt of his pistol against the side of her skull, knocking her aside then yanking Salto out of bed and dragging the moaning prisoner away.

Ignoring the hole in her gut, Lucia crawled after them. She saw the Twi'lek get halfway down the hall before he was shot in the back by another bounty hunter looking to claim the reward. And then she blacked out.

Official reports put the number of bounty hunters at the hospital that day at somewhere between six and ten. Unlike Lucia, most of them had no qualms about killing innocent civilians—or one another—to claim their prize. By the time the bloodbath was over Salto was dead, along with two other patients, one member of the hospital nursing staff, three security guards, and four bounty hunters.

The only reason Lucia's name wasn't on the list of casualties was because of Serra. The healer had dragged her back into the room and performed emergency surgery while the gun battle raged outside. She managed to save Lucia's life despite being freshly pistol-whipped . . . and despite the fact that Lucia had stuck a gun in her face only minutes earlier.

Lucia owed her life to the young healer, and from that day forward she had vowed to keep Serra safe, no matter where she went or what she did. It wasn't easy. Before marrying Gerran, Serra had moved around a lot. Never content to stay in the same place, she seemed to travel to a different world every few weeks. It was as if she was searching for something she could never find, or running from something she could never escape.

At first the healer had been reluctant to have someone constantly watching over her, but she couldn't stop Lucia from following her as she moved from planet to planet. Eventually, she came to appreciate the value of having a trained bodyguard on hand. Serra was willing to go anywhere and try to help anybody, and the Outer Rim could be a violent and dangerous place.

Over the years, however, Lucia had become more than just the princess's protector: she was her confidante and friend. And when Gerran had proposed to Serra, she accepted his offer only on the condition that Lucia still be allowed to serve at her side.

The king hadn't liked it, but in the end he had relented and made Lucia an official member of the Doan Royal Guard. But though she had sworn an oath to protect and serve the king and all his family, her true loyalty would always be to Serra.

That was why she was so nervous as they approached the throne room. Though she hadn't admitted anything to the princess, she had a pretty good idea of why the king wanted to see them.

When they reached the entrance Lucia was required to hand over her blaster; by custom only the king's personal guard could possess weapons in his presence. Though she did so without comment or protest, she always felt uneasy when she didn't have a weapon within easy reach.

She had accompanied the princess to enough audiences with the king to become accustomed to the magnificent blue-and-gold decorations of the throne room. But it looked different this morning: larger and more imposing. The typical crowd of retainers, servants, dignitaries, and honored guests were nowhere to be found. Except for Serra's father-in-law and four of his personal guards, the room was empty—what was said in this meeting was not meant to go beyond these walls.

If the yawning chasm of the strangely empty throne room bothered Serra, she gave no outward sign as she approached the raised dais where the king was seated on his throne. Lucia followed a respectful three steps behind.

Physically, the king resembled an older version of his dead son— tall and broad-shouldered, with strong features, golden shoulder-length hair, and a closely trimmed beard that was slightly darker in color. But while Lucia had come to know Gerran during his marriage to Serra, she knew little of his father's personality. She only saw him from a distance at official functions, and in these settings he had always been formal and reserved.

At the foot of the blue-carpeted stairs Serra stopped and dropped to one knee, bowing her head. Lucia remained standing at attention behind her.

"You sent for me, Your Majesty?"

"The terrorists who orchestrated the attack on my son's airspeeder were killed last night."

"Are you certain?" she asked, looking up at the king seated in his throne above her.

"A security patrol responding to an anonymous tip found their bodies this morning in an old cave they were using for their headquarters."

"This is glorious news," Serra exclaimed, her face lighting up as she rose to her feet.

She took a half step toward the throne, perhaps to embrace the king. But her father-in-law stayed in his seat, unmoving. Puzzled, Serra pulled back as his guards glared at her with suspicion.

Seeing the king's reaction toward the princess, Lucia felt her stomach twist into a knot. She hoped none of the others could sense her anxiety.

"Is there something you're not telling me, Sire?" the princess asked. "Is something wrong? Are they sure it was Gelba?"

"They've positively identified her body. Two of her bodyguards and three of her top lieutenants were also killed . . . along with a Cerean named Medd Tandar."

"A Cerean?"

"He was a Jedi."

Serra shook her head, unable to make sense of the information. "What was a Jedi doing on Doan?"

"A member of the Council contacted me and asked that I allow one of their people to make contact with the rebels," the king informed her. "I agreed to their request."

The princess blinked in surprise. Still standing rigidly at attention, Lucia gave no outward reaction, though she was just as stunned as her mistress.

"We've always tried to keep the Jedi and the Senate out of our business on Doan," Serra protested.

"The politics of our world are under attack," the king explained. "Support for the rebels is building within the galactic community. We need allies if we want to preserve the Doan way of life. Working with the Jedi will make them and the Senate less willing to take action against us."

"What did he come here for?" Serra demanded, her voice cold.

The king scowled; Lucia realized he didn't like being interrogated in his own throne room. But, possibly out of respect for his lost son, he didn't take the princess to task.

"The Jedi had news that the rebels may have uncovered a cache of ancient talismans—objects imbued with the power of the dark side. The Cerean was sent to investigate these claims and, if true, bring the talismans back to the Jedi Temple on Coruscant where they could do no harm."

Lucia could see the logic behind the king's decision to grant the Jedi leave for their mission on Doan. The last thing the nobility wanted was for their enemies to gain possession of potentially devastating weapons. If the reports were true, the best way to nullify the threat would be to have the Jedi deal with it. Unfortunately, the death of the Cerean was not part of the plan.

"You think the Jedi will blame you for Medd's death," the princess noted, her sharp mind putting all the pieces together. "You knew he was making contact with the rebels; it will look like you hired the assassin to follow him to their hideout."

The king gave a solemn nod.

"Gelba's death has dealt a great blow to our enemy, but others will surely rise to take her place. Terrorists breed like insects, and our war with them is far from over.

"So far the Senate has not interfered in our efforts to cleanse our world of these criminals. But if they believe I used the Jedi to further my personal desire for vengeance, they will not sit idly by."

The king rose from his throne, standing up to his full height. He towered over Serra where she stood on the steps below the dais.

"But this assassin was not acting on my orders!" he pronounced in a voice that echoed off the throne room walls. "This was done without my knowledge or consent . . . a clear violation of Doan law that may cost us everything!"

"Is that why you brought me here, Sire?" Serra asked, refusing to be cowed by his anger. "To accuse me of betraying you?"

There was a long silence as they stared at each other before the king spoke again.

"When my son first declared his intention to marry you, I opposed the union," he replied. He was speaking casually now, almost as if they were chatting over a meal. But Lucia could see his eyes were fixed on the princess, studying her intently.

"Yes, Sire," Serra answered, giving away no hint of emotion. "He told me as much."

"You have secrets," the king continued. "All my efforts to learn about your parents or your family turned up nothing. Your past is well hidden."

"My past is of no consequence, Sire. Your son accepted that."

"I have watched you these past three years," the king admitted. "I could see that you loved my son. I could see you were devastated by his death."

Serra didn't say anything, but Lucia could see moist tears beginning to form in her eyes as she thought back on memories of her husband.

"Over the years I have come to appreciate those qualities my son saw in you. Your strength. Your intelligence. Your loyalty to our House.

"But now my son is dead, and I cannot help but wonder where your true loyalties lie."

"I swore an oath to serve the Crown when I married Gerran," Serra told him, her voice firm despite the tears in her eyes. "Even though he is gone, I would not dishonor his memory by abandoning my duties."

"I believe you," the king said after several seconds, his voice suddenly weary. "Though this brings me no closer to finding out who was behind the attack."

Silently, Lucia let out the breath she hadn't even been aware she was holding.

The king sat back down on his throne, his expression troubled by doubt and lingering grief over his son. Serra stepped forward and knelt by her father-in-law, close enough to put a comforting hand on his arm, ignoring his guards as they took a menacing step forward.

"Your son was beloved by all the nobles of Doan," she said. "And the rebels are universally despised. Anyone could have hired the assassin, with no knowledge whatsoever that the Jedi would be there. The Cerean's death was an unfortunate accident, not some sinister plot."

"I fear the Jedi may not be so easily convinced," the king replied.

"Then let me speak to them," Serra offered. "Send me to Coruscant. I will make them understand that you had no part in this."

"I have seen you in the halls these past months," the king told her. "I know the pain you still carry over my son's loss. I cannot ask you to do this while you are still mourning his death."

"That is why I must be the one to go," Serra countered. "The Jedi will be more willing to show compassion to a grieving widow. Let me do this for you, Sire. It's what Gerran would have wanted."

The king considered her offer briefly before nodding.

Serra rose and took her leave with a bow. Lucia fell into step behind her as she left the throne room, only pausing at the doors long enough to collect her weapons.

Only when they were back in the privacy of the princess's chamber with the door closed carefully behind them did either of them dare to speak.

"Take this somewhere and burn it," Serra spat as she ripped the mourning veil from her head and cast it down to the floor. "I never want to see it again."

"I have something to confess," Lucia said as she scooped the discarded garment up from the floor.

Serra turned to look at her, but Lucia couldn't read the expression on her face.

"I'm the one who hired the assassin that killed Gelba," she said, speaking quickly to get the words out.

She wanted to say so much more. She wanted to explain that she had known nothing about the Jedi being on Doan. She needed Serra to understand that she had done it only for her sake.

Lucia had always sensed a darkness in the healer, a shadow on her spirit. With Gerran's death that shadow had grown. She had seen her friend slipping into bleak despair as the weeks turned to months, listlessly wandering the halls of the castle in her black mourning garb like some tormented ghost.

All she wanted was to try to ease the princess's suffering. She thought that maybe if those responsible for Gerran's death were made to pay, Serra could find closure, could move on and come out from the shadow that had fallen over her.

She wanted to say all this, but she couldn't. She was just a soldier; she wasn't any good with words.

Serra stepped forward and wrapped her arms around her in a long, gentle hug.

"When the king spoke of someone hiring an assassin to avenge Gerran's death, I thought it might be you," she whispered. "Thank you."

And Lucia knew she didn't have to tell the princess all the things she wanted to say. Her friend already knew.

"I think you should tell the king," Lucia said when the princess finally broke off her embrace.

"He'd have you arrested," Serra said with a firm shake of her head. "Or at the very least dismissed from your post. I can't have that. I need you at my side when I go to Coruscant."

"You still plan to speak with the Jedi?" she asked, mildly surprised. "What are you going to tell them?"

"Medd's death was an accident. The king was not involved. That is all they need to know."

Lucia had her doubts, but she knew the princess well enough to realize that arguing the point would be a waste of time. Serra had no intention of turning her in to either the king or the Jedi. But she couldn't just let it go at that.

"I never meant to cause any trouble for you. Or the king. I'm sorry."

"Don't ever apologize for this!" Serra shot back. "Gelba and her followers got exactly what they deserved. My only regret is that I wasn't there to see it myself."

The venom in her words—the raw anger and hatred—caught Lucia off guard. Instinctively, she took a step back, recoiling from her friend. But then Serra smiled, and the awkward moment was gone.

"We need to leave as soon as possible," the princess noted. "It won't do to keep the Council waiting."

"I'll make the arrangements," Lucia replied, though she knew it would be several days before their actual departure. As the princess, it wasn't easy for Serra to simply leave Doan—there were diplomatic protocols and bureaucratic procedures that had to be followed.

"This will all work out," Serra reassured her, coming over to place a comforting hand on Lucia's arm. "Gelba is dead. My husband is avenged. A quick meeting with one of the Jedi Masters and this whole incident will be behind us."

Lucia nodded, but she knew it wouldn't be that simple. This wasn't just going to go away. The death of the Jedi had set in motion a chain of events—one she feared might end very badly for both of them.

3

The cantina was almost empty at this time of day; the crowds wouldn't start arriving until the late evening. Which was exactly why Darth Bane had arranged this meeting for early afternoon.

His contact—a balding, slightly overweight man of about fifty named Argel Tenn—was already there, seated at a private booth in the back of the establishment. Nobody paid any special attention to the Dark Lord as he crossed the room; everyone here, including Argel, knew him only as Sepp Omek, one of the many wealthy merchants who lived on Ciutric.

Bane sat down in the seat across the table from the other man and summoned a waitress with a discreet wave of his hand. She came over and took their order, then slipped away to leave them to their business. On Ciutric it was common for merchants to make deals in the backs of bars and clubs, and the serving staff knew how to respect the confidentiality of their customers.

"How come we never meet at your estate?" Argel said by way of greeting. "I hear you have one of the best-stocked wine cellars on the planet."

"I'd rather not have my sister learn about our transactions," Bane replied.

Argel chuckled slightly. "I understand completely."

He stopped speaking while the waitress returned and set their drinks on the table, then continued in a quieter voice once she was gone.

"Many of my clients are reluctant to let friends and family know of their interest in the dark side."

Dealing with Argel always left a sour taste in Bane's mouth, but for this there was no one else he could turn to. The portly dealer was the sector's leading procurer of banned Sith manuscripts; he had built a small fortune by discreetly seeking them out, purchasing them, and delivering them in person to his clients while keeping their names from ever being linked to the transaction.

Of course most of his clients were nothing but collectors or Sith fetishists who simply longed to possess a work that had been officially banned by the Jedi Council. They had no real understanding of the dark side or its power. They bought and sold the manuscripts in blissful ignorance, unaware of what they were truly dealing with.

This, more than anything, was what brought the bile to Bane's throat each time he met with Argel. The man portrayed himself as an expert in the dark side. He bartered and traded the secrets of the ancient Sith like cheap rugs at an open-air bazaar. It galled Bane to think of what treasures had passed through his hands into the possession of those too weak and common to ever make use of them.

He had occasionally fantasized about revealing his true identity to Argel, just to see his terrified reaction. Bane wanted to watch him grovel, begging for mercy at the feet of a real Sith. But petty revenge against an insignificant speck of a man was beneath him. Argel was useful, and so Bane would continue to play the part of a Sith-obsessed merchant.

"I hope you were able to find what I was looking for," he muttered. "The details you provided were rather vague."

"I promise you this, Sepp," the other man replied with a cunning smile. "You will not be disappointed.

"But you have no idea how hard this was," Argel added, throwing in an exaggerated sigh. "What you're after is illegal. Banned by the Jedi Council."

"Everything you deal in is banned by the Jedi Council."

"This was different. I'd never even heard the name Darth Andeddu before. None of my suppliers had. I had to go outside the normal channels. But I came through, like I always do in the end."

Bane scowled. "I trust you were careful. I wouldn't want word of this to make its way back to the Jedi."

Argel laughed. "What's the matter, Sepp? Some of your business practices not quite on the up-and-up? Afraid the Council will come after you for cheating on your taxes?"

"Something like that."

"Don't worry, nobody will ever know you were involved. I only brought it up because I may have to renegotiate our original price."

"We had a deal."

"Now, now—you know my initial quote is only an estimate," Argel reminded him. "I had to outlay triple my normal expenses to track this particular item down.

"But I'm willing to give you a bargain and only charge you double my original offer."

Bane gritted his teeth, knowing his hopes of a quick end to their conversation would remain unfulfilled. He had the funds to simply pay, of course. But this would arouse suspicion. He had a role to play: that of a savvy merchant. If he didn't negotiate down to the last credit, it would seem strange.

"I'll give you a ten percent bonus. Nothing more."

For the next twenty minutes they haggled back and forth, finally settling on 40 percent above the starting price.

"A pleasure doing business with you, as always," Argel said once payment was agreed upon.

From inside his vest he produced a long, thin tube roughly thirty centimeters long. The tube was sealed at one end, and the other was capped with a tightly screwed-on lid.

"If the item proves unsatisfactory," he noted as he handed it over, "I will be happy to take it back and return your funds . . . less a reasonable commission of course."

"I highly doubt that will be necessary," Bane replied as he wrapped his fingers tightly around the tube.

With the transaction complete there was no point in staying at the cantina. Bane was eager to open his prize, but he resisted until he was safely back inside the privacy of the library annex on his personal estate. There, beneath the pale glow of the lonely overhead light, he carefully unscrewed the lid. He tipped the tube, allowing the single sheaf of paper rolled up inside to slide out.

His instructions to Argel had been simple: be on the lookout for any book, volume, tome, manuscript, or scroll that made mention of a Sith Lord named Darth Andeddu. He couldn't say any more than that for fear of raising suspicions or awkward questions, but he had hoped it would be enough.

For two months his supplier had turned up nothing. But then, just as Bane was beginning to fear the Jedi had successfully buried all trace of Andeddu and his secrets, Argel had delivered.

The scroll was yellow with age, and Bane gingerly unfurled the dry, cracked page. As he did so, he marveled at the long and untraceable chain of events that had allowed the scroll to not only survive across the millennia, but eventually make its way into his hands. He had chosen to seek the scroll out, yet on some level he felt his choice had been preordained. The scroll was part of the Sith legacy; a legacy that by all rights now belonged to Bane. It was almost as if he had been destined to find it. It was as inevitable as the dark side's eventual triumph over the light.

The page had been fashioned from the cured skin of an animal he couldn't identify. On one side, it was rough and covered with dark splotches. The other side had been bleached and scraped smooth before being covered with handwritten lines in a language Bane immediately recognized.

The letters were sharp and angular, aggressive and fierce in their design; the alphabet of the original Sith, a long-extinct species that ruled Korriban nearly one hundred thousand years ago.

That didn't mean the document was that old, of course. It only meant that whoever wrote it had revered and respected the Sith culture enough to adapt their language as their own.

Bane began to read the words, struggling with the archaic tongue. As Argel had promised, he was not disappointed with the contents. The scroll was a religious proclamation declaring Darth Andeddu the Immortal and Eternal King over the entire world of Prakith. To commemorate the momentous event, the proclamation continued, a great temple would be built in his honor.

Satisfied, Bane carefully rolled the scroll up and slid it back into the protective tube. Despite being only a few paragraphs scrawled across a single sheet of parchment, it had given him what he needed.

Andeddu's followers had built a temple in his honor on the Deep Core world of Prakith. There was no doubt in Bane's mind that this was where he would find the Dark Lord's Holocron. Unfortunately, he had to think of a way to acquire it that wouldn't raise Zannah's suspicions.

Andeddu's Holocron offered the promise of immortality; with it he could live long enough to find and train a new successor. It was unlikely his current apprentice would know the significance of the Holocron, but he wasn't willing to take that chance. Though she was loath to challenge him directly, if she learned that he planned to replace her Bane had no doubt she would do everything in her power to stop him.

He couldn't allow the fear of being replaced to become the catalyst that compelled Zannah to finally challenge him. Fighting back simply because she knew she was about to be cast aside was nothing but a common survival instinct. His successors would need to do more than just survive if the Sith were ever to grow powerful enough to destroy the Jedi. Zannah's challenge had to come from her own initiative, not as a reaction to something he did. Otherwise, it was worthless.

This was the complex paradox of the Master–apprentice relationship, and it had put Bane into an untenable position. He couldn't send Zannah after the Holocron, and if he went after it himself she would almost certainly suspect something. He rarely traveled off-world anymore; any journey would immediately put her on her guard. She might try to follow him, or prepare some type of trap to be sprung on his return.

Even though she had disappointed Bane by not challenging him, Zannah was still a dangerous and formidable opponent. It was possible she might defeat him, leaving the Sith with a leader who lacked the necessary drive and ambition. Her complacency would infect the Order; eventually it would wither and die.

He couldn't allow that to happen. Which meant he had to find something to occupy Zannah's attention while he made the long and arduous journey into the Deep Core.

Fortunately, he had already had something in mind.

———

Bane's personal study—unlike the secluded private library tucked in the back corner of the estate—was a buzzing hive of endless electronic activity. Even when unoccupied, the room was illuminated by the flickering images of HoloNet news feeds, the glow of data screens showing stock tickers from a dozen different planetary exchanges, or blinking readouts on the monitors indicating private communications filtering in from the network of informants he and Zannah had assembled over the years.

For all the opulence and extravagance throughout the mansion, more credits had been spent on this room than any other. With all the terminals, holoprojectors, and screens, it looked more like the communications hub of a busy starport than a den in a private residence. Yet the study was no grandiose display of wealth; rather, it was a testament to efficiency and practicality. Every single piece of equipment had been carefully chosen to handle the staggering volume of data passing through the room: thousands of data units every hour, all recorded and stored for later review and analysis.

The study helped reinforce the illusion that he and Zannah were wealthy entrepreneurs obsessively scouring news from the farthest reaches of the galaxy in search of profitable business ventures. To some degree, this was even true. Every credit spent on the study was an investment that would eventually pay off a hundredfold. Over the past decade, Bane had used the information he had gathered to grow his wealth significantly . . . though for the Dark Lord material riches were only a means to an end.

He understood that power came from knowledge, and his vast fortune had allowed him to assemble the priceless collection of ancient Sith teachings he kept secured in his private library. Yet he was interested in more than just the forgotten secrets of the dark side. From the halls of the Republic Senate to the tribal councils of the most backrocket planets on the Outer Rim, the lifeblood of government was information. History was shaped by individuals who understood that information, properly exploited and controlled, could defeat any army.

Bane had seen proof of this firsthand. The Brotherhood of Darkness was destroyed not by the Jedi and their Army of Light, but by the carefully laid plans of a single man. Ancient scrolls and manuscripts could unlock the secrets of the dark side, but to bring down the Jedi and the Republic, Bane first had to know everything about his enemies. The network of agents and go-betweens he had assembled over the years were a key part of his plan, but they weren't enough. Individuals were fallible; their reports were biased or incomplete.

Whenever possible, Bane preferred to rely on pure data plucked from the web of information that wove itself through every planet of the Republic. He needed to be aware of every detail of every plan put forth by the Senate and the Jedi Council. If he ever hoped to shape and manipulate galactic events to bring about the downfall of the Republic, he had to know what they were doing now and anticipate what they would do next.

The complexity of his machinations required constant attention. He had to react to unexpected changes as they happened, altering his long-term plans to keep them on course. More important, he needed to seize upon unexpected opportunities as they arose, using them to their fullest advantage. Like the situation on Doan.

Bane had never paid this small mining world on the Outer Rim much attention before. That had changed three days ago when he noticed an expense claim submitted to the Senate for approval by a representative acting on behalf of the Doan royal family.

It wasn't unusual for Bane to be reviewing Senate budget reports. By law, all financial documentation filed through official Republic channels was available for public viewing . . . for a price, of course. The cost was high, and typically all it resulted in was an onerous list of customs regulations, taxes levied in accordance with economic treaties, or funding appeals for various projects and special-interest groups. Occasionally, however, something of true significance would filter through the clutter. In this case, it was a line-item request for the reimbursement of costs incurred by the Doan royal family to transport the body of a Cerean Jedi named Medd Tandar back to Coruscant.

There were no further details; budget reports were rarely interested in the *why*. Bane, however, was very interested. What was a Jedi Knight doing on Doan? More importantly, how had he died?

Ever since first seeing the report, Bane had been mining his sources to try to find the answers. He had to tread carefully where the Jedi were concerned; for the Sith to survive they had to remain hidden in the shadows. But through a long chain of bureaucrats, household servants, and paid informants, he had assembled enough facts to realize the situation was worthy of more thorough investigation.

And so he had sent for Zannah.

Seated behind the desk at the center of the screens and holoprojectors, he could hear her coming down the hall, the hard heels of her boots clacking against the floor with each stride. Resting on the left side of the desk was a data disk containing all the information he had compiled on Medd Tandar and his visit to Doan. He reached out for it without thinking and froze. For a brief instant his hand hovered in the air, trembling involuntarily. Then he quickly snatched it back, hiding it beneath the edge of the desk just as Zannah entered the room.

"You sent for me, Lord Bane?"

She made no acknowledgment of the tremor, yet Bane was certain it had not gone unnoticed. Was she playing him for a fool? Pretending not to see his weakness in the hope he would become careless and let his guard down? Or was she silently gloating while she bided her time, waiting for the dark side to simply rot his body away?

Zannah was only ten years younger than Bane, but if the dark side was extracting a similar physical toll on her it had yet to show itself. Unlike her Master, she had never been infested with the orbalisks. It would still be many decades before the corruption of the dark side caused her body to wither.

Her curly golden hair was still long and lustrous, her skin still smooth and perfect. Of average height, she had the figure of a gymnast: lean, lithe, and strong. She wore fitted black pants and a sleeveless red vest embroidered with silver, an outfit that was both stylish by current Ciutric standards and practical, in that it would not hinder movement.

The handle of her twin-bladed lightsaber hung from her hip; over the past few years she had never come into her Master's presence without it. The hooked handle of Bane's own weapon was clipped to the belt of his breeches . . . it would have been foolish to leave himself unarmed and vulnerable before the apprentice who had sworn to one day kill him.

I'm still waiting for that day, Bane thought. Out loud he said, "I need you to make a trip to the Outer Rim. A planet called Doan, where a Jedi was murdered three standard days ago."

"Anyone powerful enough to kill a Jedi is worthy of our attention," Zannah admitted. "Do we know who is responsible?"

"That is what you need to find out."

Zannah nodded, her eyes narrowing as she processed the information. "What was a Jedi doing on an insignificant planet in the Outer Rim?"

"That is something else you need to find out."

"The Jedi will send one of their own to investigate," she noted.

"Not right away," Bane assured her. "The Doan royal family is calling in political favors to delay the investigation. They've sent a representative to meet with the Jedi Council on Coruscant instead."

"The royal family must be rich; those kinds of favors don't come cheap. Small world, but not widely known—yet with wealthy royals. Valuable resources? Mining?" she guessed.

Zannah had always been able to grasp bits of information and put them together into something meaningful. She would have been a worthy successor, if only she had possessed the ambition to seize the Sith throne.

"The planet's been carved down nearly to the core. There are only a few habitable kilometers of land left on the surface; all food has to be shipped in. Most of the population live and work in the strip mines."

"Sounds charming," she muttered, before adding, "I'll leave tonight."

Bane nodded, dismissing her. Only after she was gone did he dare to place his still-quivering hand back on top of the desk.

The death of a Jedi was always of interest to him, but in truth he cared about finding Andeddu's Holocron far more than he did about the outcome of Zannah's mission.

Fortunately, the incident on Doan offered the perfect distraction. Investigating the Outer Rim world would keep his apprentice occupied while he braved the dangerous hyperspace routes into the Core to retrieve the Holocron. If things went as he hoped, he would be back long before she returned to give him her report, with Zannah none the wiser.

Confident in his plan, Bane focused all his concentration on calming the tremor that still gripped his hand. But for all his power, for all his mental discipline, the muscles continued to twitch involuntarily. In frustration, he balled up his fist and slammed it once hard upon the surface of the desk, leaving a faint impression in the soft wood.

4

Ciutric IV's twin moons shone brightly down on Zannah's air-speeder as it zipped through the night sky. The evening's rain clouds were just beginning to build; they were still no more than wispy veils that simply tore apart as her vehicle ripped through them. On the ground below, still a few kilometers ahead, she could see the lights of Daplona's primary spaceport.

A light on the nav panel blinked a warning, indicating she was approaching the two-kilometer limit of restricted airspace that surrounded the port. Her hands moving with casual precision over the controls, she brought the speeder in for a landing at the section reserved for those wealthy enough to afford private hangars for their personal shuttles.

As the vehicle gently touched down on the pad located on the starport's perimeter, three men scurried out to meet her. The first, a valet, tended to her speeder, whisking it away toward the secure lot where it would be parked until she returned. The second man, a porter, loaded her luggage onto a small hoversled then waited patiently as the third man approached.

"Good evening, Mistress Omek," he greeted her.

From their first arrival on Ciutric, Zannah and Bane had worked hard to build up their identities as Allia and Sepp Omek. After nearly a decade, she was able to slip into the role of the wealthy import–export trader without even thinking about it.

"Chet," she said with a nod to the customs official as the young man handed her an official-looking form.

For the common masses, arrivals and departures at the Daplona spaceport were a long and arduous process. Because the world was built on commerce and trade, the government required copies of trip itineraries, verification of ship registration, and a host of forms and permits to be filled out before the port authority would clear a vessel, its contents, or its passengers. This frequently involved a thorough inspection of the ship's interior by customs personnel, with the official explanation being increased planetary security. However, everyone knew inspections were actually meant to discourage merchants from trying to transport undeclared merchandise in the hope of avoiding interstellar taxes and tariffs.

Fortunately, Zannah didn't have to worry about any of that. She simply signed the departure form and handed it back to Chet. One of the chief benefits of maintaining a private hangar at the port was the ability to come and go at will. In exchange for their substantial monthly hangar fees, the government kept its nose out of her and Bane's business . . . a bargain at nearly any price as far as she was concerned.

"You'll be taking your private shuttle, I assume."

"That's right," she replied. "The *Victory* over in hangar thirteen."

"I'll alert the control tower."

Chet gave a curt nod to the porter, who headed off with the hoversled in the direction of the hangar.

"Just a moment," the customs official said softly to Zannah, causing her to hang back.

"Heard some news I thought you might be interested in," he continued once the porter had disappeared around the corner. "Argel Tenn touched down a few days ago to meet with your brother."

Zannah had never met Argel, but she knew who he was and what he did. Over the past few years she had slowly been gathering information on all the members in Darth Bane's network of contacts; they could prove useful to her once she took over the Sith. She didn't know if Argel's arrival was relevant or not: Bane was always looking to acquire rare Sith manuscripts, and it could just be a coincidence. Nevertheless, she filed the knowledge away in case it should ever prove handy.

"Thanks for the update," she said, slipping Chet a fifty-credit chip before heading off toward her private hangar.

The porter was already there, waiting with her bags by the shuttle. Zannah punched in the security code, causing the boarding ramp to lower.

"Put everything in the back," she instructed, smiling and handing the porter a ten-credit chip.

"Right away, mistress," he replied, the tip disappearing instantly into a pocket somewhere on his uniform as he hustled to load her baggage.

Zannah kept the smile plastered on her face while he worked. She made a point of being friendly with everyone at the spaceport. She saw it as an investment in the future—the cultivation of a potential resource. The members of the Senate and other powerful individuals might shape galactic policy, but it was the bureaucrats, government officials, and various other low-level political functionaries who actually made things run . . . and they were so much easier to deal with than the political elite. A few kind words and a handful of small bribes, and Zannah could get anything she needed without attracting unwanted attention. Just as she had done with Chet.

This was one advantage she had over Bane. She knew she was attractive. Men in particular were drawn to her because of her looks;

they wanted to help her, to please her. Zannah wasn't above encouraging them with a soft laugh or a subtle touch—it was a small price to pay to establish a relationship that might eventually prove useful. Her Master's appearance, on the other hand, would never inspire anything but fear in those who didn't know him.

Only once the porter was gone and she was alone in the cockpit of the vessel did she let the façade drop. Settling into the custom-molded seat, she punched in the navigation coordinates. Through the cockpit viewport she could see the *Triumph,* Bane's personal shuttle, in the adjacent hangar.

Like her own, it was a Cygnus Spaceworks *Theta*-class T-1 vessel: the latest, and most expensive, personal interplanetary transport shuttle available on the open market. Everything about their life here on Ciutric—the mansion, their clothes, even their social calendar—was a part of their disguise. They surrounded themselves with luxury and material comforts; a far cry from the austere life they had lead during their years on Ambria.

There were times when Zannah missed the simplicity of those early days. Life on Ambria had been hard, but it had kept her strong. And she couldn't help but wonder if the lavish lifestyle here on Ciutric had made her—and Bane—soft.

The *Victory*'s engines roared to life, and the shuttle rose up a few meters off the ground. Zannah piloted by instinct while her mind continued its train of thought.

Life was a constant struggle; the strong would survive and the weak would perish. That was the way of the universe, the natural order. It was the philosophy embraced by the Code of the Sith. But here on Ciutric it was easy to be lulled into a sense of peace.

Peace is a lie, there is only passion. Through passion, I gain strength. Through strength, I gain power. Through power, I gain victory. Through victory, my chains are broken.

Zannah understood that chains were not always made of iron and durasteel; they could sometimes be woven of expensive shimmersilk. The easy life they enjoyed on Ciutric was a trap as dangerous as any the Jedi could ever set for them.

She had continued her study and training even after Bane had moved them into their magnificent estate outside the city. But the sense of urgency and the threat of danger that had spurred her on during her early years had faded, replaced by the ennui of security and contentment.

It was time to stake her claim as Dark Lord of the Sith. She would already have challenged him by now, if not for two things.

The first was the tremor she had noticed in his left hand several months ago. He tried to hide it from her, but she noticed it more and more. She didn't know the cause of the tremor, but regardless, it was an obvious sign of his degenerating skills.

Perhaps too obvious. Bane was a master manipulator. Zannah couldn't dismiss the idea that he was faking it. What if the tremor was just a ruse meant to lure her into the confrontation before she was truly ready—one final test to see if the apprentice had learned the lesson of patience he had worked so hard to ingrain into her?

I will strike at a time of my choosing, Zannah vowed to herself. *Not his.*

But in order to make her move, she had to be ready with an apprentice of her own. *Two there should be; no more, no less. One to embody the power, the other to crave it.* The Rule of Two was inviolate. If she was going to seize the mantle of Master from Bane, she would need to find an apprentice. So far, despite her best efforts, she had failed to locate even a single potential candidate.

Bane had recognized her own potential when, as a young girl, she had killed the Jedi who had mistakenly slain her friend. Now she was going to investigate the mysterious death of another Jedi. Might she find her successor the same way Bane had found her?

But if she was thinking along these lines, it was a sure bet that

Bane had thought of it, too. He was rarely caught unprepared or off guard. So . . . why would Bane send her on a mission that could end with her finding the individual who might become the next Sith apprentice? Did her Master want her to challenge him? Was he trying to help her? Or was he looking to replace her? Maybe he had decided she was unworthy of assuming his title. Maybe he was hoping this mission would provide him with someone new to train in the ways of the dark side, and he planned to cast her aside.

If that's true, Master, you might be surprised at how this ends. Underestimate me at your peril.

A beep from the nav screen notified her as the shuttle broke Ciutric's atmosphere. A few seconds later she felt the unmistakable surge as the ship made the leap into hyperspace.

Zannah eased her seat back and closed her eyes. There was no point in dwelling on all the possibilities of what Bane might or might not be thinking, or what his secret motivations for sending her on the mission might be. The web of his machinations could be too impossibly tangled to unweave.

But she knew one thing for sure: something was about to change. For twenty years she had served as his loyal apprentice, learning the ways of the Sith. Now her time as a pupil was about to end. Whatever the mission might bring, she had decided this would be the last time she answered to Darth Bane.

5

Coruscant was unlike anything Serra had ever seen. As a child she had known nothing but the simple isolation of her father's camp. When he had sent her away, she'd visited dozens of other worlds before settling on Doan, but all of them had been less populated planets on the Outer Rim. Her entire life had been spent on the fringes of civilization. Here, on the planetwide metropolis that was the Republic capital, she had been hurled into the madness of the Galactic Core.

Caleb had made sure his daughter's education was well rounded; she had read descriptions of Coruscant, she had memorized all the relevant facts and figures. But knowing a world had a population approaching one trillion individuals and seeing it in person were entirely different.

Serra simply stared out the window of the airspeeder, speechless as it darted and dived, fighting its way through the heavy traffic of the skylane. Below, an endless ocean of durasteel and permacrete stretched off to the horizon in all directions, shining with the permanent glow of a million lights. The effect was overwhelming: the crowds, the vehicles, the dull cacophony of sounds that could be heard over the hum of the engines—the sheer magnitude of it was almost more than her mind could grasp. It made her feel small. Insignificant.

"There it is," Lucia said, nodding out the window.

In the distance Serra could just make out a massive structure that towered high above the rest of the cityscape: the Jedi Temple. The swift-moving speeder was bringing them rapidly closer, and it wasn't long before she could make out the unique details of the Temple's construction.

The foundation was a pyramid of successively smaller blocks, creating a stepped or ziggurat effect. On the top of the uppermost level was a tall central spire, surrounded on each corner by smaller, secondary spires. Scattered among the spires were open plazas, wide promenades, vast natural gardens, and a number of smaller buildings that served as dorms or administrative centers.

As the speeder dropped out of the main line of traffic toward their destination, the structure's true scope became apparent. Everything on Coruscant was grand and magnificent, but the Temple dominated the skyline. Serra recalled that it had been built on top of a mountain. Not on a mountain, like the small settlements the nobles had constructed on the plateaus of Doan, but actually *over* the mountain—the stepped pyramid covered the entire surface, swallowing the mountain so completely that it was no longer visible.

Their vehicle banked in a wide circle around the Tranquillity Spire, the tall central tower, before touching down on a landing pad in the shadow of the smaller tower on the northwest corner.

"Let's get this over with," Lucia muttered, standing quickly and offering her hand to help Serra up from her seat.

The princess realized Lucia was as uncomfortable as she was, though she suspected her bodyguard's unease had less to do with the overwhelming sights and sounds of Coruscant and more to do with her days as a soldier fighting against the Army of Light. Even after twenty years, Lucia still harbored a resentment toward both the Jedi and the Republic.

That, and the fact that she still probably felt guilty for hiring the assassin who had killed the Jedi emissary. Serra, on the other hand, felt nothing but gratitude for what her friend had done. And she had no intention of letting anyone—not the king, and not the Jedi—find out that Lucia was responsible.

"Remember what I told you," she said, placing a comforting hand on her friend's shoulder. "I have dealt with the Jedi before. I know how to handle them. I know their weaknesses. Their blind spots. We will get through this."

The bodyguard took a deep breath and nodded. Serra did the same, centering herself in anticipation of the coming confrontation.

———

Lucia was amazed at how calm and composed the princess appeared as they prepared to leave the shuttle.

She had always carried herself with a quiet but firm resolve. It gave her an air of confidence and authority that drew others to her. When she spoke, people gave her words careful consideration . . . even people like the king of Doan. But this was different. They were about to meet a Jedi Master, and Serra intended to lie right to his face.

Lucia had no intention of letting her friend get into trouble, however. At the first sign the Jedi knew Serra was being dishonest, she intended to confess everything, no matter the consequences.

Steadied by her decision, she was able to maintain her own exterior of composure as they disembarked. Outside the shuttle they found an escort of three Jedi waiting for them. Two were human, a man and a woman. The third was a female Twi'lek. Each wore plain brown robes with the hoods thrown back to reveal their features;

their simple garb a sharp contrast with Serra and Lucia's more formal outfits.

The princess was wearing a long, flowing, sleeveless dress of blue silk; a finely woven gold stole covered her shoulders and upper arms. Her long black hair hung loose from beneath the elaborate golden tiara she wore, and around her neck was an elegant gold chain and a sapphire pendant signifying her station within the Doan royal family.

Lucia was also dressed in blue and gold—the royal colors—but she wore the dress uniform of the Doan military: dark blue pants with a gold stripe running up the leg and a tight, light blue shirt covered by a short blue jacket with gold trim buttoned up to the collar. Like the three Jedi, however, her head was bare.

The Twi'lek stepped forward with a bow. "Greetings, Your Highness. My name is Ma'ya. My companions are Pendo and Winnoa."

Serra returned the bow with a tilt of her head. "This is Lucia, my companion," she returned.

Ma'ya's eyes flicked down to the blaster prominently displayed on Lucia's hip, but all she said was, "Please, follow us. Master Obba is waiting to speak with you."

From the briefings she had reviewed during the trip to Coruscant, Lucia knew that Obba was a member of the Council of First Knowledge. As keepers of ancient Jedi lore, they often provided advice and guidance to the Jedi High Council. He had also been the Master of Medd Tandar, the Jedi who had died on Doan.

The three robed figures led them from the landing pad through a well-tended garden, dotted by a number of memorials and statues. A small crowd of children rushed past them at one point, laughing.

"Younglings from the trainee dorms," Ma'ya explained. "During afternoons they are given time away from their studies to play in the gardens."

Serra didn't reply, but Lucia could see the flicker of sorrow in her eyes. She knew the young couple had been trying to start a family in the weeks before Gerran's death, and seeing the children no doubt brought back painful memories.

They continued on in silence, the Jedi leading them to the foot of the northwest tower and then inside. They climbed up several flights of winding stairs; toward the end Lucia noticed that the princess had become short of breath, though neither she nor the Jedi had the same problem.

And then, somewhere roughly a quarter of the way up the tower, they stopped outside a large door. Ma'ya knocked, and a deep voice from inside called out, "Come in."

The Twi'lek opened the door, then stepped to the side with another bow. Serra entered the room, Lucia following a single step behind. Their escorts stayed outside, closing the door.

At first glance, the interior of the room might have been mistaken for a greenhouse. A single large window on the far wall allowed sunlight to stream through, making it exceedingly bright and overly warm. Potted plants of at least a dozen different species lined the walls; another half a dozen grew from boxes along the windowsill, while still more hung from planters affixed to the ceiling. There were no chairs, no table, and no desk. It was only when she noticed a small, straw-woven sleeping mat rolled up in the corner that Lucia realized this was the Jedi Master's personal chambers.

"Welcome, Your Highness. You honor us with your visit."

Master Obba, an Ithorian, was standing with his back to them looking out the window. In the elongated fingers of one hand he held a watering can. Setting it down on the floor, he turned to face them.

Like all Ithorians, he was taller than the average human—easily over two meters in height. His rough, brown skin looked almost like bark, and his long neck curved down and forward before looping up again, making it seem as if he was leaning toward them. Looking at the eyes bulging out from either side at the top of his tall, flat head made it easy to see why the nickname Hammerhead was often applied to the species.

"This is my adviser, Lucia," Serra told him, sticking with their planned cover story. "Thank you for agreeing to meet with us, Master Obba."

"It was the least I could do, given your circumstances," the Ithorian explained, his voice deep and resonant. "My condolences on your husband. His death was a terrible tragedy."

Lucia was no expert in the subtleties of politics, and she couldn't tell if Obba was simply a compassionate soul expressing real sympathy, or an expert negotiator trying to put the princess emotionally off balance by mentioning Gerran.

"My tragedy is mirrored by your own," Serra replied in the formal tone of a practiced diplomat. Whatever the Jedi's intentions, his words had no visible effect on her demeanor. "Allow me to apologize on behalf of the royal family for the unfortunate passing of Medd Tandar."

The Ithorian's head dipped in acknowledgment. "I grieve for his death. And it is of critical importance that we learn the identity of the person or persons responsible."

Lucia felt her heart skip a beat, though she gave no outward sign of her anxiety.

"I understand," Serra assured him. "The authorities on my world are doing everything in their power to bring those responsible to justice."

"I want to believe you," Obba replied, "but you can understand if I have my reservations. Medd was killed during an attack on your enemies. There are some who believe your father-in-law was behind the attack."

"That makes no sense," Serra objected. "The king wants to improve our relationship with your revered Order. That was why he agreed to let Medd come to our world in the first place."

"There are some who believe the king used Medd to help find his enemies," Obba countered. "They claim that was his plan all along."

"Medd's death was a tragic coincidence, not a part of some devious plot to exploit the Jedi," the princess insisted. "He was simply in the wrong place at the wrong time. As for the king, he had no knowledge of the assassination whatsoever. I give you my word."

"Unfortunately, your word will not be proof enough to allay the fears of those in my Order."

"Then let them use logic," Serra argued. "My father-in-law is not a fool. If he wanted to use the Jedi to seek revenge, he would have been smart enough to cover his tracks. He would have waited until after Medd had left before ordering the attack."

"Sometimes when we are blinded by grief, we aren't able to look past our immediate desires," the Jedi noted.

"Is that what you really believe, Master Obba? Or are you just looking for someone to blame for the death of your former Padawan?"

The Ithorian sighed. "I admit my own judgment in this may be clouded by my personal feelings. That is why I must trust in the Force and allow it to guide my thoughts and actions."

"There is no emotion, there is peace," the princess remarked.

"You have studied our Code."

"Only informally."

"I should have suspected as much," the Master told her. "I can feel the Force is strong in you."

Lucia's eyes popped open in surprise, though Serra took his observation completely in stride.

"I fear I am too old to be recruited into your Order, Master Obba," she said with a faint smile.

"Even so, the words of our mantra can serve you well," he admonished her. "You must be ever wary of the temptations of the dark side."

"Like the talismans Medd was sent to find?" Serra countered. "That is what this is really about, isn't it?"

The Ithorian nodded gravely. "As much as I grieve over his death, I must put those feelings aside and focus on the purpose of his original mission."

Lucia was impressed. So far the encounter had gone almost exactly as Serra had predicted. During their preparations for the meeting, the princess had told her the Jedi cared more about ideology and the battle of light and dark than about living people. She had planned to exploit that knowledge to turn the conversation away from discussions of who had hired the assassin . . . with a little help from Lucia.

The Jedi love to feel superior, Serra had explained during the shuttle ride. *They consider it their duty to educate and inform the ignorant masses. If you ask one of them a question, they can't help but answer it. We can use this to our advantage during our meeting.*

"Forgive my interruption, Master Obba," Lucia said, recognizing the opportunity he had given her, "but are these talismans really that important?"

"I believe they are," the Ithorian replied.

"But . . . how can you be so sure?"

"I am a member of the Council of First Knowledge," he explained, launching into a lesson just as Serra had said he would. "We are keepers of the wisdom of the Jedi. We maintain the Great Library, we oversee the teachings of the younglings, and we seek out the ancient histories and Holocrons that will bring us greater knowledge of the light side of the Force. But we are more than just caretakers. We are also guardians.

"Not all knowledge is pure; some is touched by evil. There are secrets that must remain hidden; forbidden teachings that should remain forever buried. There is a dark side to the Force. Unchecked it brings death and destruction."

Lucia nodded as if absorbing every word, but inside she felt nothing but scorn. The arrogance of the Jedi knew no bounds. As a soldier serving in Kaan's Brotherhood of Darkness, she had developed a rather different view of the dark side. The Sith taught that emotion—fear, anger, and even hate—should be embraced. She had learned to draw strength from the so-called evil of the dark side, and it had helped her survive through war and years of suffering.

The Jedi would never understand this. They lived in isolation, meditating in great towers at the center of the galaxy. They had no idea what it was like for the outcasts, the disenfranchised, and the forgotten people forced to live on the fringes of society.

"The Council of First Knowledge is sworn to keep this terrible power from being unleashed," Master Obba continued, oblivious of her true feelings. "But the influence of the dark side is scattered throughout the galaxy, as are the tools it uses to spread: ancient texts of Sith sorcery; amulets imbued with malevolent energy; tainted crystals that can corrupt the minds of the innocent.

"Sometimes these artifacts are discovered by accident, and they fall into the hands of unsuspecting victims. They become agents of the dark side, wreaking havoc across the galaxy . . . unless we get to them in time. We are trained in the handling of dark side artifacts. Some can be destroyed, but others are too powerful and must be safeguarded."

"How would something like that end up on a remote world like Doan?" Lucia asked, still playing her part.

"Humans have been living on your world for at least ten thousand years," Obba was only too willing to explain. "When the mining operations began several centuries ago, ancient burial mounds, crypts, and grave sites were often dug up, as were the remains of primitive villages abandoned long ago. On rare occasions entire cities had even been discovered, entombed millennia earlier in mudslides or ancient volcanic eruptions.

"Some of these early civilizations worshiped the Sith and followed the ways of the dark side. When the people disappeared, the artifacts of their faith were often left behind."

"How did you first hear about these artifacts?" the princess suddenly asked, seizing on an idea.

"Nothing but a rumor," Obba admitted. "We heard word that a mining team had discovered a cache of items and was offering them for sale to offworld collectors. Based on the descriptions, we felt the items might have been Sith talismans. So I sent Medd to investigate."

"If you heard about these items," Serra speculated, "then it's possible others could have heard of them as well. Medd's killer might not have been an assassin sent to avenge my husband's death. It could have been someone interested in finding the talismans."

"I have considered that possibility," the Jedi Master confessed. "Though I had hoped it was not so."

The Ithorian turned his back on them, clearly troubled. He began to pace slowly back and forth in front of his plants, as if to calm himself before speaking again. Once again Lucia was amazed at how easily the princess had controlled and directed the encounter.

Obba had commented on Serra being strong in the Force. That might help to explain the commanding presence she seemed to carry. But, Lucia wondered, was it possible the princess was so powerful she was able to manipulate a Jedi Master?

"Those who are trained in the ways of the Jedi are taught to live by the rules and tenets of our Order," Obba said at last. "We believe in self-sacrifice, and we believe that the power of the Force must only be used when it serves the greater good. Unfortunately, despite our best efforts, there are those who fall away from our teachings. They give in to weakness. They succumb to ambition and greed. They use the Force to satisfy their own base wants and desires. They reject our philosophy and fall to the dark side."

"You're talking about the Sith," Serra whispered. Lucia thought she heard fear in the princess's voice, but she couldn't tell if it was real or simply part of the game she was playing with their host.

"Not the Sith," he corrected. "I am speaking of the Dark Jedi."

"What's the difference between a Sith and a Dark Jedi?" Lucia asked.

The Ithorian stopped pacing and turned to face them, instinctively addressing his audience like a teacher giving a lesson.

"The Sith were the sworn enemies of the Jedi and the Republic. They sought to wipe us from existence; they sought to rule the galaxy. They united their strength in the Brotherhood of Darkness, drawing countless followers to their cause with false promises. They amassed an army of individuals foolish and desperate enough to believe their lies, and they plunged the galaxy into a war that threatened to destroy us all."

Lucia remained silent as Obba spoke, though she tensed involuntarily at his description of her and her fellow soldiers.

"A Dark Jedi, on the other hand, has much smaller ambitions. He—or she—thinks only of himself. He acts alone. The ultimate goal is not galactic conquest, but personal wealth and importance. Like a common thug or criminal, he revels in cruelty and selfishness. He preys upon the weak and vulnerable, spreading misery and suffering wherever he goes."

"And you think such a one might be involved here," Serra noted. "You have someone in particular in mind."

Obba bowed his head in shame. "Set Harth. As a Padawan he lost his Master to the thought bomb on Ruusan. I took him under my wing, and eventually I recommended him to the other members on the Council of First Knowledge. Like Medd, he became one of our agents, scouring the galaxy for dark side artifacts and lore.

"But the temptation of the dark side proved too strong for Set. He rejected the Jedi teachings to pursue wealth and personal gain at the expense of others. Too late we learned that he had kept many of the artifacts he uncovered for himself. By the time I realized what he had become, he was gone, vanished into the galactic underbelly of lawless mercenaries, bounty hunters, and slavers."

"So you fear that Set Harth, this *Dark Jedi,* may have killed Medd Tandar on Doan?"

"If the killer was not an assassin hired by someone on Doan, then this seems to me to be the most likely possibility. If Set somehow learned about the artifact cache on Doan, he would have sought to claim it . . . and he would have killed anyone who got in his way."

"He sounds like a dangerous man," Serra noted.

"Now that the Sith are extinct," Obba proclaimed, "Set Harth may be the most dangerous individual in the galaxy."

Serra stared at him. She thought of the black-armored man who had haunted her dreams for the past twenty years, and remembered the words of her father:

The Jedi and the Sith will always be at war. They are each wholly uncompromising; their rigid philosophies make no room for mutual existence. But what they fail to realize is that they are merely two sides of the same coin: light and dark. You cannot have one without the other.

"How can you be so sure the Sith are gone?" she demanded. "Weren't there rumors that some of the Sith Lords survived the thought bomb that destroyed the Brotherhood of Darkness?"

"That is true. One did survive," Obba explained. "But now he, too, has fallen . . . though his defeat came at a terrible cost."

"I don't understand."

The Ithorian sighed, an anguished, mournful sound. "Come. I will show you."

With slow plodding steps he crossed the room and opened the door leading back out to the hall. The three Jedi who had escorted them there were all sitting cross-legged on the ground, silently meditating. They scrambled to their feet upon seeing the Ithorian emerge.

"You may return to your regular duties," he informed them.

"Yes, Master," they replied, bowing in unison. Dismissed, the Jedi headed up the stairs to whatever tasks awaited them in the higher floors of the tower.

Moving at a pace so languid it bordered on maddening, Obba led the way back down to the base of the tower and out into the gardens where, at long last, he stopped.

They stood before one of the many monuments raised in the garden. This particular one was a white block of stone a meter and a half high and nearly twice as wide. The handles of five lightsabers were inlaid on the face of the stone; beneath each was a small engraved portrait—presumably an image of the lightsaber's owner. Beneath this, in larger letters, was the following:

> *In honor of those who fell beneath the blade of*
> *the last Dark Lord of the Sith.*
> *May their memories live on, to remind us of what is lost.*
> *There is no emotion; there is peace;*
> *There is no death; there is the Force.*
> *Jedi Master Valenthyne Farfalla*
> *Jedi Master Raskta Lsu*
> *Jedi Master Worror Dowmat*
> *Jedi Knight Johun Othone*
> *Jedi Knight Sarro Xaj*
> *Caleb of Ambria*

When her eyes fell upon the last name of the list, Serra felt her knees grow weak. Speechless, she could only stare at the monument, her mind unable to make sense of what she was seeing.

"What is this?" Lucia asked, echoing her mistress's confusion. "Why'd you bring us here?"

"Ten years ago, Master Valenthyne Farfalla learned that a Dark Lord of the Sith had somehow survived the thought bomb on Ruusan. Acting on a tip, he quickly assembled the team of Jedi you see honored on this monument to try to apprehend the Dark Lord. They followed him into the Deep Core and confronted him on the world of Tython. None of the Jedi survived."

"Did you know them well?" Lucia wondered aloud, still following Serra's instructions to ask questions at every opportunity.

"I knew Master Worror and Master Valenthyne back when we were all Padawans. We served together in Lord Hoth's Army of Light during the war against Lord Kaan's Brotherhood of Darkness."

For several seconds there was silence, Obba lost in his memories and Serra still too stunned to speak. It was Lucia who broke the spell, asking yet another question.

"The last name, Caleb of Ambria—I remember hearing it back during the war. He was a healer, wasn't he?"

"He was. In the battle against the Jedi on Tython, the Dark Lord was grievously injured. He went to Ambria in search of the one man with the knowledge to heal his wounds. But Caleb refused to help him."

In her mind's eye, everything became clear to Serra. As her father had predicted, the man in black armor had returned. As before, he had come to try to compel Caleb to work his art. As before, Caleb had resisted. This time, however, her father had the upper hand. Having sent his daughter away, there was nothing the Sith could do to compel him to cooperate.

"What happened when the healer refused?" she whispered, her eyes still transfixed on her father's name etched into the base of the stone.

"Nobody knows for certain. What we do know is that shortly after the Dark Lord arrived, Caleb sent out a message alerting the Jedi Council. He told them the last of the Sith was at his camp on Ambria, injured and virtually helpless. He wanted the Jedi to come capture him."

"Why would he do that?" Lucia wondered. "I seem to remember hearing that Caleb refused to take sides in the war. Didn't have much use for the Jedi or the Sith."

"He did not always agree with the philosophies of our Order," Obba admitted. "But he was a good and moral man. The war was long over by this point, and his conscience would not suffer evil to endure without taking action. He knew if he let the Sith leave, sooner or later more innocents would suffer.

"Upon receiving the message, the Council sent a team led by Master Tho'natu out to Ambria. I was one of the Jedi chosen to accompany him. Unfortunately, by the time we arrived at the camp, Caleb was dead."

"How?" Serra asked, her voice low and devoid of all emotion.

"The Dark Lord learned about the message. Driven mad by Caleb's betrayal, his injuries, and the corruption of the dark side, he butchered the healer, hewing him limb from limb.

"By the time we arrived, the Dark Lord had gone completely insane. He was still lurking around the camp and he rushed out to attack us, one man against an army of Jedi. Master Tho'natu was forced to cut him down to protect his own life."

Serra's father had been right. He had known the black-armored man would return. He had sensed the danger, and he had sent his daughter away. He had saved her life, at the cost of his own. And in so doing, he had helped destroy the man Serra feared more than any other.

A flood of emotions swept through her. Relief. Guilt. Sorrow. Shame. But drowning them all out was a fierce, primal anger. More than anything she wanted revenge. She wanted to strike out at the monster who had terrorized her as a child and then, years later, killed her father. Yet that was impossible. The Jedi had stolen that from her.

"What was he like?" Lucia asked. "The last Sith, I mean."

"He was a tragic, pathetic figure," Obba answered. "Thin. Frail. You could see the madness in him when he charged us. His eyes were as dark and wild as his hair."

No, Serra thought. *That's not right.* "He had hair?" *The black-armored man's head was shaved.*

"Yes. Hair like an animal's. Long. Unkempt. Matted with blood."

An unthinkable suspicion was worming its way into Serra's brain.

"Was he a big man?" she demanded, straining to keep the urgency from her voice. "Tall, I mean?"

The Ithorian shook his head. "No, not overly so. Not for a human."

The dark-armored man was a giant. At least as tall as you, Master Obba.

Oblivious to Serra's inner turmoil, the Ithorian continued his tale. "The lightsabers of the fallen Jedi were found in Caleb's camp; the Dark Lord had kept them as trophies. Master Tho'natu brought them back, along with the healer's remains, so they could be laid to rest in a place of honor.

"This monument represents one of the greatest triumphs of the Jedi Order, but also one of its grimmest chapters. The Sith are no more, but only at the cost of many lives that will be sorely missed. This was the price we had to pay to rid the galaxy of the Sith forever."

Serra's mind was churning, trying to put all the pieces together. She needed time to think, to figure it out. But she couldn't do that here—not with her father's name staring up at her from the stone. She needed to leave before she said or did something that would expose her secret and reveal her true identity.

"You have given us a lot to think about, Master Obba," Serra said stiffly. "I will be sure to relay all of this to the king."

Master Obba cleared his throat apologetically. "I have every confidence you will do so, but I would still like to send one of my own people to investigate and see if the talismans are still there."

When Serra hesitated before answering, Lucia came to her rescue.

"What would be the point of that? I mean, if you're right about Set Harth being the killer, wouldn't he be long gone by now? He's not going to hang around after he gets his hands on those talismans, right?"

"You are probably correct," the Jedi admitted after considering her words.

"Then I see no reason for the Jedi to follow up on this matter," Serra said, collecting herself enough to seize the opportunity Lucia's quick thinking had provided her. "Given the delicate political situation on Doan, it would probably be best for all concerned if the investigations were conducted by the local authorities."

She could see the Ithorian wasn't pleased with the arrangement, but he had been backed into a corner. Caught in the web of galactic politics, he was now helpless to take action without turning this into an official diplomatic incident—something the Senate would not look kindly on.

"If we learn any news about Set or the talismans," the princess promised, "you have my word that we will inform you right away."

"Thank you, Your Highness," the Ithorian replied with a stiff bow, only now realizing how he had been outmaneuvered.

Serra gave Master Obba a curt nod as a final farewell, then quickly turned to take her leave, anxious to return to the privacy of her shuttle. Lucia immediately fell into step beside her. Neither of them spoke as they crossed the gardens to the waiting airspeeder; the silence continued as the speeder whisked them up and away, turning the buildings and swarming crowds of Coruscant into a blur beneath them. Serra was still thinking about the black-armored man from her nightmares. She knew her dreams were more than just memories or subconscious fears bubbling to the surface. Caleb had been neither Sith nor Jedi, yet he had believed in the natural power of life and the universe and had taught Serra to listen to the power within her, to draw on it when she needed wisdom, courage, or strength of spirit. Most important, he had taught her to trust her instincts.

In the same way Caleb had known that the black-armored man

would return, Serra knew he was still alive. She knew he was somehow involved in her father's murder. The Jedi who had come to Ambria had been tricked. She was certain of it. It wouldn't have been
hard; they wanted to believe the Sith were extinct. It was always easier to make people accept a lie they had hoped and wished for.

A plan began to form in Serra's mind. For too many years, she had
been tormented by the terrifying figure from her childhood. Now,
with Caleb's death as the catalyst, she was going to do something
about it. She would avenge her father. She was going to find the
black-armored man, and she was going to kill him.

She didn't speak again until she and Lucia were alone on board
the private shuttle that would take them back to Doan. Here she
knew they were safe, that whatever was said would stay between the
two of them. Even so, she wasn't ready to confess everything. She
would keep the secrets of her past—her father, her nightmares—a
little longer yet.

"The assassin you hired. I need you to contact her again" was all
she said. "I have another job for her."

6

Set Harth had been on Doan for two days. He was determined not to still be here by the end of the third. In part, he wanted to be gone before any more Jedi showed up to investigate Medd's death, or to try and claim the artifacts the Cerean had come for in the first place. But beyond that, Set was just sick of being surrounded by miners.

They were all beginning to look the same: squat and stout, their common thickness a result of generations spent at hard manual labor. Their skin was brown and weathered, not to mention caked with the dust and grime that hung over everything. They all had the same hair—short and dark—and they all wore the same clothes, drab and ratty. Even their features all looked the same: grim and sullen, despondent and broken by a lifetime of grinding in the quarries.

To say he didn't fit in was the epitome of understatement. Set was thin and wiry, with long, silver hair flowing down over his shoulders. His skin was creamy white and unblemished by the elements; his handsome features conveyed a mischievous charm and just a touch of arrogance. And, unlike the miners, Set dressed with style.

He wore a tailor-fitted combat suit, the material a shade some-where between black and violet. The lightweight outfit gave him full mobility, yet was also durable enough to afford some protection if, as so often happened around Set, events took a violent turn. Atop this he wore a pale yellow vest; both the combat suit and vest were sleeve-less to leave his arms bare. A fashionable violet band of woven veda cloth encircled each ripped bicep, and his boots, belt, and fingerless gloves were made from the finest Corellian leather.

Typically he also carried a GSI-24D disruptor pistol holstered on his right thigh and a conventional blaster strapped to his left. Here on Doan, however, disruptors were banned, so he had tucked both weapons—along with his lightsaber—into the various pockets lining the inside of his vest.

It was obvious he didn't belong with the rest of the crowd in the cantina, but Set wasn't trying to blend in. It was common knowledge that mercenaries could find high-paying jobs here on Doan. Set fig-ured anyone who saw him would assume he was just one more soldier-of-fortune hoping to cash in on the escalating violence be-tween the rebels and the nobility.

They'd be wrong, of course. Set *was* here hoping to cash in, but it had nothing to do with Doan's inevitable civil war. Less than a week ago his former colleague Medd Tandar had been on this world, and there was only one reason he would ever come to a pit like this.

Master Obba sent you here to find some dark side talisman, didn't he? Only you got more than you bargained for. Always suspected you were soft.

Whatever Medd had come in search of, he had died before retriev-ing it. That meant the item was still here, just waiting for someone to claim it. Someone like Set.

For the past two days he had traveled the scarred surface of Doan, moving from one cantina, barracks, or work site to another. At each stop he asked questions, trying to find someone—anyone—who knew something about the Cerean who had been killed along with the rebel leaders. More importantly, he needed to find someone who knew what Medd had been looking for.

To anyone who asked, he explained that he was interested because he was a collector of rare artifacts. But the people here were wary. Some of them suspected he was working for the royal family. It wasn't easy to get the answers he needed. Still, over the years Set had learned that everyone had their price . . . or their breaking point.

His investigations had led him here, to this nameless cantina owned by a Rodian bartender named Quano, one of only a handful of nonhumans who chose to try to make a living on Doan.

Eager to get away from the blowing dust clouds rolling across the surface, Set pushed open the door and entered the cantina. He immediately began to regret his decision. It was clear that the crowd in this particular establishment comprised the lowest dregs of Doan mining society. Most of the people here were bent and twisted; the hard-timers, hunchbacked and half crippled by a lifetime of digging up ore for the profit of others. Their clothes weren't just shabby, but filthy, and the acrid stench of sweat and unwashed bodies nearly brought tears to his eyes. Exactly the kind of people Set would expect to find in a Rodian's bar.

The furniture was as wretched and broken-down as the clientele: glasses disfigured by chips and cracks; discolored tabletops tottering on three rickety legs; rusting stools that looked as if they would crumble if given one good kick. Against the far wall was a long, wide bar covered by a slap-dash coat of peeling paint that did little to hide the rotting wood beneath. The row of bottles perched on the shelf behind the bar were covered in a thick layer of dirt and grime, but Set didn't need to read the labels to guess they were all brands that readily sacrificed quality for price.

He noticed two heavyset thugs loitering on either side of the door and quickly sized them up: typical goons—big, strong, and stupid.

He could tell from the awkward way they stood that each had a small pistol jammed down the front of his respective belt.

Leaning against the wall behind the bar was the green-skinned proprietor himself, his arms crossed in front of his chest. His insect-like eyes glared at Set from across the room, his tapirlike snout twisted into what the former Jedi could only assume was meant to be a sneer.

Ignoring the uninviting greeting, Set made his way slowly toward the Rodian. Two dozen eyes gave him the once-over as he passed the bar, their collective gaze cold, appraising, and ultimately uncaring as the owners turned their attention back to the brackish sludge swirling around in their mugs.

"Bar for miners only," Quano muttered in heavily accented Galactic Basic once Set was close enough to rest an elbow on the bar. "You not drink. Go away."

Set reached out and casually dropped a pair of hundred-credit chips on the counter. The Rodian tried to act nonchalant, but Set could sense that he was suddenly holding his breath.

"I was hoping we could have a little chat," Set told him, getting right to the point. "Alone."

In a flash the chips disappeared and Quano was standing on top of the bar.

"Cantina closed!" he shouted at the top of his lungs. "Time to go! Back to work! Everybody out!"

Most of the crowd rose grudgingly from their seats, muttering darkly as they shuffled to the door. One stubborn soul stayed sitting, doing his best to keep his wobbly chair from being knocked over by the other patrons heading for the exit. The bartender clapped his hands together twice, and the bouncers by the door quickly moved in.

They grabbed the man, each one seizing an arm, and yanked him from the chair. Too drunk to even struggle, the customer hung like deadweight between the two hulking brutes, his feet dragging limply on the floor as they forcibly ushered him out. Upon reaching the exit, the bouncers rocked their human cargo back and forth several times in a surprising display of coordinated effort, building momentum before hurling him through the doorway and onto the hard ground outside. It would have been a lie for Set to say he wasn't impressed by the distance they achieved.

With the last customer gone, one of the bouncers slammed the door and latched it shut. Then they both turned to face Set, grinning as they resumed leaning against the wall on either side of the room's only exit.

Set couldn't help but admire the Rodian's utter and complete lack of subtlety. Most proprietors would have invited Set into a back room to chat rather than shutting down their entire establishment for only two hundred credits. Judging by the general décor, however, the establishment was barely profitable.

Not that Set really cared. He wasn't trying to keep a low profile. He was used to leaving memorable stories in his wake; if anyone ever came to investigate he would be long gone, so what did it matter if he had another tale to add to his legend? Over time the details would in-evitably become exaggerated, and one day people would marvel at how Set had been so wealthy that he had paid thousands of credits to shut down an entire cantina just so he could speak to the owner.

"Nobody bother us now," Quano said from behind him, hopping back down onto the floor. "You want drink?"

"I'm a collector interested in rare artifacts," Set replied, ignoring the question and cutting right to the chase. He wanted to spend as lit-tle time here as possible. "Rings. Amulets. That kind of thing."

Quano shrugged. "Why you tell Quano?"

"Word around the camp is you sometimes have these kinds of items for sale."

The cupped antennae on the bartender's head twitched ever so slightly. "Maybe," he whispered, leaning forward so Set could hear him. "Miner finds things. Him wants to sell it offworld. Maybe Quano help him."

"Then this is your lucky day," Set replied, somehow managing to flash a dazzling smile despite the pungent aroma of alien phero-mones wafting off the Rodian. "Like I said—I'm a collector. A wealthy collector."

Quano cast a quick glance around the empty room, almost as if he expected someone to be listening in on their conversation. Set recog-nized it as a nervous reflex developed after years of making shady deals in public places.

"What you interested in?"

"I think you know what I'm looking for. The same thing as the last collector who came here. The Cerean."

"Him not collector. Him Jedi. You Jedi, too?"

Set sighed. This was going to drive the price up. *Never did under-stand the value of keeping a low profile, did you, Medd?*

"Do I look like a Jedi?"

The Rodian tilted his head from one side to the other before an-swering. "No. Look more like bounty hunter."

"Does it really matter? I want to buy what you're selling. And I've got plenty of credits . . . if you've got the merchandise."

"Stuff not here. Quano just middlebeing. Miner have it."

"Can you take me to whoever has it?"

Quano shook his head. "Miner change his mind. Not for sale no more."

"Everyone has a price. I'm a wealthy man. If you take me to him, I'm sure we can come to some agreement."

Another shake of the head. "Last time Quano take someone to meet miners, everyone end up dead. Too risky."

"I'm willing to take that chance."

The Rodian snorted. "Quano not care about risk for you. Miners say if Quano show up again, they kill him."

"They don't have to know you were involved," Set promised. "Just show me where to find them. I'll make it worth your while."

To emphasize his point he produced his small drawstring purse, reached in, and pulled out an entire handful of high-value chips. He held them up for Quano to look at before letting them spill through his fingers back into the satchel.

The Rodian's tongue poked out and swirled around his snout, his reluctance to take Set to the miners doing battle with his greed.

"You pay one—no, two!—thousand, yes?"

"Seven hundred. Or I go find someone else who can help me."

"Okay, deal," the bartender blurted out, unwilling to barter for fear he might let a small fortune slip through his fingers.

To seal the deal, he extended his hand. Gritting his teeth Set returned the gesture. He clasped the other's palm for one quick shake then pulled back, mildly repulsed by the feel of the Rodian's scaly skin against his own.

"You have drink to celebrate," Quano declared. "On the house."

"Pass," Set replied.

"You got credits with you, right?" the bartender wanted to know. "You pay now, right?"

Set nodded. "I'll pay you as soon as we go."

"We go now. Quano just grab something first."

As the Rodian ducked back behind the bar, Set realized there was something off about his voice. Too eager.

So it's going to be like that, is it?

Slipping his hand into his vest, the Dark Jedi whipped out his lightsaber. He ignited it as Quano popped back up into view, just in time to deflect the bolt from the blaster pistol that was now pointing at him. The Rodian let out a shriek of surprise and disappeared back behind the cover of the bar.

He'd dealt with Quano's type before. Set would have been perfectly content to honor the terms of their agreement, but the Rodian had obviously come up with a different plan. Why risk your life and take someone to a hidden base for seven hundred credits when you can murder him in cold blood and take all his money instead?

Set respected the sentiment; after all, he lived by similar self-serving principles. But the bartender had made an unforgivable error by trying to use those principles against a Dark Jedi.

Keeping one eye on the bar, Set turned to face the two burly miners guarding the door. They had probably been expecting Quano's betrayal, but they were caught completely off guard by the failure of his plan. Now the grins had fallen from their faces, and they were clumsily scrambling to draw their own weapons.

Why are the big ones always so kriffing slow?

Set could have stopped them any number of ways: He could have used the Force to yank their weapons from their grasp, or unleashed a wave that would send the guards flying across the room. Given how long it was taking them, he could have leapt forward and sliced them both in half with his lightsaber before they ever fired a shot. Instead, he chose to simply hold his ground, waiting for the inevitable barrage of blasterfire.

His adversaries didn't disappoint him. Set easily caught the first round of bolts with his shimmering blade, sending them ricocheting harmlessly away. At this point a smart opponent would have made a break for the door. Quano's two thugs, on the other hand, simply kept firing, too dumb to realize the sheer futility of their attacks.

Set picked off a few more shots before growing bored with the game. Using the Force to anticipate the precise location of the next two incoming bolts, he angled his lightsaber so that they deflected straight back toward their point of origin.

The first miner was hit in the chest, the other in the stomach. Both died instantly.

Killing his enemies with their own blaster bolts was a long-standing tradition for Set. There were occasions when he needed to keep a low profile, and lightsabers tended to leave very distinctive wound patterns. This wasn't one of those times, but why pass up a chance to keep his skills sharp?

All this time, Quano hadn't reappeared. Set was unsurprised.

"Might as well come out. Don't make me come get you."

The Rodian's green head slowly rose up into view. He was still holding his blaster, pointing it at Set. But his hands were trembling so much he couldn't even keep the barrel steady.

Set shook his head. "If you're going to kill somebody so you can steal their credits, at least go after an easy target."

"You liar," Quano replied, his voice rising defensively. "You said you no Jedi."

With a flick of his wrist, Set used the Force to slap the pistol from Quano's hand. Another gesture lifted the helpless bartender off the ground and yanked him across the room, where he landed in a crumpled ball at Set's feet.

Reaching down to seize one of the Rodian's antennae, Set used it to pull his whimpering victim up to his knees. His free hand brought the blade of his still-ignited lightsaber to within a few centimeters of Quano's scaly face.

"Let's get one thing clear. I'm *not* a Jedi."

To emphasize his point, he flicked his blade, caressing it against the Rodian's cheek for a fraction of a second. The sizzle of smoldering flesh was drowned out by Quano's scream.

"No kill, no kill!" he blubbered.

The damage was minor; a burn that would heal within a week while leaving only a faint scar. But Set was satisfied his point had been made. Shutting off his lightsaber, he released his grip on the antenna and took a step back, giving Quano room to stand.

The Rodian stayed on his knees, his hand reached up gingerly to examine his wound.

"Now why would I want to kill you?" Set asked him. "You're the only one who can take me to the miners and their talismans. Until I have them in my hands, I'll do everything I can to keep you alive."

"What happen after you get them?" Quano asked, suspicious.

Set flashed him his most charming smile. "At that point, we'll just have to play it by ear."

———

Set could hear the voices of the miners echoing down the tunnel. He estimated they were only a few hundred meters away; from the tone of the echoes he suspected they were in a large, high-roofed cavern.

They live like vermin, huddled in underground warrens, afraid for their lives. Pathetic.

Ahead, his unwilling guide suddenly stopped and turned to look back at him. It wasn't easy to read a Rodian's expression, but it was clear what Quano was asking: *I brought you this far—can I go now?*

Set simply shook his head and pointed farther down the tunnel. Shoulders sagging, Quano continued to shuffle forward.

They were close enough now that Set could actually make out what the miners were saying to one another.

"You can't be serious!" a deep-voiced man shouted. "The nobles murdered Gelba! We have to make them pay!"

"If they got Gelba, they can get anyone," another man protested. "I think we should lay low for a while. Let things simmer down."

"I agree," a woman chimed in. "I know Gelba was your friend, Draado. But you're talking madness!"

Set could see light from the entrance to the cavern spilling around a bend in the tunnel just up ahead. Quano crept around the corner silently and crouched behind a rock that gave him a clear view of their quarry. He might have been a coward, Set noted as he moved up to join him, but he had a natural talent for sneaking and spying.

From their vantage point he could clearly see the cave. It was dotted with dozens of large stalagmites protruding up like ugly brown spires from the floor. Stalactites hung from the ceiling, looking ominously like the teeth of some ancient stone monster waiting to chomp down on the people below.

He counted an even dozen miners gathered in a loose semicircle near the center of the chamber. All of them were armed, just like the four guards he had dispatched at the tunnel's entrance not ten minutes earlier. A few of the miners were sitting on short, flat-topped rock formations. Others paced nervously back and forth. One leaned against a nearby stalagmite. Two men and a woman appeared to be engaged in a heated argument. Four others were standing guard on the edges of the group, blaster rifles drawn while they nervously scanned the cavern's entrance, as if trying to pierce the shadows in anticipation of an attack.

Whoever killed Medd and your friends made you paranoid.

"With Gelba gone, I call the shots," a bearded man was saying to one of the women. "And I say Gelba's death calls for blood!"

"Draado," Quano whispered, speaking so softly Set had to lean in to hear it. "Him one who dig up stuff you want."

Looking closer, Set noticed an amulet draped around Draado's neck, and he caught the glint of a ring on his finger—the only jewelry he had seen on any of the miners since he'd set foot on this destitute world.

"You want to start a war that will get us all killed," one of the men objected.

"At least we'll take a few of the nobles with us!" Draado snapped back.

Draado was standing less than ten meters from where Set was hiding, close enough that he could sense the power emanating from the talismans. The amulet seemed to call out to him; the ring beckoned with its dark heat.

"What happened to you, Draado?" the woman asked. "You always used to be the one who said we could get what we want without violence and bloodshed."

"I've changed. Now I see the truth." Draado pounded his chest for emphasis as he spoke, his fist striking the amulet.

"The nobles won't respect us until they learn to fear us," he insisted, turning to look at everyone scattered about the cavern. "We need to make them scared for their very lives. We need to strike terror into their hearts!"

Clearly Draado was under the influence of the talismans; they were corrupting his mind and his thoughts. The power of the dark side had taken hold of him.

No wonder Quano said he wouldn't want to sell them.

The Dark Jedi considered his options. Bargaining with the miners was out of the question; Draado would never willingly give up his newfound treasures. Given the tension in the room and the itchy trigger fingers on the guards, it was pretty clear that any attempt to negotiate would probably end up in a firefight no matter what he did.

He drew out his twin pistols and took a deep breath, bracing for the confrontation. He needed the target practice anyway.

Leaping from his hiding place, he charged into the cavern with guns blazing. He dropped all four of the rifle-carrying guards before anyone had a chance to react. With the Force guiding his hand, he easily picked them off with four clean shots as he sprinted toward the cover of a large stalagmite on the far side of the cavern.

He skidded in behind it just as the miners began to return fire. They peppered his hiding place, sending up fine clouds of dust as the bolts disintegrated small chips from the stone. Poking his head out, Set fired twice more, reducing the number of opponents to six before ducking back behind the safety of the stalagmite.

The sound of enemy blasterfire reverberated off the walls of the cavern. Set smiled, enjoying the glorious clamor of battle. *Halfway done already. This might be easier than I thought.*

Behind him, he sensed Quano making a break for freedom back up the tunnel. Set could have taken him out with a single shot in the

back, but he decided to let him go. He always preferred to leave someone behind to tell the tale of his exploits, anyway.

A sharp crack suddenly echoed across the cavern. Glancing up, Set
saw one of the large stalactites from the ceiling plunging down to impale him. He rolled out of the way at the last instant, the deadly rock
spear exploding into fragments as it hit the unyielding cavern floor.
He ducked his head as the shower of jagged stone shards washed over
him, scoring the exposed skin of his neck and bare arms with hundreds of superficial, stinging cuts.

Blasterfire opened up again, but Set was already on his feet. Darting and weaving erratically, he managed to sidestep the shots as he
made a mad dash for cover behind another of the prominent rock
formations.

Momentarily safe, he took a second to catch his breath, glancing
up to make sure another potentially deadly stalactite wasn't poised
above him. He had no doubt who had fired the shots that had dis-
lodged the last one. He'd gotten sloppy, underestimating Draado and
the talismans.

It wasn't necessary to be trained in the ways of the Force to benefit from its power. It heightened the senses, made an individual
quicker to react and anticipate. What some saw as expertise with a
weapon or luck in battle was often really a manifestation of the Force.
Even if he wasn't aware of it, Draado was drawing on the power of
the dark side. And that made him dangerous.

Putting his pistols away, Set unclipped his lightsaber. *Playtime's
over.*

Leaning out from behind his rock, igniting his lightsaber, he
hurled it with a sidearm throw, sending it spinning horizontally on a
wide, looping trajectory. It circled the room once, easily slicing
through stalactites and miners before returning to Set's waiting grasp.

It had taken Set years to fully master the devastating power of the
lightsaber throw, but the attack was virtually unstoppable. Five of his

remaining opponents had been caught in the lethal arc it traced around the room. Only Draado had been quick enough to duck out of the way, saved by the power of the talismans he wore. But even with these artifacts, he was no match for a former Jedi Knight.

Set simply stood up and reached out with his free hand in Draado's direction, his fingers forming into a claw. The miner dropped his blaster, his hands flying up to his throat as he gasped for breath.

Set crossed the room, increasing the pressure on his helpless victim's windpipe. Draado collapsed to his knees, his face turning purple. The Dark Jedi stood above him, watching coldly as his life was slowly choked away.

When the miner's struggles finally stopped, Set bent down and stripped him of both the amulet and the ring. He resisted the temptation to put them on right away. From his apprenticeship under Master Obba he had learned that it was wise to study the artifacts of the dark side carefully before using them—their power often came with a cost.

He had what he came for, and he was eager to get off this civilization-forsaken world and back to the luxury of his home on Nal Hutta. Besides, the longer he stayed on Doan, the greater the chance he would run into another Jedi sent to investigate Medd's death. If he left now all they'd find would be the sniveling bartender he'd left behind, and he wouldn't be able to tell them anything they couldn't figure out for themselves.

So long, Quano. You better hope we never meet again.

As he made his way back up the long, winding tunnel toward the surface—the amulet and the ring firmly in his possession—he couldn't help but wonder if the Rodian would ever appreciate just how lucky he was.

7

In Zannah's opinion, of all the worlds she had been to—including the war-torn fields of Ruusan, the lifeless deserts of Ambria, the desolate gray plains of Tython—Doan was by far the least hospitable.

The entire surface of the planet had been gashed open in the endless quest for new minerals. Flora and fauna were nonexistent; everywhere she looked she saw nothing but dirt and rock. It was an ugly, ravaged world: by all rights it should have been devoid of all life. And yet the mining camps teemed with desperate beings scratching and clawing to carve out a meager existence for themselves.

Watching them, she couldn't help but compare them with her Master, whom she knew had grown up on a place like Doan: Apatros, a world rich in nothing but cortosis mines, owned by Outer Rim Oreworks, a corporation notorious for treating its indentured employees like slaves. But where Bane's brutal childhood and savage upbringing in the mines of Apatros had taught him to fight to survive, had helped forge his indomitable spirit, the miserable curs she had encountered on Doan were weak, deserving nothing better than servitude. Bane had ambition. Bane had strength. He had managed to rise above his surroundings. Through sheer force of will, he had cast off the shackles of his childhood and forged a new destiny for himself. He had risen from nothing to become the Dark Lord of the Sith.

It was time for Zannah to do the same. She would not allow herself to be like these pathetic wretches: weak, afraid, and enslaved.

Through power, I gain victory. Through victory, my chains are broken.

There was still the problem of finding her own apprentice, of course. But for now, she needed to focus on why she was here. Her investigations had revealed that she wasn't the only one interested in the dead Jedi. A man with long, silver hair—some called him a mercenary, others a bounty hunter—had been here not two days earlier, asking the same questions she was. Since then, she had been following his tracks: talking to the people he spoke to, and charming, bribing, or threatening them into giving her the same information they had given him.

She now suspected she knew why Medd Tandar had come here in the first place. It was common knowledge among the miners that a small cache of jewelry had been uncovered during a dig, and that the Jedi had come to Doan in the hope of acquiring the find. Zannah could only think of one reason why a Jedi would be interested in a few trinkets discovered in a long-forgotten tomb on an insignificant Outer Rim world—her Master wasn't alone in his obsessive efforts to locate ancient Sith artifacts scattered across the galaxy.

At first she had assumed the man who had been asking about Medd before her had been another Jedi sent to complete the original mission. However, it quickly became clear from the reports of his use of terror and torture to extract information that he was not a Jedi or even someone working for the Jedi Order. The trail of these reports had ended at a dilapidated cantina in one of the seemingly infinite mining camps. But she found the establishment closed, and Quano, the Rodian proprietor, nowhere to be found. With no more eyewitnesses, Zannah decided to have a look around herself, hoping for further clues.

Night had fallen, casting everything in near blackness. She tried the door and discovered that someone had smashed the lock. Not surprising, given the poverty she had seen. Pushing her way in, she picked up the faint odor of decaying flesh. She cracked a glow stick from her belt, filling the room with its pale green light. She was just able to make out two bodies on the floor.

Crouching by the first one, she made a quick examination. Doan's dry, dusty heat—combined with the general lack of airflow through the cantina—had partially mummified the corpse, slowing the decomposition process. The cause of death was obvious: a blaster bolt to the chest. His own blaster was still clutched in his hand.

It was obvious he wasn't Quano; the body was plainly human. And he didn't fit the descriptions she had been given of the man she was following. Based on his clothes and large muscles, he was probably one of the miners. She found the second body the same: a dead miner, shot in the chest.

Continuing her examination of the scene, she noticed that the shelf behind the bar was empty—but clear circles in the dust showed that until very recently, dozens of bottles had stood there. Whoever had broken in must have stolen all the alcohol . . . and left the two bodies where they lay on the floor.

A thorough search of the room turned up no trace of either the Rodian or the silver-haired man.

At the sound of someone fumbling at the door, Zannah covered her glow stick with her cloak and crouched low to the ground, a perfect statue hidden—she hoped—by the darkness.

The door creaked open and a shadowy figure slowly picked its way through the tables toward the bar in the back. Zannah waited to make sure the intruder was alone, then stood up and cast her cloak aside, bathing the room in the light of her glow stick.

A Rodian stood frozen, staring at her with wide, fearful eyes.

"Quano, I presume?"

"Who you?" he asked, his barely passable Basic made even harder to understand by the panic in his voice. Then he noticed the empty shelf behind the bar, and his face scrunched up in sullen anger. "You steal all Quano's booze."

"I didn't steal anything. I just came here to ask you some questions," she assured him.

The Rodian's shoulders slumped. Sighing, he sat down cross-legged on the ground, his head hanging despondently.

"More questions. You Jedi, too? Like other one?" He spoke with a tone of utter hopelessness, as if he realized he was doomed and had given up any hope of escaping his fate.

"A Jedi? You mean Medd Tandar? The Cerean?"

"No. The other one. Human. Long, white hair."

"I'm looking for him," Zannah admitted. "But what makes you think he was a Jedi?"

"Him got lightsaber. Use it to give Quano this."

The Rodian turned his head and pointed to his cheek. Moving slowly so as not to startle the obviously distraught fellow, Zannah approached until she was able to make out his scar. In the dim light of the glow stick she couldn't be sure, but the burn did appear to be consistent with that made by a lightsaber's blade.

She knew how to read people. The Rodian was like an abused pup, cowering as he waited for the next blow. Show him a little compassion, however, and he would react as if she had saved his life.

"He tortured you. You poor thing," she cooed, feigning sympathy even as her mind churned on the identity of the mysterious white-haired man.

A Jedi would never harm someone without just cause. Whoever

had done this wasn't one of the Order, but he did have a lightsaber. And he was skilled enough to wound Quano without accidentally slicing off half his head. She had heard tales of Dark Jedi—Jedi Knights who had fallen away from the teachings of their Masters to embrace the power of the dark side. Was it possible the man she sought was one of these?

More importantly, did Bane already know this? Her Master often kept secrets from her, and she had learned to always assume he knew more than he said. But if he knew there was a Dark Jedi on Doan, why had he sent Zannah to investigate? Was it some type of final test? Was she supposed to prove herself by finding and killing this potential rival? Or was Bane testing the white-haired man? If he proved strong enough to defeat Zannah, would he become her Master's new apprentice?

"Him wanted information," Quano whimpered.

"I'm sorry, Quano," she said, speaking softly as she gently placed a hand on his shoulder, "but I need information, too. I need to know what you told him."

As she did so, she reached out with a gentle push of the Force, nudging the bartender's will ever so slightly so he would be more inclined to tell her what she wanted.

"Him you friend?"

"No," Zannah assured him, using words to reinforce her subtle mind manipulation. "He's not my friend."

Maybe Bane was trying to force her hand, she thought; pushing her to act. Was he providing her with a suitable apprentice in the hope it would compel her to challenge him for leadership of the Sith?

"You want kill him?" Quano asked, his voice rising excitedly.

"That is a possibility," she answered, giving him a warm smile. *That, or make him my apprentice . . . assuming he doesn't kill me.* "But I've got to find him first."

"Him no here no more. Him go two days ago. Leave Doan."

"He came here looking for something, didn't he?"

Quano nodded. "Stuff miner dig up. Him take it. Kill miners. That when Quano escape."

"And you've been hiding ever since," Zannah guessed. "So why did you come back to the cantina?"

The Rodian hesitated, his bug eyes darting nervously between Zannah's face and the small wrist-mounted blaster peeking out from beneath the sleeve of her cloak.

"I'm not going to hurt you, Quano," she promised. "I'm not like him." *He enjoys hurting people. I only hurt people if I see some way to profit from their suffering.* "I don't think he's coming back." *Not if he's got the talismans.* "But I need to know something else, Quano. When that man left Doan, where did he go?"

She saw the Rodian flinch before answering. "Quano not know. For trueness."

"I believe you," she said, reaching out to gently pat his hand. "But I bet you know people who could help me find out, don't you?"

The bartender shifted uncomfortably, but another gentle push with the Force overcame his reluctance. "Quano has friend at spaceport. Him maybe find out."

"Can we go see him?"

"You want go now?"

Zannah smiled again, knowing it would help sustain the rapport she had established. "You can grab your credits from the safe first, if you want."

It was a two-kilometer walk from Quano's cantina to the nearest ground-shuttle station, a fifteen-minute wait for the shuttle to arrive, and then a forty-minute ride before they reached the spaceport. By the time they arrived it was well past midnight, and the Doan spaceport—never busy even during peak hours—was empty except for a few individuals assigned to work the graveyard shift.

Unlike the highly regulated ports on Ciutric, the authorities at the

Doan docks didn't bother doing any registration checks on incoming vessels. In fact, their only job seemed to be collecting the landing fee.

"Your friend," Zannah asked as she and Quano walked into the unstaffed gate, "what does he do here?"

"Cleaning crew," the Rodian answered.

Zannah wasn't quite sure how a janitor was going to be able to help her track down a ship that had left nearly two days ago, but she held her tongue as he led her into the arrival/departure area then out to the landing pad at the back.

The pad was small, barely large enough to accommodate a dozen midsized passenger shuttles. The vast majority of Doan's interstellar traffic was made up of either the personal vessels of the wealthy nobles, who all docked at private landing pads on their estates, or cargo vessels affiliated with the mining operations, which were handled at a different location. Individuals landing here at the communal spaceport were few and far between.

The landing pad was poorly lit by a handful of floodlights set on tall lampposts, but even so Zannah could clearly see there were only three ships on site, one of which was her own shuttle. Half hidden in the shadows near the edge of the landing pad was a young man slumped backward in a chair. He wore a crumpled custodian's uniform and an ID badge, his arms hung limp at his sides, and he was snoring loudly.

Quano walked over and kicked the leg of his chair, startling him out of his sleep.

"Pommat. Get up."

Looking around with the bemused expression of one only half awake, the young man shifted his position and sat up straighter in his chair. When his gaze settled on Zannah, his eyebrows arched suggestively.

"Hey, Quano. Who's your pretty friend?"

"My name is not important," Zannah said, speaking before the

Rodian could reply. "I was told you could help me track down a ship that passed through here two days ago."

When the man looked at Quano, the Rodian said, "Is okay. She nice. She friend."

The young man turned back to Zannah, crossing his arms and giving a derisive snort. "Yeah, right. A friend who won't tell you her name."

She could sense that his will was stronger than the bartender's, but still malleable. The fact that Pommat obviously found her attractive would help, too, if she was willing to flirt with him a little.

"I'm a friend who has credits," she replied coyly. "If you have what I need."

The man bobbed his head back and forth a few times before uncrossing his arms and running his fingers through his shaggy, sleep-ruffled hair.

Zannah arched one eyebrow playfully and reached out with the Force. "Come on, Pommat. I'm not looking for the strong, silent type."

"Yeah, all right," he relented. "Maybe I can help. What do you need?"

"A few days ago a man with long white hair arrived on Doan. Did he come through this port?"

She already knew the answer: unless the man had some connection to one of the noble families, this was the only port for a thousand kilometers. But a basic tactic in negotiations was to get the other person to start giving you affirmative answers to simple questions. It made them more likely to agree with you on more important matters later on.

"Oh, yeah. I remember him. Nice ride. State-of-the-art shuttle. Custom interior. Top of the line. Even nicer than yours."

"How would you know what the interior of my shuttle is like?" Zannah asked suspiciously.

There was a brief pause, then both Quano and Pommat burst out laughing.

"Him smuggler," the Rodian explained when he caught his breath.

"Not exactly," Pommat clarified. "It's just a little side racket I've set up. Something to help pay the bills, you know?"

"No," Zannah said darkly. "I don't know. Why don't you tell me."

"Whoa, you got a little fire in you, doll," Pommat said appreciatively. "Let me break it down for you. At night, I'm the only one working here. I can pretty much do anything I want. Including breaking into somebody's shuttle."

"You're not worried about security systems?"

"Never ran across one I couldn't slice," he said, puffing out his chest. "It's one of my many talents. Maybe if you're lucky, I'll show some of the others later on."

"So you break into people's shuttles and steal from them?" Zannah clarified, ignoring his clumsy come-on.

"Nah. That'd be stupid. People would notice if stuff was missing. They'd report it to my boss. Wouldn't take long to figure out who was behind it."

"So what do you do, exactly?"

"You're going to love this," Pommat said with a sly wink. "Once I'm inside, I slice into their nav computer and download all the info onto a datapad. It gives me everything: the owner, any planets the ship is registered with, commonly plotted hyperspace routes. I know who owns it, where they've been, and which world they use as a home port."

"Clever," Zannah admitted. "But what use is that?"

"This is where it gets good," he promised, obviously pleased with himself. "I've got an arrangement with a guy on Kessel. Every month he sends me a shipment of glitterstim."

Glitterstim, or spice, was a powerfully addictive drug banned on most worlds. Doan, however, had no laws against importing it. *And nobody at the spaceports to enforce the laws, even if they did exist,* Zannah silently noted.

"I don't sell the spice here," Pommat continued. "Nobody has any money except the nobles. And they won't deal with the lower classes. But I've got contacts at the spaceports on a bunch of other worlds here on the Outer Rim.

"So let's say I slice into a ship's nav computer and I find out it's from Aralia. I reach out to my contact on that world, and I see if he wants me to send him a shipment. After we work out a price, I sneak onto the vessel while the owner's not around and I hide a stash of spice somewhere on board.

"I tell my contact where I hid it, give him the ship's registration, and he tells one of his buddies at the spaceport to let him know when it returns to Aralia. Then he waits until the coast is clear, sneaks on board, takes the stash, and transfers the credits into my account back here on Doan. The owner never has a clue!"

"Spice smuggling is a capital offense on Aralia," Zannah remarked.

"That's the best part. If the customs officials ever decide to search one of these ships, the owner goes down for the crime, not us. It's foolproof!"

The whole operation seemed rather petty and ill thought out to Zannah. She wasn't bothered by the fact that Pommat was willing to have innocent people suffer horrible fates just so he could make a handful of credits from time to time. What bothered her were the technical details. The operation had obviously been thrown together out of simple opportunity, but it struck her as inefficient and unreliable. But she wasn't about to ruin the rapport she had established by saying so out loud.

"I didn't realize I was dealing with a criminal mastermind," she teased, bringing a cocky grin to Pommat's face. "So when the white-haired man left, you snuck onto his ship and copied everything from his nav computer?"

"Got it all right here on my datapad," Pommat replied, patting his hip pocket.

"So you know his name? You know where he's from?"

"I do . . . but it's going to cost you."

Zannah smiled, and tilted her head in acknowledgment. "Of course. Name your price."

"Go big," the Rodian chimed in. "Remember, Quano get half."

Pommat shot his friend a disapproving look before stammering out his opening offer. "Uh . . . four hundred credits?"

She was in no mood to negotiate. "Deal." From the crestfallen expression on the smuggler's face, she knew he was suddenly wishing he had asked for a lot more.

Reaching into her cloak, she produced four hundred-credit chips and handed them over to the young man. "Start talking."

"Ship's registered to someone named Zun Haako," Pommat answered glumly as he flipped two of the chips to Quano and slipped the remaining pair into his pocket.

"Haako's a Neimoidian name," Zannah pointed out. "The man I'm looking for is human."

Pommat shrugged. "Maybe the shuttle's stolen."

"I'm starting to think this information isn't worth what I paid for it."

"The registered owner might be fake, but the nav data's real," the young man assured her. "That ship came from Nal Hutta."

"You're certain?"

"No doubt about it."

"Just out of curiosity," Zannah asked, "is he carrying a shipment for you?"

"No," he replied, almost regretfully. "I don't do any business there. The Hutts don't like small-timers cutting in on their action, you know?"

"Probably a wise decision."

Quano barked out a laugh.

"What about my ship?" she asked, keeping her tone light. "Any hidden surprises on board?"

"Nah. You're the first ship that ever came here from Ciutric," Pommat replied. "I don't have any contacts back on your world.

"Unless you're interested in establishing a more long-term relationship?" he added, leering at her.

Zannah answered by whipping out her lightsaber handle and igniting the red three-quarter-length blades protruding from each end. She moved with the blinding speed of the Force, her first vicious slash severing Pommat's outstretched arm at the elbow and carving a lethal furrow across his chest while the second cleanly removed Quano's head from his body. Both were dead before they even had a chance to register an expression of surprise.

The deed done, she shut off her weapon, the twin blades disappearing with a low-pitched hum. She didn't kill without reason, but once Pommat revealed that he knew she was from Ciutric she had no choice but to eliminate both him and Quano. The Jedi might still come to investigate Medd's death, and she couldn't risk having them trace the shuttle back to her and Bane's estate. She didn't like loose ends.

Crouching down, she removed the datapad from Pommat's pocket, along with the credit chips she had given him. Then she did the same with Quano before loading the bodies, along with the dismembered bits, onto a nearby hoversled used to move heavy baggage around the spaceport. If any Jedi did come snooping around she didn't want to leave any signs that someone with a lightsaber had killed the two men.

Loading the corpses onto her shuttle, she took a last look around to make sure she hadn't left any witnesses behind. Satisfied, she made her way to the cockpit to prepare for liftoff.

The remains of her victims could be jettisoned into Doan's

sun just before she made the jump to hyperspace, leaving behind no physical evidence that could connect her to the world. After that, it was off to Nal Hutta, though whether she was going to eliminate a rival or recruit an apprentice, Zannah couldn't say for sure.

8

A soft beep from the console alerted Bane that the *Triumph* was at last approaching its final destination.

The journey to Prakith had taken longer than he had anticipated. Travel into the Deep Core was always dangerous; the densely packed stars and black holes at the galaxy's heart created gravity wells capable of warping the space–time continuum. Under such extreme conditions, hyperspace lanes were unstable, shifting or even collapsing without warning.

The last known route to Prakith had collapsed nearly five hundred years ago, and nobody had bothered to plot a new one since. This happened frequently with worlds in the Deep Core: if they weren't rich in resources or mineral deposits, the dangers of trying to find new hyperspace lanes simply didn't justify the effort.

In the centuries since the collapse of the hyperlanes, Prakith had basically been forgotten by the rest of the Republic. Even travel from nearby systems was risky, and Bane expected to find a planet that had stagnated after being cut off from the rest of society. Interplanetary trade was the lifeblood of galactic culture; without it populations dwindled and technology levels tended to regress to varying degrees.

Prakith's isolation had also allowed the Jedi to effectively purge all mentions of Darth Andeddu and his followers from galactic records, though Prakith itself was still mentioned in a handful of older sources. Bane had compiled all the known sources, including several hopelessly out-of-date navigational charts, in the hope of relocating the lost world.

It wasn't impossible to travel through unmapped hyperlanes, but it was both slow and dangerous. Bane was forced to plot and replot his course multiple times, making hundreds of small jumps, moving from one star to its nearby neighbors, picking and choosing from a list of potential hyperspace routes generated by the *Triumph*'s state-of-the-art nav computer.

Despite being the best program credits could buy, the computer was far from foolproof. It operated on probabilities and theoretical assumptions derived from previously reported data and complex astrogational measurements made on the fly. There was no way to predict the stability or inherent safety of a given route until a ship charted it by going through; as a result each stage of the journey had the potential to end in disaster.

Traveling through uncharted space was more art than science, and Bane relied as much on his instincts as the mathematical calculations of the nav computer. By sticking to shorter jumps he prolonged the journey, but he was able to minimize the risk of the *Triumph* being torn apart by an unexpected gravity well or being crushed out of existence by a collapsing hyperlane.

This wasn't the first time he had braved the perils of the Deep Core. Ten years ago he had traveled to the lost world of Tython to reclaim the Holocron of Belia Darzu. The fact that he was now going to Prakith to retrieve another Holocron—this one created by Darth Andeddu—didn't strike him as mere coincidence, however.

What the ignorant dismissed as chance or random luck was often the work of the Force. Some chose to call it destiny or fate, though these terms were far too simple to convey the subtle yet far-reaching influence it wielded. The Force was alive; it permeated the very fabric of the universe, flowing through every living creature. An energy that touched and influenced all living things, its currents—both light and dark—ebbed and flowed, shaping the patterns of existence.

Bane had spent a lifetime studying these patterns, and he had come to realize that they could be manipulated and exploited. He had come to understand that as the power of the dark side waned, the talismans created by the ancient Sith tended to become lost. But in time the cycle would turn, and as the power of the dark side waxed full the chance for these lost treasures to be found again would bubble up to the surface. During these windows of opportunity, all that was required was an individual with the wisdom to recognize them and the strength to take action.

Bane had mastered these talents, yet he was unsure if he could say the same of his apprentice. Zannah was smart and cunning, and her powers in the dark side might be even greater than his own. But did she have the vision to guide the Sith through the invisible tides of history as they rose and fell?

He wondered how her investigation on Doan was progressing. He had hoped to return to Ciutric before her, but he had underestimated the difficulty of navigating through the Core. By the time he got back, it was likely she would already be there waiting for him. She would realize he had sent her away as a distraction, and she would be expecting betrayal on his return. The confrontation he had been anticipating would finally come to pass.

The nav console beeped again, and the view outside the cockpit changed from the blinding white field of hyperspace to reveal the Prak system: a small red sun surrounded by five tiny planets. Taking manual control of his vessel, Bane descended on the third—a forbidding world largely covered by active volcanoes, burning lakes of magma, and dark fields of sulfuric ash.

As he entered the atmosphere, the scanners picked up several small cities scattered across the inhospitable surface. The nearest was several hundred kilometers to the north, but Bane turned his ship in the opposite direction, heading for the vast mountain range that ran east–west along the planet's equator.

He didn't know whether Andeddu's cult still existed or not, but from the moment he had come out of hyperspace he had been confident their stronghold still survived. He could feel its presence on the surface of the world—a nexus of dark side energy pulsing like a beacon from the heart of the mountains.

As he drew closer, the ship detected a small settlement on the edge of the range. Surprisingly, an automated landing beacon was emitting a signal on standard channels. That meant there was still an active spaceport, though it was probably used by shuttles traveling from one location on the planet's surface to another, rather than visitors from offworld.

Bane's theory was confirmed when he brought his shuttle in to touch down at the small landing pad on the edge of the settlement. The only other person on site was an old man sitting in a chair outside a small, dilapidated customs booth. He watched curiously as Bane emerged from the ship, but made no effort to rise.

"Don't see too many visitors lately," he said as Bane approached. "You from Gallia?"

From his research, Bane knew that Gallia was one of Prakith's larger cities. The man was assuming he was a native of Prakith; the idea that someone from outside their system would come to visit obviously hadn't even crossed his mind.

"That's right," Bane said, seeing no reason to complicate the situation by revealing the truth. "I flew in from Gallia. I'm looking for information on Darth Andeddu's followers."

The man leaned forward in his chair and spat on the ground. "We don't like to talk about them." He fixed Bane with a suspicious stare, spat again, then sat back in his chair and crossed his arms defiantly. "I got nothing else to say to you. Go back to Gallia. You aren't welcome here."

Bane could have pressed the issue, but he saw no benefit in intimidating or torturing an insignificant, irritable old man. Instead, he turned away and began walking in the direction of the buildings on the horizon. He was confident that someone there would be willing to tell him what he wanted to know.

————

A few hours later Bane was back in his shuttle, armed with the information he needed. Despite the old man's declaration, he'd found people were only too eager to share what they knew about the strange, insular cult deep in the neighboring mountains.

It was clear that Andeddu's followers were still active; occasionally some of them even came into the small town in need of supplies. It was also clear that the people in the mountain village regarded their mysterious neighbors with a combination of fear and loathing. Estimates of their numbers ranged from a few dozen to more than a thousand, though Bane suspected the truth was somewhere closer to the low end. Beyond that, everything else fell under the headings of wild speculation or illogical superstition.

Drawn by the unmistakable power of the dark side emanating from his target, Bane dropped the *Triumph* lower and began to weave in among the tall black peaks. As he flew deeper into the range, he began to notice increased signs of recent seismic activity. Some of the mountains were over twenty kilometers tall but most were half that height, their tops blown off when the molten lava at their core erupted in a shower of smoke and fire.

It wasn't long before the stronghold itself came into view, a towering structure built on the flat plain of a valley hidden deep within the heart of the range. A four-sided, flat-topped pyramid chiseled from black obsidian, the two-hundred-meter tall building was part fortress and part monument to a self-proclaimed god.

From the stories of the townspeople, Bane had learned that Andeddu had been worshiped as a deity during his long, long life before being overthrown. Yet even after his betrayal and death, a small cult of devoted followers believed his spirit still existed. They had continued their loyal service, preparing themselves for the day their Master would return.

Prakith's long isolation from the rest of the galaxy had only served to strengthen his followers' resolve. Those who lived in the temple now were described by everyone he spoke to as fanatics, and Bane suspected each would be willing to sacrifice his or her life to protect Andeddu's Holocron.

Bane throttled back his shuttle, searching for a place to touch down. Ribbons of lava crawled down from the surrounding peaks and crisscrossed their way across the valley. The malevolent power emanating from the stronghold kept the deadly streams at bay, but any landing site he chose on the ground would be at risk. He had no intention of acquiring the Holocron, only to return and discover that his ship had disappeared beneath a slow-flowing river of magma.

There was one option: the flat top of the stronghold, no doubt constructed in the first place as a landing site. He would have preferred not to risk alerting anyone inside the pyramid by landing on it, but it seemed he had no choice. There was a time for subtlety, and a time for strength. He circled the pyramid once, then brought the shuttle in for a perfect landing on the landing pad.

Moving quickly, he sprang from the cockpit and raced outside, lightsaber already drawn. Through the Force, he could sense the chambers in the building beneath his feet explode in a flurry of activity as the cultists rallied to meet the unexpected intruder.

He glanced quickly around, taking stock of his surroundings. The roof was square, thirty meters across on each side, with a small hatch built into one corner. At that moment, the hatch burst open and beings he assumed were cultists began to pour out—nearly two dozen in total, all armed with vibroblades and clubs.

Despite their numbers, Bane instantly realized they posed no real threat. Though they worshiped one of the ancient Sith, these were ordinary men and women. The Force did not flow through their veins; they were nothing but fodder. Their fury might be fueled by the dark side energies emanating from the temple, but Bane could just as easily draw upon the same power, letting it build until he unleashed it against his foes.

A decade earlier he would have eagerly engaged them in physical combat, his body pumped full of adrenaline released by the orbalisks that had covered his flesh. Swept up in a mindless rage, he would have carved a bloody swath through their numbers, hacking and slashing at his helpless enemies while relying on the impenetrable shells of the orbalisks to protect him from their blows.

But the orbalisks were gone now. He was no longer invulnerable to physical attacks, yet he was also no longer a slave to the primal bloodlust that used to overwhelm him. Free from the parasitic infestation, he was able to dispatch his enemies using the Force rather than relying solely on brute strength.

Bane extinguished his weapon and stood perfectly still, allowing the swarming horde to close in on him as he gathered his strength. He called upon the power of the temple itself, feeding on it to bolster his own abilities as he created a deadly field around his body. It began as a tight circle, but quickly spread outward until it extended to a radius of ten meters, with the Sith Lord at the center. The air within the circumference of the field suddenly became darker, as if the light from the red sun above had been suddenly dimmed.

Cloaked in the shadowy gloom, Bane simply held his ground

against the enemy assault. The front ranks of onrushing cultists shrieked in agony as they entered the field, their life essence violently sucked out of their bodies, aging them a thousand years in only a few seconds. Muscles and tendons atrophied instantaneously; their skin withered and shrank, pulling tight across their bones. Eyes and tongues shriveled, turning them into mummified husks before their desiccated flesh crumbled away, leaving only skeletal remains and a few strands of hair.

The effort of creating an aura of pure dark side energy would have quickly exhausted even Bane. However, as his enemies fell he was able to draw their essence into himself, feeding on their energies to revitalize his fading strength and reinforcing the field in preparation for the next wave of victims.

The mass of cultists continued to charge forward. Those in the middle ranks had seen the fate of their companions and tried desperately to stop. But the momentum of those behind swept them forward into the field to suffer the same agonizing death as those who had already fallen.

Only those at the very rear of the crowd were able to see the danger and pull up in time to save themselves. Of the more than twenty cultists who had attacked him, only a handful were able to save themselves. They stood at a safe distance, hovering on the edge of the deadly field with weapons raised, uncertain how to proceed.

Bane ended their confusion by letting the field drop and drawing his lightsaber. His opponents were too slow and too few to challenge him, and their crude vibro-weapons couldn't even parry his glowing blade. Completely helpless against a superior foe, their mindless devotion to Andeddu still compelled them to attack the invader of the sacred temple. Bane cut them down like dogs.

No more cultists emerged from the hatches to attack him, but Bane could sense nearly a hundred more in the temple below him. The ones he had slain on the roof were the warriors, guardians sent up by the priests and attendants still huddled in the rooms and corridors of the pyramid.

The remaining enemies were potentially more dangerous: the priests of Andeddu had no doubt ascended to their positions because of their affinity for the Force. Their training was probably limited, and Bane knew no single one among them was powerful enough to stop him. Together, though, they might have the potential to overwhelm him. However, he didn't intend to give them time to organize so they could attempt to unite their strength.

Moving quickly, Bane strode over to the hatch. Sometime during the battle it had been closed, and he discovered it had been locked from the inside. Letting the Force flow through him, he clipped his lightsaber and crouched down to grip the handle with both hands. Bracing his massive shoulders, he wrenched the metal hatch open, yanking it off its hinges and tossing it aside.

He jumped down the steep staircase revealed below, landing in a sloping corridor that led deeper into Andeddu's stronghold. Igniting his lightsaber again, he moved with long, quick strides as he made his way unerringly through the labyrinthine halls, drawn by the power of Andeddu's Holocron calling to him from the lower chambers.

The interior architecture reminded him of the Sith Academy on Korriban: ancient stone walls, heavy wooden doors, and narrow halls dimly lit by torches sputtering in sconces along the wall. As he marched through the corridors, Bane sensed the occasional presence of one or two individuals on the other side of the doors he passed. Most simply cowered in their rooms, allowing him to continue on unhindered; they could sense his power, and they knew that interfering with his quest would only result in their pointless deaths. Every so often, however, a cultist whose devotion to Andeddu outweighed all sense of self-preservation would spring out to try to stop him.

Bane responded to each of these attacks with brutal efficiency. Some he sliced in two with a single swipe of his lightsaber; with others he used the Force to cleanly snap their necks, never even breaking stride. By the time he reached the central chamber of the stronghold, all pretense of resistance was gone. Anyone still left in the temple had retreated to the lowest chambers, fleeing his wrath.

Here at the heart of the pyramid Andeddu's followers had built a shrine to their Master. Glow lamps in each corner illuminated the room with their eerie green light. The walls were covered with murals depicting images of the God-King unleashing his power against the armies of those who opposed him, and a great stone sarcophagus lay in the center, its lid carved with a relief of the long-dead Sith Lord.

In the Valley of the Dark Lords on Korriban, Bane had searched the ancient burial sites of the Sith who had come before him. Each of these, however, had been empty. Over the centuries the Jedi had stripped away anything of value or dark side power from the world, secreting the treasures away in their Temple on Coruscant for safe-keeping.

Here, however, Bane had found what had been lost on Korriban. The isolation that had allowed the Jedi to purge Andeddu from the galactic records had kept his resting place safe from their looting. The sarcophagus on Prakith had been undisturbed for centuries. Inside, the Dark Lord's most prized possession waited to be claimed by one worthy of its secrets.

Entering the room, Bane noticed the cloying smell of sickly-sweet incense in the air. As he approached the sarcophagus, he could feel the scent crawling over him like a fine mist, clinging to his clothes. Finding a grip on one corner of the sarcophagus's lid, he leaned in and shoved. Muscles straining, he used all his great strength to slide it out of the way, the sound of grinding stone echoing in the chamber as the heavy lid grudgingly succumbed to his efforts.

Inside, Andeddu's mummified corpse lay on its back, hands clasped around a small crystal pyramid clutched against his chest. Reaching into the casket, Bane seized the pyramid and pulled. For a moment it felt as if the corpse inside was resisting him, its bony fingers refusing to relinquish their grip.

He pulled harder, wrenching the Holocron free from the hold of its dead creator. Then he turned and left the room.

On his way back to his ship, only a few of Andeddu's followers made any effort to stop him; those who did he brushed aside like gnats. He half expected to find a few dozen amassed on the roof against him in a last desperate stand, but except for his shuttle the roof was empty. Apparently wisdom and self-preservation had prevailed over their loyalty to Andeddu.

As it should be, Bane thought to himself. The leaders of the cult had realized a fundamental truth: the strong take what they want, and the weak can do nothing about it. They were not powerful enough to stop him from claiming Andeddu's Holocron, therefore they did not deserve it.

Bane climbed into his shuttle and prepared for liftoff. He couldn't help but think that if any of the cultists had been worthy, he would have left with more than just a Holocron: he would have taken a new apprentice, as well.

As it was, the search for Zannah's replacement would have to wait. He had what he'd come for. It would take many days to traverse the hyperspace routes leading out of the Deep Core, but Bane welcomed the journey. It would give him time to explore the Holocron in greater detail. And if all went as planned, by the time he arrived back home all of Andeddu's secrets would be his.

9

Paradise was anything but what it promised. The ironically named space station was located along a small hyperspace route branching off from the Corellian Trade Spine. Although technically under Republic jurisdiction, the quadrant was largely neglected by most major shipping corporations; it was known more for pirates and slavers than the transport of commercial goods. But, realizing that even criminals needed somewhere to spend their ill-gotten credits, a group of Muun investors had pooled their resources to create an orbital platform catering to a segment of Republic society shunned on more civilized worlds.

Lucia had been to Paradise more than enough times in her life. After her release from a Republic POW camp she had spent several years as a freelance bodyguard, and many of her clients had contracted her specifically to provide protection during their visits to the station. The jobs always paid well, but she only took them when there was nothing else available.

Though Paradise officially billed itself as a "full-service entertainment lounge," the reality of what transpired there was far more sordid than that innocuous term implied. Pleasure slaves, gambling, and illegal narcotics were available on hundreds of worlds and orbital platforms, most of them promoting themselves as hedonistic retreats for the rich and powerful—but generally law-abiding—citizens of the Republic. This was not the case with Paradise. The clientele here could best be described with a single word: scum.

Lucia's dislike of the station had been formed on her first visit, and each time she returned her opinion was further reinforced. As she made her way through the crowd at the Stolen Fortune—the largest of the six casinos on the station—she didn't see anything to change her mind.

Music was pumped in through overhead speakers, mingling with the general din rising up from the crowd. Humans, near-humans, and aliens all mingled freely, drinking, laughing, shouting, and tossing credits away on various games of chance. Pirates and slavers made up the bulk of the crowd, along with a few mercenaries, bounty hunters, and a handful of personal security personnel. Virtually everyone was armed. Pleasure slaves, both male and female, made the rounds offering drinks and other, more powerful indulgences for purchase. For the right price, anything could be bought on Paradise . . . even the pleasure slaves themselves.

The potential threat of sudden, lethal violence was an inevitable and generally accepted element of Paradise's culture. There were no security forces on board, and no official representative of Republic law had ever set foot on the station—not openly, at any rate. Autotargeting blasters mounted in the ceiling could be used as an extreme method of crowd control if anyone ever attacked the casino staff, but when it came to individual safety, patrons were expected to fend for themselves. Those able to afford the expense typically hired an entourage of bodyguards, but the average visitor had to rely on a prominently displayed blaster at the hip and the threat of retribution from friends to make others think twice about starting something.

Lucia didn't have any friends with her on this trip, but she had been here enough to know how to avoid trouble. She carried herself with an air of confidence, an unspoken challenge in the set of her shoulders and the tilt of her head that dissuaded others from approaching her. Besides, most of the conflicts started near the gaming tables, and Lucia wasn't here to gamble.

She was here because the princess had sent her to find the Iktotchi assassin known as the Huntress. The last time Lucia had come here she had also been looking for the Huntress, though that had been her decision, not Serra's.

At the time, Lucia hadn't known about the king's arrangement with the Jedi. She never suspected the assassin would kill Medd Tandar and set off a diplomatic incident. Yet even if she had, she would still have come for Serra's sake.

She had seen her mistress grieving for her husband. His death had torn a hole in the princess's heart, and after two months with no signs of improvement, Lucia couldn't bear to watch her friend suffer any longer without doing something.

The princess needed closure; she needed to see those responsible pay for their crimes. But though the king had sent his troops in search of Gelba and her followers, they had made no progress in tracking her down. And so Lucia had taken matters into her own hands.

Going behind the king's back to hire an assassin was a clear breach of Doan law and a direct violation of the oath she had taken when she was sworn into the Royal Guard. But this went beyond any oath or vow. Serra was her friend, and her friend had been wronged. She couldn't bring her husband back, but she could see that those responsible for his death were punished. That was what you did as a friend: you put the needs of each other above everything else. You were loyal to your own.

That was the reason Lucia had joined Kaan's armies in the New Sith Wars twenty years ago. She didn't care one way or the other about the dark side, or the Sith, or even destroying the Republic. She had been a young woman with no family or friends. No prospects. No future. When the Sith recruiter came to her world, he offered her something nobody else had: a chance to be part of something greater than herself; a chance to belong.

She had found that sense of belonging during her time as a sniper with the Gloom Walkers. The other members of the unit became like her family. She would have given her life to save any one of them, and she knew they would have done the same. And if she couldn't save someone, she would do the next best thing and honor their memory by avenging their death.

That's what happened with Des. Although Lieutenant Ulabore was the official commander of the Gloom Walkers, everyone knew Sergeant Dessel was the real leader of the squad. A miner from Apatros, he had been a giant of a man: two meters tall and 120 kilograms of pure muscle, with an instinct for battle and a knack for keeping his fellow soldiers alive in impossible situations. Des had risked his own life to save the unit more times than Lucia could even remember.

Thinking back on what had happened to Des still filled her with anger. While stationed on Phaseera, the Gloom Walkers had been given orders to attack a heavily fortified Republic installation before sundown . . . a suicide mission that would have seen the entire unit get slaughtered. When Des suggested to the lieutenant that they wait until after nightfall, Ulabore had refused to listen. The kriffing coward would have sacrificed them all rather than tell his superiors that they were making a mistake.

Unwilling to march his friends into certain death, Des took charge of the situation. He knocked Ulabore out and took command of the unit, changing the plan so they would strike under cover of darkness. The mission turned out to be a complete success: the enemy forces were wiped out with minimal casualties, securing a major victory for the Sith war effort.

Des should have been hailed as a hero for his actions. Instead, Ulabore had him arrested and court-martialed for insubordination. Lucia could still remember the military police leading Des away in cuffs. She would have shot Ulabore right then and there if Des hadn't seen her slowly raising her weapon and shaken his head. He knew there was nothing anyone could do to save him; there were too many MPs around, all with weapons drawn. Anyone trying to help Des would be killed, and he would still end up getting court-martialed. Even as he was being led away to face certain execution, Des was still looking out for his friends.

Lucia never saw Des again; never heard what happened to him, although she could easily guess. Insubordination was a capital offense, and the Sith weren't known for leniency. But though she couldn't save him, she could still do something to repay him.

It took almost a month before she got the chance, but she wasn't about to forget. It came during a skirmish against Republic troops on Alaris Prime. The Gloom Walkers were on patrol when they stumbled into an ambush—something that never would have happened if Des had still been with them. But their sergeant had taught them well, and even without him the Gloom Walkers were still one of the best units in the Sith army. The encounter only lasted a few minutes before the Republic soldiers broke ranks and fled.

The intense, close-quarters fighting resulted in several casualties on both sides. Among them was Lieutenant Ulabore. His status was officially registered as killed in action, and nobody in the Gloom Walkers ever bothered to report that he had been shot in the back from point-blank range.

There were some who might consider her a bad person for what she had done, but Lucia never regretted her decision. To her, it was simple. Des was her friend. Ulabore was responsible for his death. It had been the same with Serra. The princess was her friend. Her husband was dead. Gelba was responsible. It was all about loyalty.

And so Lucia had made the trip to Paradise. A few discreet inquiries, along with significant sums of credits changing hands, led her to the Huntress. Two weeks later, Gelba was dead. Now Serra wanted her to hire the assassin again . . . though Lucia had no idea why.

Something had happened to Serra during their visit to the Jedi Temple on Coruscant. She had seen something upsetting, something she hadn't wanted to talk about. Lucia knew there were secrets in the princess's past, but she had always respected her right to privacy. After all, there were things in her own past she didn't want people poking their noses into, either.

Yet even though she had agreed to help, she was worried about her mistress. Serra was basically a kind and gentle person, but there was another side to her as well. She had nightmares, and sometimes she would go into dark depressions. Lucia suspected she had been scarred by some traumatic event in her childhood—a memory so intense, it had damaged her in a deep and fundamental way.

The sight of the Huntress seated at one of the viewing tables near the edge of the casino refocused her thoughts on the task at hand. The Stolen Fortune, like all the casinos on Paradise, overlooked the arena built at the center of the orbital platform. Through the large transparisteel windows patrons could watch combatants—typically beasts or slaves—fight to the death.

While it was common for bettors to wager on the outcome of each battle, Lucia realized that couldn't be the case with the Huntress. Iktotchi were rumored to have telepathic and precognitive powers, and as a result they were barred from gambling at virtually every casino in the galaxy. Lucia realized she had to be enjoying it purely for the brutality of the kill.

The Huntress was seated in the farthest corner, her back to one wall. She was dressed in the same black cloak she had worn during their previous encounter. Her heavy hood was thrown back to reveal the horns that curled down to her shoulders, framing her sharp features.

Lucia could only see her in profile, the black tattoos tracing down from her lips hidden by the angle and the shadows in the corner. From this perspective there was something striking about the red-skinned Iktotchi, a grace and elegance she had never noticed before.

She could have been beautiful, she thought with some surprise. *But she chose to turn herself into a demon.*

The Huntress glanced up as she approached, and Lucia froze—fixed in place by her piercing yellow eyes.

"I've been expecting you," the Iktotchi said, her voice barely audible over the music and crowd.

"Expecting me?" Lucia replied, too stunned to say anything else. Maybe she really could read minds and see the future.

"There was collateral damage during my mission on your world," the Huntress explained. "The Jedi. I expect your mistress was displeased."

Lucia shook her head. "That's not why I'm here."

"Good. Because I don't give refunds."

"I want to hire you again."

The Iktotchi tilted her head, considering for a second before nodding. Lucia took a seat at the table across from her. Out of the corner of her eye she could see into the arena, where two monstrosities covered in fur and blood tore at each other with claws, tusks, and teeth. One appeared to be an Endorian boarwolf; the other was some type of three-headed canine abomination.

"A terbeast," the Huntress explained, though whether she read Lucia's mind or simply the confusion on her face wasn't clear.

Lucia turned her head away in disgust.

"You have other rebels you want me to eliminate?" the assassin guessed.

"No." *At least I don't think so.* "My mistress wishes to meet with you in person. On a world called Ambria."

The assassin's eyes narrowed suspiciously. "Why Ambria?"

"I don't know," Lucia answered honestly. "She wouldn't tell me. She only said she wants to meet you there, alone. She is willing to pay triple your normal rate."

She slid a datapad across the table. "Here is the location."

Lucia was certain she would refuse. It sounded too much like a trap. But the Huntress simply sat back in her chair and didn't speak for a very long time. She almost seemed to slip into some type of trance.

Waiting patiently, Lucia did her best to ignore the bloody show playing out in the arena. She didn't approve of killing for sport or pleasure—it seemed pointless and cruel. Despite her refusal to watch, a roar from the tables along the viewing windows told her the match had ended; one of the animals must have dealt a fatal wound to the other. Instinctively, she turned her head to see the result and was greeted with the sight of the terbeast's three heads burrowing into the torn belly of the boarwolf in a race to feast on its organs.

She turned away quickly, struggling to control her rising gorge.

"Tell your mistress I accept her offer," the Huntress said, reaching out to seize the datapad with the thick, stubby fingers that were common to her species.

Their business done, the assassin turned her attention back to the arena, the hint of a smile playing across her painted lips as she watched.

Disgusted, Lucia stood up and gave a curt nod before turning to go, eager to leave the station as quickly as possible. The Huntress, seemingly enraptured by the gruesome spectacle below, didn't seem to notice her departure.

10

Zannah had never actually set foot on Nal Hutta before, but she knew the world well enough by reputation. While the ruling Hutt clans had entirely covered the surface of Nar Shaddaa, the nearby moon, with a sprawling cityscape, Nal Hutta remained largely undeveloped. The planet's predominant natural terrain of marshland had been poisoned by the pollution spewing unchecked from industrial centers scattered across the world, turning the surface into a cesspool of fetid swamps capable of supporting only mutated insect life. The capital city of Bilbousa huddled beneath a perpetual sky of greasy-gray smog punctuated only by dark clouds drizzling acid rain on the stained and pockmarked buildings below.

The physical ugliness of the world was mirrored by its moral corruption. Hutt space had never been a part of the Republic, and the laws of the Senate held no sway here. What few rules there were had been handed down by the powerful Hutt clans that controlled nearby Nar Shaddaa, making Nal Hutta a haven for smugglers, pirates, and slavers.

But protection from Republic law enforcement came with a price. The Hutts considered other species to be inferior, and all resident aliens on both Nar Shaddaa and Nal Hutta had to pay a hefty monthly fee to one of the ruling clans for the privilege of living under their protection. The exact price fluctuated wildly, depending on the rising and falling fortunes of the respective clan, and it wasn't unusual for it to double or even triple without warning. In such cases, those who were unwilling or unable to meet the new price tended to disappear, with all their possessions and assets being claimed by the sponsoring clan, in accordance with Hutt law.

The bias against other species would have made it difficult for Zannah to get the information she needed. The port authorities on Nal Hutta had a deeply ingrained mistrust of outsiders asking questions, and it was unlikely any amount of credits could have convinced them to overlook their prejudices to tell her anything useful. Fortunately for her, however, Bane's network of informants and agents included several high-ranking members of the Desilijic clan, one of the most prominent, and stable, Hutt factions. In the familiar guise of Allia Omek, Zannah was able to use these contacts—along with the ship registration stored in the late Pommat's datapad—to track down the silver-haired man she had followed here from Doan.

She'd learned his real name was Set Harth, and there was a persistent rumor that he had once been a Jedi. She'd also discovered that he was incredibly wealthy. And while nobody she spoke with seemed to know the exact source of his vast fortune, all agreed his gains were almost certainly ill gotten. On Nal Hutta, that was generally seen as something to be admired.

One other interesting fact had also surfaced during her investigations: Set Harth was a fixture on the thriving Nal Hutta social scene. Despite the fact the city was a grimy, greasy pit ruled over by the oppressive clans of Nar Shaddaa—or maybe because of it—the non-Hutt residents of Bilbousa were prone to throwing lavish and extravagant parties, each one a celebration of hedonistic excess. Set Harth never failed to receive an invitation to these functions, and he was even known to host them several times a year.

By good fortune he was at one of these galas tonight, giving Zannah an opportunity to break into Set's mansion to try to gain a better understanding of the man who could possibly become her apprentice.

Her first impression was that, in many ways, his mansion resembled the estate Bane had set up on Ciutric IV: it was less a home than a temple of elegance and luxury in which no expense had been spared. A chandelier fashioned from Dalonian crystal dominated the entrance, reflecting the light from Zannah's glow stick with soft turquoise hues. The halls were lined with marble tiles, and several of the rooms Zannah inspected contained Wrodian carpets, each one woven over several generations by a succession of master artisans. The massive dining room could easily seat twenty guests at a table made from crimson greel wood. The desk in Set's study was even more extravagant; she recognized it as the work of the master craftsbeings of Alderaan, hand carved from rare kriin oak.

But the furniture paled when compared with the rare and expensive works of art that accentuated each room. Set had a penchant for bold, striking pieces, and Zannah was almost certain every one was an original work. She recognized statues carved by Jood Kabbas, the renowned Duros sculptor, landscapes from Unna Lettu, Antar 4's most famous painter, and several portraits that bore the unmistakable style of Fen Teak, the brilliant Muun master.

Clearly, the owner was someone who preferred the finer things in life. Bane's estate on Ciutric was supposed to give the same impression to visitors—all the extravagant art and opulent furniture was part of a façade, key to maintaining the disguise of a successful galactic entrepreneur. In Set's case, however, she wasn't sure the lavish décor was an act. There was a vibrancy here. Things felt real. Alive.

The more she looked around, the more Zannah began to believe that the Dark Jedi wasn't just playing a part: his home was a true reflection of his personality. Set obviously enjoyed spending his fortune on material goods; he craved the attention and envy it inspired in others.

The thought gave Zannah pause. Bane had taught her that wealth was only a means to a greater end. Credits were nothing but a tool; amassing a vast fortune was nothing but a necessary step on the path to true power. Materialism—an attachment to physical goods beyond their practical value—was a trap; a chain to ensnare the foolish with their own greed. Apparently Set had yet to learn this lesson.

That is why he needs a Master. He needs someone to teach him the truth about the dark side.

Continuing her tour, Zannah mounted a large spiral staircase leading up to the second floor. Running her hand absently across the fine finish of the railing on the balcony overlooking the sitting room below, she made her way to the rear of the mansion. There she came across Set's library. Hundreds of books lined the walls, but most were novels written purely for entertainment . . . works she wouldn't consider worthy of reading herself. One shelf did give her hope, however: a collection of technical manuals and guides authored by experts in more than two dozen widely varied fields. Assuming Set had actually read and studied them all, he was a man of broad knowledge and numerous talents.

At the back of the library was a nondescript door; beyond it, Zannah could sense the power of the dark side. It called out to her, like the vibrations of a churning engine thrumming through the floor. Approaching carefully, she felt the power grow. It wasn't coming from any person or creature; she knew the sensation of a living being attuned to the Force. This was different. It reminded her of the invisible pulses of energy she had felt emanating from the Force crystals she had used to construct her lightsaber.

She tested the door and was surprised when it opened easily. Obviously, Set was confident in his privacy—but then, he no doubt had never suspected that a Sith might come to visit. Stepping into the room, she found it small and plain next to the rest of the mansion. There were no works of art, and the only furnishing was a display case set against the back wall a few meters away. By the light of her glow lamp, she could see an array of jewelry carefully arranged in the display case: rings, necklaces, amulets, and even crowns, all imbued with the power of the dark side.

Zannah had seen collections like this before. Ten years ago Hetton, a Force-sensitive Serrenian noble obsessed with the dark side, had shown her a similar trove of Sith artifacts . . . an offering he had hoped would convince Zannah to take him on as her apprentice despite his advanced age. Unfortunately for Hetton, his baubles and trinkets hadn't been able to save him—or his trained guards—when they confronted Zannah's own Master. Bane had shown Hetton the true power of the dark side, a lesson that had cost the old man his life.

Bane also collected the treasures of the ancient Sith, but he preferred the wisdom contained in the ancient texts. Zannah knew he looked on the rings, amulets, and other paraphernalia with disdain. The spark of the dark side that burned within them was like a single drop of rain falling into the ocean of power he already commanded; he saw no need to augment his abilities with gaudy jewelry fashioned centuries ago by ancient Sith sorcerers. Her Master believed true strength must come from within, and he had ingrained this belief in his apprentice. Apparently that was another lesson she would have to teach Set Harth, assuming he proved himself worthy of being her apprentice.

Zannah froze as she felt a sudden presence within the mansion. Reaching out with the Force, she confirmed her suspicions: Set had returned from his party, and he was alone. Extinguishing her glow rod, she moved in perfect darkness back toward the main entrance, letting the Force guide her path.

Slipping silently to the railing overlooking the large sitting room at the foot of the stairs, she spotted her quarry almost directly below her. By the light of the lamp on a nearby end table she could see him lounging on an exquisite leather couch, a bottle of fine Sullustan wine in one hand and a half-filled glass in the other. He was still dressed in the clothes he had worn to the party: a turquoise-blue shirt of fine Dramassian silk, tailored black slacks, and knee-high boots polished to perfection. The collar of his shirt was unbuttoned and its long, loose-fitting sleeves hung from his wrists, billowing softly as he gently swirled the wine to release its full body between each sip.

She made no attempt to mask her own presence; she was curious to see if Set would sense her through the Force the same way she had sensed him on his arrival. Much to her dismay, he seemed completely oblivious, lost in the comforts of his home and the enjoyment of his drink.

Zannah leapt over the railing and fell five meters to the floor below, landing behind him, silent save for the soft rustle of her black cape. Set shifted at the noise, twisting in his seat to fix his bleary gaze on the intruder.

"Greetings," he said with a smile, seemingly unsurprised by her arrival. "I don't believe we've had the pleasure. My name is Set Harth."

He raised his drink and tilted his head as if toasting her arrival.

"I know who you are," Zannah replied coldly.

Set carefully placed the wine bottle and his glass on the nearby end table, then turned back to Zannah and patted the cushion beside him. "Why don't you make yourself comfortable? Plenty of room for both of us."

"I prefer to stand."

Zannah was both confused and dismayed by his reaction. Instead of being guarded, wary, or even outraged at discovering an intruder in his home, Set seemed to be hitting on her. His tone was playful and suggestive. Couldn't he sense that his life hung in the balance? Couldn't he sense the danger he was in?

Set responded to her refusal with an easy shrug. "Followed me home from the party, did you?" he guessed. "Normally I wouldn't forget such a pretty face."

Zannah cursed herself as a fool. She had come here looking for an apprentice and found nothing but a womanizing fool too interested in making clumsy advances to recognize her power. Her failure was embarrassing; she knew with certainty Darth Bane would have seen Set for what he was right away.

"You still haven't told me your name," Set reminded her, waggling his finger in front of his face. "You're a very naughty girl."

The attack came the instant Zannah opened her mouth to reply. It came without any warning, Set moving with the preternatural speed of the Force. The Dark Jedi's lightsaber materialized in his hand, igniting and spiraling across the room toward her faster than thought itself.

Zannah barely managed to duck out of the way, the lightsaber's blade slicing off a section of her cape as she threw herself to the floor. By the time the weapon completed its boomerang path and returned to Set's hand, he was on his feet . . . as was Zannah.

She realized Set's initial greeting had all been an act. He had been waiting with his lightsaber up his sleeve the whole time, just looking for Zannah to lower her guard. Maybe there was hope for him yet.

"You move fast," Set noted, a hint of admiration in his voice.

His words no longer carried the light, easy tone of a guest at a party; he had dropped all pretense now. His blue eyes were sharp and focused, boring through his opponent searching for any weakness he could exploit.

Zannah braced herself for his next assault. In her mind the next few seconds played out in a thousand different scenarios, each unique in its specific details, each a vision of a possible future glimpsed through the power of the Force. The sheer number of possibilities could be overwhelming, but Bane had trained her well. Instinctively, she collapsed the matrix of probabilities into the most likely outcomes, effectively allowing her to anticipate and react to her opponent's next move even before it happened.

Set fired out a sharp burst of dark side power in a shimmering wave designed to knock her from her feet. Zannah easily countered by throwing up a protective energy barrier, the simplest and most effective way for one Force-user to defend against the attacks of another. It was a technique taught to every Jedi Padawan, and it had been one of the earliest lessons Bane had required her to master.

"You're a Jedi?" Set exclaimed.

"A Sith," Zannah replied.

"I thought the Sith were extinct," he replied, casually twirling his lightsaber in one hand, never taking his eyes off Zannah.

"Not yet." She stood still, her own lightsaber still tucked inside her belt. But she was wary now: Set had almost fooled her once, and she wasn't about to let it happen again.

"Let me see if I can fix that."

As he leapt over the couch toward her, Zannah ignited her own weapon. The twin blades sprung to life, and she fell into the familiar dance.

Set came in low to start, slashing at her legs. When she parried his incoming blade he spun away quickly, moving out of range before she could retaliate. With the Force he picked up a bronze bust on the side of the room and hurled it toward her left flank. At the same time, he dived forward into a somersault that brought him close enough to strike at her right side as he tumbled past her.

Zannah easily repelled both threats, her spinning blades slicing the bust in half even as she pivoted just enough so that Set's weapon missed her hip by less than a centimeter. For good measure she kicked him hard in the back as he rolled past, a blow meant not to disable him, but to goad him on to further aggression.

When two skilled combatants engaged each other with the lightsaber, the blades moved so quickly it was impossible to think and react to each move. Bane had taught her to rely on instinct, guided by the Force and honed by thousands of hours' training in the martial forms. This training allowed her to realize within the first few passes that Set was using a modified variation of Ataru, a style defined by quick, aggressive strikes. In only the first few moments of battle she had already evaluated her opponent, noting his speed, agility, and technique. Set was good. Very good. But Zannah also knew without any doubt that she was much, much better.

Set, however, had yet to come to the same realization. Her kick had had the desired effect: when he came at her the next time his face was twisted with snarling rage. His fury allowed him to call upon the dark side, making him even more dangerous as he unleashed his next series of attacks. Leaping high in the air, crouching low to the ground, lunging forward, springing back, spinning, twisting, and twirling, he came at her from every conceivable angle in a relentless barrage meant to overwhelm her defenses, only to have Zannah turn his efforts back with a cool, almost casual, efficiency.

Lightsaber battles were brutal in their intensity; few duels lasted more than a minute. Even for a trained Jedi, the effort of all-out combat was exhausting . . . particularly when using the acrobatic maneuvers of Ataru. It didn't take long for Zannah to sense that her opponent was wearing down. She, on the other hand, was barely winded. At Bane's urging, she had become an expert in the defensive sequences of the Soresu form. It was simple for her to parry, redirect, or evade her opponent's blows by using Set's own momentum against him, easily keeping the Dark Jedi at bay.

In their short encounter, she was presented with at least a dozen opportunities to land a lethal blow to the silver-haired man. But she hadn't come here to kill him; not yet, at least. She had come here to test him, to see if he was worthy of being her apprentice.

He didn't have to beat her to succeed in Zannah's eyes; he only had to show potential. Despite his inability to penetrate her defenses, she had seen enough to satisfy her. He may have been reckless and wild with the lightsaber, but he was also imaginative and even, at times, a little unpredictable. He had shown enough cunning when they first met to make Zannah underestimate him. And, most importantly, she could feel the power of the dark side raging within him as he grew more and more determined to take her out . . . futile though his efforts might be.

She was toying with him now, dragging the battle out. It wasn't enough for her to want Set as an apprentice; he also had to want her to be his Master. She had to prove her superiority so completely that he would be willing to serve. It wasn't enough just to beat the Dark Jedi; she had to break him.

When he was a step slow in retreating after one of his thrusts, she kicked his feet out from under him and sent him sprawling to the floor, only to back away and let him get to his feet again. When he moved back in, she twisted her lightsaber in a sharp, unorthodox move, hooking one of her blades onto his and wrenching the weapon from his hand.

Set sprang back immediately and used the Force to yank the hilt back to his palm, then stubbornly renewed his attacks. But as the seconds slipped by, the fire of the dark side was less and less able to fight off the fatigue setting into his joints and limbs.

It was inevitable that his weary body would betray him, and soon enough he came in with his blade held out too far to the side, instead of tight in front of him. Zannah stepped forward and snapped her foot straight up, catching Set under the chin. He staggered back howling in pain while a string of unintelligible profanities spewed from his mouth, along with a spatter of blood.

"Do you yield?" Zannah asked.

His only response was to spit a gob of blood onto the expensive carpet at his feet and rush forward once more.

Zannah felt a small twinge of disappointment. She had hoped he would be smart enough not to continue a battle he could not win. *Another lesson I will have to teach you.*

As he drew near, she responded not with physical violence, but rather with a powerful spell of Sith sorcery that attacked Set's mind. He tried to throw up a protective Force barrier in response, but Zannah's power shredded his defenses, leaving him completely vulnerable.

Sith sorcery was as much a part of the dark side as the deadly violet bolts of energy her Master unleashed from his hands, and when Bane had first recognized her talent for the subtle but devastating magics he had encouraged her studies into the arcane. From ancient texts she had learned to twist and torment the thoughts of her enemies. She could make them see nightmares as reality; she could cause their deepest fears to manifest as demons of the psyche. She could, and had, rip the minds of her enemies apart with a simple thought and a gesture.

With Set, however, she did not intend to destroy him completely. Instead she enveloped him in a cloud of utter despair and hopelessness. She reached into the innermost recesses of his mind and wrapped it in the nothingness of the void.

Set's eyes went blank, his jaw hung slack, and his lightsaber slipped from nerveless fingers. He slowly slumped to the ground, his eyes closing and his body trembling slightly as he curled up into a fetal position.

This was to be his final test. A weak mind would collapse upon itself to wither and die, leaving the victim forever comatose. If Set was strong, however, his will would fight back against the horror. Little by little it would tear away at the emptiness, refusing to die, clawing its way back to the surface until consciousness finally returned.

If Set was truly worthy of being her apprentice, he would recover from his current condition in a day or two. If not, she would simply have to begin her search anew.

11

The Huntress brought her shuttle in low over the desert wastelands that covered the majority of Ambria's surface. Though she had received no formal training, she was highly attuned to the Force, allowing her to feel it rising up from the sunbaked dirt as her ship skimmed across the surface.

Thousands of years ago Ambria had been a world of verdant forests, brimming with life and the power of the Force. But the lush vegetation had been devastated when a Sith sorceress tried—and failed—to bend the entire planet to her will through a powerful ritual. Unable to control the violent energies of the dark side, she was destroyed by her own spell . . . as was the landscape of the entire planet.

For centuries the corruption of the failed ritual influenced all life on Ambria, transforming the once beautiful world into a nightmare of stunted, poisonous vegetation and twisted, mutated beasts. Eventually the dark side energies released by the Sith sorceress were trapped in a great lake near the planet's equator by a Jedi Master named Thon, but the damage was too widespread for the world to ever be completely healed.

The Iktotchi knew all this not because she had studied the planet's history, however. Her connection to the Force allowed her to see things; it gave her glimpses of the past, present, and even possible futures. The ability was common to all Iktotchi in varying degrees, but the Huntress's talent went far beyond that of the rest of her species. Most Iktotchi would get nothing more than a subtle sense of danger when an impending threat was coming, or a general feeling of whether a new acquaintance might be friend or foe. On occasion they would be granted precognitive dreams, but even these were little more than random images that meant little without context.

With her, however, it was different. Over the years she had developed her skills so that she could control and direct the visions that flashed through her mind. When she concentrated on a specific person or place, she would get a rush of visual and emotional stimuli that she could often assemble into something useful and coherent.

She had meditated for several hours in preparation for her journey to Ambria, calling on the Force while thinking about her destination. In return, she had witnessed scenes plucked from the planet's history: the Sith sorceress as she was consumed by her failed spell; the Jedi Master's struggle to trap the dark side in Lake Natth.

But not all her visions were as clear, particularly those dealing with the shifting probabilities of the future. Her arrival and meeting with the princess from Doan had only been revealed in vague impressions. She was confident she wasn't walking into a trap. More importantly, she had the sense that somehow this meeting was going to have a profound influence on the rest of her life. For better or for worse she couldn't say, but she was certain the journey to Ambria would set her on a new path . . . and the Huntress was never one to shy away from her destiny.

The location for the meeting was a small abandoned camp located deep in the heart of Ambria's impassable desert. As it drew nearer, the shuttle's sensors indicated that another ship was already waiting on the ground. Readings indicated a single life-form on board; as promised, the princess had come alone.

The Huntress landed, shut down the engines, and made her way from the climate-controlled comfort of her shuttle out into the dry, suffocating heat of Ambria's midday sun. The princess was standing at the edge of the camp, facing away from her and lost in thought.

The camp itself wasn't much to look at; it was nothing but a small, dilapidated hut and an old cooking pot suspended over a ring of stones and charcoal. But despite the modest surroundings, the Huntress could feel this was a place of power: a nexus for both the light and dark sides of the Force. Despite the heat, the Iktotchi shivered. Great and terrible things had happened here; events that would one day shape the course of galactic history.

The princess—Serra, the assassin recalled—turned to face her.

"I'm glad you came" was all she said.

The Huntress sensed something dark and powerful in the other woman, a strength of will and a hatred nurtured over many years.

"Your bodyguard said you wished to hire me?"

The princess nodded. "They say you can track anyone. No matter where they hide, you can find them. They say you can see across time and space."

The statement wasn't precisely accurate, but the Huntress saw no need to explain the subtle intricacies of her talent to this woman.

"I have never failed a mission."

Serra smiled. "There was a man here. Many years ago. I don't know his name. I don't know where he is now. But I want you to find him. Can you do this?"

She didn't answer right away. Instead, she closed her eyes and reached out with her mind. She felt the Force gathering; it swirled around her like a rising storm, carrying the dust of memory imprinted on the campsite.

The captured memories encircled her; images flooded her mind. She saw a child, dressed in a frayed and tattered tunic; she saw the child blossom into a young woman; she saw the woman leave Ambria, only to return many years later as a princess.

"You grew up here," she whispered as she continued to probe even deeper.

Sometimes the history of a place was faint, washed away by the passage of mundane events and insignificant people. Here the memories were strong, preserved by isolation and trapped in the currents of the Force that permeated the camp.

"I see a man. Tall and thin. Dark hair. Brown skin."

"My father," Serra explained. "His name was Caleb."

"He was a healer. Wise. Strong. A man who commanded respect."

She didn't say this to please the princess; the Huntress never cared what her clients thought of her as long as they paid.

"There is another man," Serra told her. "He came to my father for help during the New Sith Wars. Tall and muscular. Bald. He was . . . evil."

Evil. Reaching out with the Force required intense focus and deep mental concentration. Even so, the Iktotchi couldn't help but notice the other woman's hesitation.

The Huntress had no use for words like *evil,* or *good,* or even *justice.* She killed those she was hired to kill; she gave no thought of whether they deserved their fate. Still, she found the princess's choice of labels odd. She was an assassin. She killed for profit. Was this any more evil than the man Serra spoke of? And what about the princess herself? She wanted to hire someone to take the life of another; did that make her evil?

She did not speak her thoughts aloud, however. They had no relevance to what she was doing. Instead she pushed deeper into the well of memories, submersing herself in them in search of the man Serra had described.

Hundreds of faces flashed before her. Male. Female. Human, Twi'lek, Cerean, Ithorian. Soldiers serving the Jedi, and even those serving the Sith. Caleb had healed them all. The only ones he turned away were the leaders of the armies. He saw himself a servant of the common folk. The Jedi Masters and the Sith Lords he always refused to help, with one notable exception.

The Huntress could see him now: a Sith Lord in black armor; the curved hilt of a lightsaber clipped to his belt as he towered over the healer. They were locked in a battle of wills, the big man dying from some illness she couldn't discern. Even though they were decades re-moved from the encounter, the Iktotchi sensed the raw power of the dark side emanating from him. It was like nothing she had seen or felt before, both terrifying and exhilarating.

"I see him," she told the princess. *I see what he did to you.*

"My father always said he would return. That was why he sent me away. Made me change my name."

"Your father was right."

Now that she had seen him in her visions, it was easy to skim the passing years looking for the imprint of the Sith Lord. Through the maelstrom of images, she easily picked out his next visit to the camp. Yet again, he arrived in need of the healer's aid. This time, however, he did not come alone.

"There are others with him. A young woman. A young man."

"What happened?" the princess asked, her voice trembling slightly.

A series of shocking and violent images assailed the Iktotchi's senses. She saw the healer's decapitated body, his limbs hacked from his torso and arranged in a gruesome display near the fire pit. Inside the cabin the young man crouched in a corner, a babbling idiot driven mad by the horrors that had been visited upon him. The other two—the young woman and the Sith Lord—were harder to see, though she sensed they were still there. Something concealed them; some power or spell cloaked their presence.

When she tried to pierce the veil something pushed back, snapping her out of her meditative trance and severing her connection with the past. She fell to her knees with a cry of anguish, clutching at her temples, her mind reeling.

Serra was at her side in an instant, crouching over her. "What happened? What did you see?"

The Huntress didn't speak right away. She had heard of this happening to others, but she'd never experienced it herself. It wasn't the images of Caleb's gruesome death that had caused her to recoil. It had been sorcery, Sith magic. A spell of concealment had hidden the Sith Lord and the young woman from the Jedi who had discovered the healer's body. The memories still carried the echo of the spell upon them; even after a decade it had been potent enough to momentarily overwhelm her.

How can one individual command such power?

"Tell me what you saw," the princess demanded, rising to her feet.

"Your father's death," the Huntress replied, also rising to her feet.

"He was there? The man in the black armor?"

"Yes. I think so. It wasn't clear."

"He was there," the princess said with certainty. "He was responsible for my father's death."

"There was another with him," the Huntress said. "A young blond woman."

"I only care about the man in black. Can you find him?"

"If he still lives, I will find him," the Huntress assured her.

She knew she would dream about the Sith Lord tonight, and for many nights to come. Her sleep would be filled with pictures and images from his daily life. She would see how many suns rose in the sky each morning on whatever world he called home; she would see their color and their size. Whatever moons and stars marked the night sky would be revealed to her. Familiar landmarks would bubble up from her sleeping subconscious night after night. She would cross-reference these with a database containing descriptions of all the systems and worlds in the known galaxy, narrowing her search down until she had his exact location.

It might take days, or possibly even weeks, but in the end she always found her prey. This time, however, she wasn't certain what the outcome would be. She had killed a Jedi on Doan, but this encounter would be far more dangerous. The lingering remnants of the Sith spell had been enough to thwart her efforts to peer into the past. How much stronger would the creator of that spell be in person? And who had cast the spell? The Sith Lord? Or the young woman with him?

She still intended to take the job, of course. But she was smart enough to understand that her odds of success would increase if she wasn't acting alone.

"This man is powerful," the Huntress admitted. "I don't know if I will be able to kill him without help."

"I don't want you to kill him," the princess replied. "I want you to capture him. I want you to bring him to me alive."

The assassin's lips twisted up in an angry sneer. "I'm not a bounty hunter."

"I'll pay ten times your normal price. And I'll hire mercenaries to help you. As many as you want."

"Even if we capture him, how are we supposed to keep him prisoner while we bring him back to you? Normal restraints can't hold someone who has the power to call upon the Force."

"Leave that to me," the princess replied, pushing past the Iktotchi and heading toward the small hut on the other side of the camp.

Curious, the assassin followed her.

Only a few meters on either side, the hut was little more than a crate with a doorway. On the floor inside, buried under a layer of sand that had blown in from the encroaching desert, were a tattered old curtain and a threadbare rug.

The curtain looked as if it had been torn down. The rug, on the other hand, was still spread out across the far corner of the hut, though its fibers were caked with dirt.

With the Iktotchi watching from just outside the doorway, the princess pulled the carpet aside, revealing a trapdoor built into the floor. A small ladder led down to a tiny chamber below.

"My father built this cellar to store the tools of his trade," Serra explained, climbing carefully down the ladder.

The Huntress entered the hut to get a better view, approaching the trapdoor and peering down into the darkness below. She heard a sharp crack as the princess ignited a glow lamp to dispel the gloom.

From her vantage point the assassin could just make out a series of shelves built into the cellar walls, each lined with jars, satchels, and other small containers. The princess rummaged through them quickly until she found what she was looking for: a nondescript bottle of a pale yellow liquid that she tucked into the folds of her clothes before making her way back up the ladder.

"Do you know what senflax is?" she asked once she was back aboveground.

The assassin only shrugged in response.

"It's a neurotoxin extracted from a rare plant found only in the jungles of Cadannia."

"What use could a healer have for poisons?" she wanted to know.

"It's not really a poison. Senflax is more like a sedative. One that allows the patient to stay conscious while numbing all pain and sensation. It disrupts the nerves of the primary muscles, paralyzing them, but it won't cause the heart, lungs, or other vital organs to shut down no matter how large the dose."

"Even a paralyzed Sith Lord can kill with his mind," the Huntress warned.

"Senflax also clouds the mind. It makes it impossible for the patient to focus or collect his thoughts; it takes away any semblance of free will. He can give simple answers to direct questions, but otherwise he is completely helpless.

"I saw my father give it to a pilot who had been badly burned in a chemical explosion," she continued, her eyes growing distant as she slipped back into the memories of her youth. "His friends brought him here, but by the time they arrived he had been driven mad with pain. The senflax took the pain away while leaving the pilot still able to answer questions about what chemicals he had been transporting so that my father would best know how to treat him."

"You're certain the neurotoxin will still work after all this time?"

The Huntress was aware that most people would have inquired about the fate of the injured pilot, but she wasn't most people. The only thing she cared about was the job she still wasn't sure she was going to accept.

"It should be fine as long as the bottle was sealed," Serra confirmed. "Once we get back to my ship I can test it for potency."

"Do you know how to prepare it properly?" the assassin demanded. "How to administer it? How quickly it takes effect and how long it will last?"

"I am my father's daughter," the princess proudly declared. "He taught me everything he knew about healing and medicine."

What would he say if he knew you were using his knowledge to seek revenge for his death? the Huntress silently wondered.

"I can show you how to use the senflax to keep the prisoner under your control," Serra continued. "So, will you take the job?"

The Iktotchi took her time before answering. It wasn't the money that intrigued her. It was the challenge; the knowledge that she would be pitting herself against a foe more powerful than any she had faced before. She couldn't see the outcome of the mission; too many conflicting forces were at work for the future to be clear. Yet she sensed that this was the moment she had been training for her entire life.

"I'd need at least ten well-trained warriors under my command," she said, speaking slowly.

"I'll give you twenty."

"Then we have a deal," the Iktotchi replied, her faint smile making the dark lines tattooed on her lower lip curl up like an animal baring its fangs.

12

The return trip from Prakith to Ciutric IV was taking even longer than the original journey. It should have been quicker, of course; Bane had already plotted the hyperspace routes that would lead him back out of the Deep Core. But in the hours he had spent on the volcanic world acquiring the Holocron from Andeddu's followers, several of the lanes he had used for the inbound flight had shifted and become unstable.

Two had already collapsed, forcing him to recalculate his journey. Statistically, the chances of this happening in such a short time span were astronomically small. However, statistics often fell by the wayside when events were influenced by the Force. There were too many accounts of those who had come into possession of powerful Sith artifacts falling victim to grim misfortune to dismiss the tales as mere coincidence.

Many believed the talismans of the dark side carried a curse; others claimed they were somehow alive, as if the inanimate materials used to make a ring, amulet, or Holocron could somehow achieve sentience. Those ignorant enough to believe in such superstition might have claimed that Andeddu's Holocron was fighting Bane. They would have declared the collapsing hyperspace routes were evidence of Andeddu's vengeful spirit trapped within the crystal pyramid seeking to destroy the thief who had defiled his sacred temple.

Bane knew there was no inherent malevolence in the Holocron; it was merely a tool, a repository of knowledge. Yet he also understood how far reaching the effects of the Force could be. A storm of violence swirled around items imbued with the magic of the ancient Sith; the strong could ride the storm to even greater heights, the weak would be swept up in its wake and destroyed.

Andeddu's Holocron was a talisman of undeniable power; Bane could feel the waves of dark side energy radiating from it. It was possible the fragile matrix of the Deep Core's space–time continuum had been subtly altered by these waves during his outbound journey, destabilizing the hyperlanes. He plotted a course of nearly one hundred brief jumps, minimizing the danger by spending as much of the journey in realspace as possible. It would take him nearly twice as long to get home, but it was better to be cautious than risk having his ship instantaneously crushed into a pinpoint singularity by the sudden collapse of a weakened hyperspace corridor.

Fortunately, he had a way to help him pass the time.

"Essence transfer is the secret of eternal life," the hologram told him.

Bane was sitting cross-legged on the floor of his ship, the Holocron resting on the ground in front of him. A three-dimensional image of Darth Andeddu, twenty centimeters tall, was projected just above the apex of the four-sided pyramid.

"The physical body will always weaken and fail, yet it is nothing but a shell or vessel," the hologram continued. "When it is time, it is possible to transfer your consciousness—your spirit—into a new vessel . . . as I have done with this Holocron."

Bane understood that the projection speaking to him was not the dead spirit of the ancient Sith Lord; it was only a simulated personality known as a gatekeeper. Every Holocron had one. A virtual guide programmed with the personality traits of the original creator, the gatekeeper served as a guardian of the information stored within the artifact.

The appearance of the gatekeeper often mirrored that of the Holocron's creator . . . or at least, the image the creator wanted others to see. Bane remembered how the gatekeeper of Belia Darzu's Holocron would often change appearance, reflecting her changeling heritage.

His own Holocron projected an image of Bane still clad in his orbalisk armor. Although the parasites had proven impractical in real life, the horrific appearance of his body covered by the infestation was more visually impressive and intimidating. It also hinted at the sacrifices one must make to embrace the true power of the dark side—a valuable lesson for any who would follow his teachings.

More importantly, the orbalisks masked his appearance and concealed his true identity. Should the Holocron ever fall into the hands of the Jedi while he was still alive, they would be unable to recognize him from the gatekeeper's image . . . an even greater consideration now that he was on the cusp of learning the secrets of eternal life. But first, he had to overcome the small but imposing figure who now stood before him.

Andeddu had chosen to represent himself as a heavily armored man bathed in a fiery glow of red and orange. Atop his head rested a tall, flat headdress reminiscent of a high priest, encircled by a thin gold crown inset with gems. His face was sunken and drawn, almost skeletal.

For the past four days Bane had played the gatekeeper's games in an attempt to unlock the secrets of eternal life. He had delved deep into Andeddu's Holocron, accomplishing in less than a week what would have taken others months or even years. He had suffered through the tedious lessons; he had listened to the tiresome philosophical rants of the holographic image. He had learned nothing new about the Force, though the gatekeeper's words had revealed much about Darth Andeddu's personality and beliefs.

Like many of the ancient Sith, he was cruel, arrogant, self-centered, and shortsighted. His lessons mirrored those of Bane's instructors at the Sith Academy on Korriban; lessons Bane had rejected decades ago as flawed. He had moved beyond their teachings. His understanding of the dark side had evolved. In creating the Rule of Two, he had ushered in a new era for the Sith. He had transcended the limited understanding of men like Andeddu, and he was done listening to the gatekeeper's ignorant litany.

"Show me the ritual of essence transfer," Bane demanded.

"The ritual is fraught with danger," the gatekeeper warned. "Attempting it will cause the current vessel to be destroyed; your body will be consumed by the power of the dark side."

Bane clenched his teeth in exasperation. He had heard these warnings at least a dozen times before.

"Choose your new vessel carefully. If you select a living being, be warned that their own spirit will fight you as you try to possess their body. If their will is strong, you will fail and your consciousness will be cast into the void, doomed to an eternity of suffering and torment."

The mention of the void always made Bane think of the thought bomb, and the hundreds of Sith and Jedi spirits trapped forever by its detonation. It reminded him of what he had accomplished; it reminded him of who he was.

"I am not some student cowering in fear before the unimaginable power of the dark side," Bane snapped at the hologram. "I am the Dark Lord of the Sith."

"Your title means nothing to me," the gatekeeper sneered. "I decide who is worthy to learn my secrets, and you are not yet ready. Perhaps you will never be."

Over the past few days Bane had come to this point too many times. He wasn't about to let the gatekeeper thwart him yet again.

Bane snatched the Holocron up from the floor with his right hand, ignoring the all-too-familiar trembling in his left. There was another way to get the knowledge he sought, but it was a path fraught with peril.

In the construction of his own Holocron, Bane had developed an intimate knowledge of how the talismans worked. Each was unique, a repository of everything its creator had learned during his or her long life. But there were similarities that were common to them all, including the one he now studied.

Andeddu's Holocron was a four-sided pyramid made of smooth, dark crystal. Arcane glyphs of gold and red were etched into each face, the mystic symbols focusing and channeling the power of the dark side. Inside was an intricate matrix of crystal lattices and vertices. The fine, interwoven filaments formed a data system capable of storing near infinite amounts of knowledge, as well as providing a framework for the cognitive networks required to create the gatekeeper's appearance and personality.

The entire system was controlled by the capstone, a single piece of black crystal perched atop the apex of the pyramid. Imbued with incredible power, the capstone stabilized the matrix structure, allowing the individual pieces of data to be accessed instantaneously by the gatekeeper.

However, it was possible to circumvent the gatekeeper ... but only by one strong enough to survive the attempt. If Bane's will faltered, or if the power of Andeddu's Holocron was more than he could handle, then his mind would be destroyed. His identity would be devoured by the talisman, leaving his body a mindless husk. It was a desperate gamble, but there was no other way to get what he needed. Not in time to help him against Zannah.

"If you will not give me what I want," he shouted at the gate-keeper, "then I will take it!"

Reaching out with the Force, he plunged his awareness into the depths of the pyramid's inner workings as the gatekeeper let loose a howl of impotent rage. Thrusting his consciousness directly into the capstone, Bane let his will invade the small four-sided talisman just as he himself had invaded the stronghold of Andeddu's cult back on Prakith.

For a brief instant he could feel the burning inferno of power trapped within threatening to consume his identity. Bane welcomed the pain, feeding on it and transforming it along with all the frustration and anger he had built up over the past four days into a raging, swirling storm of dark side energy. Then, bit by bit, he began to impose order on the chaos, bending it to his will.

Using the Force, Bane began to make subtle adjustments to the Holocron's crystal matrix. He began to manipulate the arrangement of the filaments, twisting, turning, and shifting them with subtle, immeasurable adjustments as he worked his way deeper and deeper into the data in pursuit of what he sought. In many ways it was like slicing a secure computer network, only a million times more complex.

With each adjustment, the gatekeeper's image flickered and cried out, but Bane was oblivious to the simulation's artificial suffering. For several hours he continued his work, his body perspiring heavily, until he finally found what he sought: the ritual of essence transference; Andeddu's secret of eternal life.

With one final push of the Force, he reached out with his mind and seized what he had been searching for. With the aid of the gate-keeper the information would have taken weeks to absorb and learn. Bane, however, had gone right to the source. The knowledge streamed directly from the Holocron into his mind, raw and unfiltered. Thousands of images flooded his consciousness, an explosion of sights, sounds, and thoughts that caused him to drop the Holocron to the floor, breaking the connection.

The gatekeeper's image vanished, leaving Bane alone in the ship, still sitting cross-legged on the floor. He was slumped forward, his breath coming in heavy gasps. His clothes were soaked in sweat; his body shivered with exhaustion.

Slowly, he got to his feet and made his way over to the pilot's seat. He walked with the stumbling gait of a man drunk on Mandalorian wine, resting his hand on the wall for support. His head was swimming, lost in the secrets he had wrenched from the Holocron's depths.

As he collapsed into the seat the control console began to beep softly. It took him several seconds to realize the latest hyperspace jump on his return journey was reaching an end . . . though there were still many more jumps to go.

He needed to plot a course for the next leg of the trip, but he was in no state to contemplate that right now. Not while his addled mind was still wrestling with what he had learned. He needed time to process the information from the Holocron, to wrap his head around it. To analyze and compartmentalize all the facts, arranging them into some semblance of rational thought.

Bane reached out and activated the autopilot, content to let the ship drift slowly through space while he recovered. Then he closed his eyes and let the darkness of sleep envelop him.

13

Consciousness returned slowly to Set Harth. It was as if his mind were swimming through a swamp, struggling to escape the murky depths of his own subconscious. Pushing up through the sludge he finally broke the surface, though the lingering memories of strange dreams and nightmares still prowled the dark corners of his mind.

On some level he was aware the nightmares had nearly driven him mad. They had been on the verge of destroying him, but Set had refused to succumb. Bit by bit he had managed to shove them back down into the hidden recesses of his mind where they belonged, separating fantasy from reality one small piece at a time.

How long was I out? he wondered, keeping his eyes closed and his breathing steady so as not to reveal he had woken up. *Feels like days.*

He was in his own room, that much he was sure of. He recognized the smell of his perfumed pillow, the soft feel of silk sheets against his skin, the luxurious comfort of his down-filled mattress. Everything else was still a blur.

Come on, Set. Let's figure this out.

Careful to avoid the horrors of his recent nightmares, Set

stretched his memory back, trying to piece together exactly what had happened to him.

The blond woman.

She had been waiting in his mansion when he returned home from the party. It wasn't the first time that had happened . . . though this was the first time his uninvited guest had tried to kill him.

Probably wasn't really trying to kill you, he reminded himself. *Seeing as how you're still alive.*

They had fought. That much he remembered clearly. They had fought and she had beaten him.

Though his eyes were still closed, Set was beginning to assemble a detailed image of his surroundings by reaching out with the Force. He was in his own bed, in his own room. But he wasn't alone. Someone else was there. The woman.

Claimed she was a Sith.

He still had no idea why she had broken into his home. He couldn't even guess why she had left him alive. But he was determined to make her regret it.

Pushing out gently with his mind, he scanned the room for his lightsaber. It was resting on his dressing table on the far side of the room. The woman was sitting in a chair at the foot of the bed, patiently waiting for him to wake up. Would he be able to use the Force to pull the lightsaber across the room and into his hand before she could react?

And then what? She already beat you once.

Maybe this time he could surprise her. Catch her off guard. Carefully, he began to gather his power.

"I thought you were smarter than that," the woman said.

Set froze. *Going to have to talk your way out of this one. Time to turn on the charm.*

He opened his eyes and gave an easy laugh.

"Can't blame a guy for trying," he said with a shrug, sitting up in bed.

He was still dressed in the same clothes he had worn to the party.

"That was quite an entrance you made last night," he said.

"Three nights ago," she corrected, returning his smile with a humorless stare. "I was beginning to wonder if you would be trapped in your nightmares forever."

Her words caused his mind to momentarily flash back to the terrors he was still struggling to suppress, and he shuddered involuntarily.

"I managed to find my way out," he answered, his voice grimmer than he intended. "What did you do to me? Some kind of drug?"

"If that's what you really think," she said, her lip curling up in disdain, "then I'm wasting my time here."

There was an implied threat in her words, and Set's survival instincts kicked into high gear.

Get on the ball, Set. You don't want to make this woman angry.

"Sorcery," he said after a second of deliberation. "You said you were a Sith. You attacked my mind with some kind of spell."

She nodded, and Set saw her shoulders relax. So she had been on the verge of killing him for his ignorance.

"Are you the assassin who killed Medd Tandar?" he asked, still trying to fit everything together.

The woman shook her head, blond curls swaying slightly.

She's attractive enough . . . if you can get past the whole Sith sorceress thing.

"You followed me here from Doan," Set guessed, desperately looking for some piece of information he could use. If he figured out what she was after, then he'd have something to bargain with. "You want the talismans."

"You're half right," she replied. "I followed you from Doan, but I'm not interested in the talismans."

Set wasn't used to being at a disadvantage. If he didn't have it, he was usually smart enough to figure out a way to get it. Here, however, he was utterly at a loss as to the woman's motives and goals. And so he had no recourse but to fall back on the one thing he hated most of all: total honesty.

"I have absolutely no idea what you want with me."

"My name is Darth Zannah," she explained, "and I am looking for an apprentice."

On one level, Set was even more confused than before. But part of his mind—the part that had kept him one step ahead of the Jedi for the past ten years—seized on her words. *Now you know what she wants. Figure out a way to use it.*

"Why are you looking for an apprentice?" he asked carefully, wary of enraging her with his lack of understanding.

"The Jedi believe the Sith are extinct," she began. "But you can plainly see by my presence that the Jedi are wrong. The Sith still exist, but now we number only two: one Master, and one apprentice. One to embody the power of the dark side, the other to crave it."

"So you want to increase your numbers," Set reasoned. "You're seeking recruits to join your cause and rebuild the Sith armies."

"That is the path to failure," Zannah replied. "The history of the Sith has proven that in greater numbers the Sith will always turn their hatred against one another. It is inevitable; it is the way of the dark side.

"The only way we can survive is by following the Rule of Two. Our numbers can never grow beyond this. The Master will train his apprentice in the ways of the Sith, until one day she must challenge him. If she proves unworthy, the Master will destroy her and choose a new apprentice. If she proves the stronger, the Master will fall and she will become the new Dark Lord of the Sith, and choose an apprentice of her own."

Set felt like things were becoming clearer now. "You are the apprentice. You think it's time to challenge your Master. And you want me to help you defeat him."

"No!" she snapped, causing Set to flinch in his bed. "That is the old way. Lesser followers would unite their inferior skills to bring down a strong leader, weakening the Order. This goes against everything the Rule of Two stands for.

"If I am to become the Dark Lord of the Sith, I must prove myself by facing my Master alone. If I am unworthy, then I will fall . . . but the Order will remain strong under his leadership.

"Do you understand?"

Set understood all too well. "The Rule of Two guarantees that each Master will be more powerful than the one who came before. It culls the weak." *Good for the Sith as a whole, but not so great if you're the one getting culled.*

Zannah may have been willing to sacrifice herself for the greater good of the Sith Order, but Set wasn't ready to do the same. Of course, he was smart enough not to say so out loud.

Instead, he asked, "What made you choose me?"

"I have been seeking an apprentice for some time now," Zannah explained. "When I stumbled across your path on Doan, I knew it was more than mere chance.

"You are strong in the Force, and you have rejected the Jedi and their teachings. You are intelligent and resourceful. But your potential is unfulfilled. You have not dedicated yourself to the dark side. In your quest for the talismans of the ancient Sith you are like a child playing with his toys.

"You have no thoughts of the future. No ambition. No plan. No vision. That will change if you agree to be my apprentice. Join me and I will show you your destiny."

"My destiny?"

"For thousands of years the Jedi and Sith have waged an endless war against each other. The Jedi believe the war is over. They think the Sith are gone. But we still exist in the shadows, planning our revenge.

"With patience and cunning, we are laying the seeds of our ultimate victory. Generation after generation our power and influence will grow until one day we will destroy the Jedi, and the Sith will rule the galaxy."

Set wasn't interested in ruling the galaxy. Or destroying the Jedi. It sounded like a lot of work. *It's not like you've got a lot of options. She's not going to just let you walk away if you refuse.*

Aloud, he said, "The Rule of Two dictates there can only ever be two Sith, so how can you take me as an apprentice if your Master is still alive?"

"If you accept my offer, you will accompany me as I go to face my Master," Zannah explained. "But you must not interfere. If he falls, then I will take you on as my apprentice."

"What happens to me if you fail?" Set wondered.

"If I die, my Master will need a new apprentice. If he judges you worthy, then you will replace me. If not . . ."

There was no need for her to finish the thought.

Set wasn't crazy about the deal, but he understood the position he was in. Refuse, and she would kill him. Accept, and there was a good chance he would die anyway if Zannah proved weaker than her Master. And even if she was victorious, he would be returning to the life of an apprentice . . . a life he had been eager to escape while he was with the Jedi.

But there was one thing worthwhile in Zannah's offer. He had been given a glimpse of what she was capable of during their one-sided battle in his living room. It might be worth a few years of following orders and calling her "Master" if he could learn to command that kind of power for himself.

"You said you can help me reach my full potential. Teach me how to unlock the true power of the dark side."

"If you follow me," Zannah promised, "you will become more powerful than you ever imagined."

———

Zannah could sense Set Harth's reluctance to become her apprentice. He lacked the burning hatred of the Jedi and what they represented; he had little interest in embracing the greater destiny of the Sith. But it was also obvious that he was tempted by her promises of individual power.

Set cared only for himself. He would accept her offer only because he saw it as a means to an end, a way to make himself stronger. Zannah knew this, and she was prepared to accept it. She would have preferred to find an apprentice eager to learn the Sith philosophies Bane had imbued in her, but in the lack of a better option she was willing to work with what she had.

She understood the risks, but nothing of importance had ever been accomplished without risk. Over the first few years of his training, she would keep a close eye on Set. She would be wary of treachery and deceit as little by little she exposed him to the greater truths Bane had taught her. She would use his lust for personal power as the bait to draw him deeper and deeper into the ways of the Sith.

In time Set would come to accept the teachings and philosophies as she had done. As his understanding of the dark side evolved, he would gain the vision to see beyond his own petty wants and desires. He would recognize their need to destroy the Jedi and he would embrace the ultimate destiny of the Sith.

And if he did not, then she would destroy him and find another to serve her.

All this was running through her mind as she watched the silver-haired Jedi rubbing his chin, contemplating the prospect of becoming her apprentice.

"I accept," he said at last. "And I am honored you have chosen me."

"No, you're not," she said. "But someday you will be."

14

"W"e should have force pikes for this job," Captain Jedder grumbled. "They've got twice the juice of these kriffing stun rifles."

"Force pikes can kill if you're not careful," the Huntress reminded him, though she was only half paying attention to the conversation. "The princess wants him taken alive. Besides, you'd never get close enough to use them."

They were inside the mansion of Sepp Omek, though the Huntress doubted that was the man's real name. Not that it mattered. She hadn't needed a name to track him here to the estate on Ciutric IV. The Sith Lord had covered his tracks well, hiding his true identity behind layers of middlebeings and go-betweens and making it virtually impossible for anyone to connect him to the events on Ambria through normal methods. But all his careful preparations couldn't guard against the Iktotchi's unique powers. Guided by the images in her dreams and her infallible instincts the Huntress had found her quarry, as she always did.

"How long till he gets here?" Captain Jedder wanted to know.

"Soon," she replied. "Tell your team to get into position."

Her visions had shown her the house would be empty when they arrived, just as they had shown her that the owner would be returning this very same night.

"Can you be more specific?" Jedder asked. "Twenty minutes? An hour? Two?"

"It doesn't work that way," she muttered absently, her eyes picking out locations for them to set their trap.

She had already scouted out the estate in detail, committing every room to memory as she had gone through and disabled every alarm and anti-intruder system on the grounds. She had even managed to slice her way past the security panel on the small building at the rear of the grounds. At first she had thought it might be some kind of arsenal or weapons bunker, but once she managed to open the door she realized it was a library. Instead of datapads or holodisks, however, the shelves had groaned under the weight of ancient leather-bound books and scrolls of yellowed parchment.

There was something else inside the building that had given her pause, however. Resting on a pedestal near the back of the library was a small, four-sided crystal pyramid. The Huntress had no need to steal from her victims; she had ignored the priceless works of art and other valuables scattered around the mansion. But there was something oddly compelling about this piece. Unsure what it could be, she had somehow felt drawn to it, and she'd slipped it into one of the pockets beneath her robe before continuing her investigation of the grounds.

Once she was done she had signaled for Jedder and the others that it was safe to come in and begin their preparations.

"Something wrong?" the captain asked.

"No," she replied, annoyed at herself for getting distracted. "Just looking for places to set your team up."

This job was unlike any the Huntress had ever taken before. It wasn't simply the mercenaries she was working with, or the fact she was supposed to take her victim alive. Ever since she had visited the small camp on Ambria, the tall, bald man and the blond woman had haunted her dreams. Some of what she had seen had helped lead her here to Ciutric, but there were other images, too: bewildering, troubling visions that she was unable to decipher.

She had been witness to dozens of battles between the pair. She had watched the man kill the woman, yet she had also seen the woman kill the man. She understood these were visions of the future, each a possible reality that might or might not come to pass. Usually when she caught glimpses of the future, however, there was purpose or meaning behind them. The visions would help direct and guide her actions. Yet this seemingly random collage of images did nothing but confuse her, and so she had done her best to ignore them and focus on the job she had been hired for.

The princess had offered her twenty well-trained mercenaries for the job, and she had been as good as her word: twelve men and eight women, all with prior military experience, had accompanied the Huntress to the world.

She had also sent along Captain Jedder, a senior member of the Doan Royal Guard. The Doan noble houses had a long history of supplementing their numbers with hired soldiers for particularly dangerous missions, and Jedder had handpicked this particular team from crews he had worked with in the past.

Technically, the mercs answered to Jedder, though he, in turn, answered to the Huntress. That was fine by her. Mercenaries had been known to cut and run if things went bad on a job, but if they had worked with the captain in the past they were more likely to stick with the battle plan right to the end.

The front entrance to the mansion was open and spacious. The door opened onto a large foyer, which flowed into an oversized sitting room furnished with two couches and a large glass table. A spiral staircase led off to one side, curling up to a balcony that over-looked the sitting room.

"We should try to take him here, when he first comes in," she said. "He'll sense that something is wrong right away, so we need to hit him fast."

"Set up a pair of sonic detonators on either side of the door," Jedder said into his radio. Instantly two of the soldiers ran over to comply with his orders.

"I fought against the Sith, you know," Jedder told her as the Huntress turned slowly in place, scoping out the rest of the room. "Twenty years ago. During the war. I was barely more than a kid."

"That's probably why the princess sent you along," the Iktotchi replied absently.

"I'm surprised she didn't send Lucia with us," Jedder noted. "She fought for the Sith during the war. Probably knows their tactics better than anyone."

She cares for Lucia, the Huntress thought. *She knows how danger-ous this mission will be. She's not expendable like the rest of us.*

Out loud she told him, "Position two of your team with the stun rifles up on that balcony at the top of the stairs. That should give them a clear shot down here into the foyer."

"I wish we had carbonite guns," Jedder lamented. "Freeze him solid."

The Huntress had already considered and discarded that idea.

"Same problem as the force pikes. You have to get in too close for them to be effective. And the carbonite will only freeze him for a few minutes. What are we supposed to do when he thaws out?"

"The tangle guns aren't any better," he countered. "A lightsaber will slice through the webbing like it was made of flimsi."

"They aren't meant to hold him," the Iktotchi explained. "They only have to slow him down long enough for me to administer the senflax."

She held up a long, thin blade to illustrate her point. The edge was coated with the potent neurotoxin. According to the princess, any wound deep enough to draw blood would get the poison into his system.

"After the toxin is introduced, we'll have to keep the pressure on," she reminded the captain. "If we even give him a chance to breathe, he'll recognize that the drug is in his system. He might have some way to counter it with the Force."

"How long after you cut him before that stuff starts to take effect?"

"Thirty, maybe forty seconds." *Assuming Serra knows what she's talking about.*

"That's a long time for a bunch of soldiers to go toe-to-toe with a Sith."

There really wasn't anything she could say to reassure him, so she didn't bother with an answer.

"Make sure your unit remembers that this is a two-stage attack," she told him. "The first stage needs to distract him long enough to give me an opening. After that, hit him with everything we've got."

"Can you really see the future?" the captain asked after passing on her instructions to the team.

"Sometimes. The future is always in motion. It's not always clear."

"Are we going to get out of this alive?"

"Some of us might," she replied, not mentioning the vision she had of Jedder's broken body lying lifeless on the mansion's marble floor.

———

When Bane returned to Ciutric, he was surprised to find Zannah's ship still gone, but he was grateful that she wouldn't be waiting for him back at the mansion. He was in no shape to do battle with her now; he was even too tired to come up with a lie to explain his absence without raising her suspicions. Yet as his airspeeder approached his mansion on the horizon, he knew that even if Zannah had been waiting for him, his journey would still have been worthwhile. Andeddu's knowledge was his now; over the past few days his brain had processed the raw information he had stolen to the point of full comprehension. He fully understood the ritual of essence transfer; he had learned the techniques that would allow him to move his consciousness from his own failing body into another. He just needed to select an appropriate victim.

Finding a new body to inhabit was the most difficult part of the ritual. He needed someone physically strong enough to withstand the massive quantities of dark side energy he would call on over the coming years, but at the same time he needed someone mentally vulnerable enough for him to overpower their will. The best candidate would be an engineered clone body, an empty shell with no thoughts or identity of its own. But creating a suitable clone could take years, and Bane wasn't convinced he had that much time left.

He would have to try to possess the body of a living victim . . . a very dangerous course of action. He would only have one chance: no matter the outcome, his own body would be destroyed in the process. And if his target possessed a will strong enough to resist his assault, the attempt would fail, banishing his spirit to the void for all eternity.

He brought the airspeeder in for a landing and climbed from the vehicle, pausing only to grab his travel pack—a simple duffel bag with the Holocron tucked safely away inside. With slow, heavy steps he approached the front door of the mansion.

Has to be someone young. Under thirty.

He opened the door and stepped inside, letting it swing shut behind him.

Naïve and inexperienced. Maybe—

He froze. Someone else was in the mansion. He could feel the intruders everywhere: hiding around corners in the hallways, crouched on the stairs, ducking behind the furniture, perched on the balcony above.

All this flashed through Bane's mind in less than a tenth of a second—just enough time for it to register before the sonic detonators on either side of him went off.

Their earsplitting shriek staggered Bane, causing him to stumble forward into the room and away from the door and possible escape. His hands instinctively flew up and clutched at his ears, his travel pack dropping to the floor. And then the enemy fell upon him.

They poured out like a swarm of insects, bursting into view from every side. Four soldiers armed with stun rifles sent a barrage of bolts raining down from the balcony; Bane—still reeling from the sonic detonators—barely had enough time throw up a protective barrier to shield him from the assault.

As he did so, he felt something fighting him. Some power was trying to block his ability to call upon the Force to shield himself. It wasn't strong enough to stop him, but it did hinder his efforts just enough so that a flicker of energy passed through the barrier.

His muscles seized as he was hit; his back arched and his arms and head were thrown back. Every nerve in Bane's body lit up as if it were on fire. The pain lasted only an instant, but it was enough to knock him to the floor in a crumpled heap.

He didn't stay down, however. He sprang back to his feet, simultaneously drawing his lightsaber with his right hand as he sent a blast of lightning out from the fingertips of his left. The violet bolts should have incinerated all four of his targets on the balcony, yet again the strange power interfering with his ability to draw upon the Force hindered his efforts.

Three of the victims were electrocuted, dying before they even had a chance to scream. The fourth, however, managed to throw herself back from the balcony's edge, evading the deadly attack.

Bane never got a chance to finish her off. A pair of soldiers emerged from a hallway on the left, and three more appeared from the hall on the right. They opened fire with tangle guns, sending out long streams of sticky, synthetic webbing.

The soldiers were smart; they coordinated their efforts. Two fired at his feet, looking to glue him to the floor. The others aimed for the chest and torso, looking to pin his arms to his sides with the viscous strings. But Bane wasn't about to let himself become immobilized.

Leaping up, he grabbed onto the chandelier hanging from the ceiling, holding himself with his free hand. Swinging his legs to build momentum, he launched himself up over the railing and onto the balcony, giving him the advantage of higher ground.

He came down with a heavy thud, the inexplicable power that still impeded his connection to the Force robbing him of a graceful landing. The bodies of the three dead soldiers were scattered about him. To his right were the stairs leading back down to the foyer; straight ahead was a long hall leading to another wing of the mansion.

A female Iktotchi stood at the far end of the hall, a long, thin knife held in each hand. She grinned at Bane, and in that moment he knew who was interfering with his ability to use the Force.

She broke into a run, charging down the hall toward him. Bane dropped into a fighting crouch to meet her attack, knowing her knives were no match for his lightsaber. It was only then that he noticed the flash grenades lying by the dead bodies at his feet.

They exploded with a burst of intense light and chemical smoke that blinded Bane. Disoriented, he fell back against the balcony's railing. An instant later he felt the sole of the Iktotchi's boots strike him hard in the chest, sending him tumbling backward over the banister to the marble floor four meters below.

He hit the ground hard enough to knock the breath from his body, leaving him gasping for air. The impact jarred his lightsaber from his grip, sending it skittering across the floor. An instant later his prone form was enveloped by the webbing from the tangle guns, pinning him to the ground.

Blind and immobilized, Darth Bane's fury saved him. Years of training allowed him to focus all his pain and rage in one single instant, drawing on it so he could unleash the full power of the dark side. Once again he felt the Iktotchi's barrier opposing his efforts, but this time he tore through it like it wasn't even there.

For a moment it was as if the world around him was frozen in place. Though his eyes were still suffering the effects of the flash grenade, the Force rushing through his body gave him an otherworldly awareness of his surroundings—the scene was burned into his brain in exquisite detail.

The soldiers were scattered about the foyer, scrambling to take up new positions in preparation for the next stage of the battle. They were well trained, but he could still sense their fear: they knew the fight was far from over. The Iktotchi had leapt over the railing in pursuit of him. She hung poised in the air above him, her twin blades held out to the either side as she braced for landing. Bane could even see himself lying on the floor, buried beneath a thick, wet blanket of rapidly drying chemical adhesive.

The frozen tableau lasted only a fraction of an instant, but it told the Dark Lord everything he needed to know. And then the instant was gone, and everything became a blur of motion again.

The Iktotchi landed just as Bane unleashed a wave of crackling electricity that burned away the webbing of the tangle guns. She dropped to one knee and tried to stab her knives into him as he lay on the floor, but through the Force Bane saw her coming. He managed to roll aside, escaping with only a long, deep cut along one of his forearms as he scrambled back to his feet.

In response to his call, his lightsaber flew up from the floor and into his waiting hand, but the Iktotchi was already retreating. Now that he was no longer helpless, she was eager to fall back and let others step in.

Several more flash grenades exploded around him, but Bane was unaffected; he was no longer relying on his physical sight to guide him. Fresh streams of webbing arced across the room toward him, but this time he incinerated them while they were still in the air. Half a dozen concussion grenades tossed in from every side clattered on the floor at his feet. As they exploded, Bane simply enveloped himself in the Force, creating a protective cocoon that absorbed the impact and left him standing completely unharmed.

Two men popped up from behind a nearby couch and fired at him from point-blank range with their stun guns. Bane slapped the incoming bolts away with his lightsaber, then thrust out a hand to send the couch slamming straight back into the wall, crushing the men who had been using it for cover.

Then he was on the move, bearing down on two of the soldiers carrying tangle guns. He sliced them both in half horizontally with a single blow from his lightsaber, carving a perfect line just above their belts. Another volley of stun bolts came too late to save them; Bane was already gone.

A single flip and he was back on the balcony again, face-to-face with the Iktotchi.

"You can't escape," he told her.

"I wasn't trying to," she hissed back at him, lunging forward with her knives.

She was quicker than Bane expected, coming in low and fast. He didn't have time to simply chop her down; instead he had to spin out of the way.

He tried to take one of her arms with his lightsaber on a counterthrust as she slipped past, but the Iktotchi anticipated his move and managed to contort her body so that his blade caught nothing but air.

They had switched positions from their first engagement; she was now the one standing with her back to the balcony railing. Bane thrust out with the Force, the impact sending her hurtling backward over the railing as her kick had done to him less than a minute earlier.

Somehow the Iktotchi managed to turn in the air so that she landed on her feet. Because of this, she was able to spring to safety when Bane sent a blast of lightning hurtling down toward her. Instead of her charred corpse, it left only a smoking circle on the floor.

Soldiers were firing their stun guns at him again from the stairwell. Bane didn't even bother to strike back at them; he simply dodged their attack by vaulting over the railing and dropping back down to the floor below. The soldiers were nothing to him; it was the Iktotchi he was interested in now. She was the only opponent who posed any real threat. Eliminate her and he could deal with the soldiers at his leisure.

He landed on the floor in a crouch, absorbing the impact. And then everything went black.

———

The Huntress couldn't say how long it had been since she'd carved her senflax-coated blade through the flesh of the Sith Lord's forearm, but the neurotoxin had to take effect soon.

Jedder was dead, crushed against the wall by a piece of flying furniture. At least five other soldiers were already down, too. The Sith Lord was focusing his efforts on her.

The Iktotchi knew she couldn't beat him. He was too strong. The tricks she had used against the Jedi had slowed him down at first, but now they had no effect at all. The senflax was her only hope of surviving.

She saw the Sith leaping down from the balcony, coming after her. He hit the floor, turned toward her, and collapsed. The big man lay on his side, eyes open and seeming to stare right at her. The pupils were bloodshot from the chemicals in the flash grenades.

The Huntress waited until he blinked. Then, seeing no other signs of movement, she held up her hand and shouted, "Cease fire! Cease fire!"

She thought briefly that his paralysis might be a trick, then discarded the notion. The Sith didn't need subterfuge to win the battle; it was obvious he had them overmatched. The only explanation was that Serra's drug had finally worked its magic. According to the instructions she had been given, they had four hours before they needed to administer the next dose.

With Jedder dead, the hired soldiers were staring at her, waiting for their next orders. The Huntress closed her eyes and reached out with her mind, seeking guidance. Someone else was coming: the blond woman from the camp on Ambria.

"You three go bring the airspeeders around to the front of the house," the Huntress barked. "The rest of you gather up the bodies. Don't leave anything behind that could link this to the princess."

The survivors hustled to follow her commands.

She didn't bother to tell them to hurry; they were already moving as fast as they could, eager to get away from this place where so many of their comrades-in-arms had fallen.

On an impulse, she bent down and retrieved the now extinguished lightsaber from where it lay on the floor beside the fallen Sith. She turned the curved handle over, inspecting it carefully.

She ignited the weapon and was surprised by its weightlessness.

"What about this?" one of the soldiers asked, holding up the duffel bag the Sith had dropped in the first few seconds of the attack.

"Take it with us," she said absently, not even bothering to look over. "Give it to the princess."

Infatuated with her new toy, she made a few slow, experimental swings with the unfamiliar weapon before extinguishing it and secreting it away in one of the pockets inside her robe, just as she had done with the strange crystal pyramid from the library out back.

Five minutes later they had the prisoner and their casualties in the back of the speeders, and they were heading to the drop shuttle that would take them back to Doan.

15

As Zannah brought the *Victory* in to touch down in her designated hangar at the Ciutric IV starport, she felt a sudden sense of uneasiness.

"Something wrong?" Set asked from the passenger's seat, picking up on her discomfort.

I'm about to challenge my Master in a battle to the death, and I'm still not sure if I made a mistake picking you as my apprentice.

"It's nothing."

Set shrugged. He was sitting with his chair reclined, his legs stretched out, and his feet resting on the dash. If he was feeling any anxiety himself, it was well masked.

With the ship on the ground, Zannah cut the engines. She couldn't shake the feeling that something was very wrong, but she had come too far to turn back now.

Is this a premonition of my own death? Will Bane end my life tonight?

"What now?" Set asked, sitting up and swinging his legs down to the floor.

When he had first accepted Zannah's offer, she had sensed a clear reluctance in him. Over the course of the trip to Ciutric, however, he seemed to have warmed to the idea. Now he appeared almost eager . . . though Zannah was aware this could all be an act.

"When we arrive at the estate you need to wait outside," she said out loud. "My Master doesn't like uninvited guests."

"I'll hide in the bushes like a scared little Kath pup," he promised.

"This isn't a game," she warned him.

"Everything's a game," he replied. "This is just one you really can't afford to lose."

"If I lose, you might end up dead, too."

"Or I could end up as your Master's new apprentice," he countered with a sly grin.

"You wouldn't find him nearly as tolerant of your impertinence."

"Then I truly hope you win. Is that all, Master?"

When Zannah nodded, Set rose from his seat and executed a deep bow, his head dipping down so low his long hair tumbled forward to hang like a silver curtain covering his head and face.

"Lead and I will follow," he offered, though there was something almost mocking in his tone.

She couldn't help but wonder what Bane would have done in response to Set's irreverent behavior. The consequences would no doubt have been harsh. Zannah, however, was content to let the Dark Jedi have his fun. She had wounded his ego, humiliating him by so easily overpowering him during their confrontation. It was important to let him regain his confidence. And if his jests made it easier for him to accept his role as apprentice, she was willing to put up with them . . . to a point.

Set understood all this, of course. She knew he was pushing her, testing the limits and boundaries of their relationship. At the same time, Zannah had been testing him. So far he had been smart enough to know where to draw the line.

Leaving their bags on the ship, Zannah and Set made their way from the hangar to the small customs building at the front of the starport. Chet, the young customs officer who had spoken to her the last time she'd left Ciutric, was on duty again.

"Good evening, Mistress Omek," he said with a tilt of his head. "I'll have someone bring your speeder around."

"Thank you, Chet."

"Want me to send someone for your bags?"

"I'll pick them up in the morning." *If I'm still alive.*

"Aren't you going to introduce me to your friend?" Set chimed in.

Zannah silenced him with a glare.

Chet obviously caught the exchange, but what he made of it Zannah wasn't sure. A few seconds of silence passed before the customs official said, "May I speak with you alone for a moment, Mistress Omek?"

Curious, Zannah nodded at Set, who turned and walked away in the other direction, looking mildly offended.

"Had an unregistered drop ship enter atmosphere a few hours ago," Chet whispered once Set was out of earshot. "Touched down in the jungle about a hundred kilometers east of the starport."

Odd, Zannah thought.

Ciutric IV was located at the nexus of several key trade routes, but the tariffs and taxes charged by the customs stations were minimal. No legitimate merchant would incur the risk of landing in the untamed jungle just to avoid some paperwork and save a handful of credits. And there weren't any smuggling operations active in the region; if there were, she and Bane would have known about them.

"Any idea who they were?"

Chet shrugged. "They landed outside our jurisdiction, and they didn't send off an emergency beacon, so nobody bothered to send a patrol to investigate."

She wasn't surprised at the lack of official urgency generated by the unregistered vessel. Ciutric was generally a law-abiding world; as a result planetary security was somewhat lax. It was one of the reasons Bane had chosen to take up residence here.

She was intrigued, however. Did the drop ship have anything to do with the unease she'd felt upon landing?

"You said they touched down to the east?" *Our estate is on the eastern edge of the city.*

"Yeah. Showed up on the sensors a couple of hours before your brother got back."

"My brother?"

"Oh," Chet said, mildly surprised. "I just assumed you knew. He left the day after you did. Just got back tonight."

"Any idea where he went?"

The customs official shook his head. "Sorry."

Zannah's mind was spinning with a thousand possibilities as the valet arrived with her speeder. Bane almost never left Ciutric. If he had business, people came to him . . . or he sent Zannah. Something must have come up that was too important for him to wait for her to get back. Either that, or he had business he wanted to deal with personally. And if that was the case, was it possible he had sent her to Doan as a way to get rid of her temporarily?

She could think of only one reason Bane would have wanted to keep her from knowing about his journey: he was looking for someone to replace her!

"Trouble?" Set asked, wandering over to see what was going on.

"It's fine," Zannah replied, not wanting to reveal her apprehension to either of the men.

She climbed into the speeder and nodded at Set to do the same.

"Thanks for the update, Chet."

As the speeder roared to life and took to the air, she began to consider her options. If Bane was alone, she would challenge him as she planned. However, if Bane had found someone else to become his heir things would get more complicated.

If Bane had cast her aside, did the Rule of Two still apply to her? Or would Bane and his new apprentice combine their strength to defeat her as an enemy of the Sith? If that happened, she wouldn't be able to survive alone.

If things went bad, she didn't really know if the Dark Jedi sitting beside her would come to her aid, but she didn't have any real choice. She had decided to confront Bane tonight, and she wasn't about to turn back now. She'd waited too long for this moment, put it off too many times before.

"Be on your guard when we land," she warned Set.

"I'm always on guard," he assured her.

Zannah's apprehension continued to mount as she approached the estate, but as she drew nearer she realized she couldn't sense her Master's presence. Puzzled, she brought the speeder in to land and saw that the front door was wide open.

"Wait here," she instructed Set.

With one hand on the hilt of her lightsaber, she approached the open door cautiously and peeked inside. At first glance the damage was almost more than she could comprehend. The plaster on the walls was cracked and burned in at least a dozen places; the marble floors were scratched and scorched. Sticky strands of synthetic webbing and flakes of ash were everywhere.

Every piece of furniture she could see was either smashed or overturned. Carefully, she made her way upstairs, still wary despite not sensing anyone else in the building.

A quick inspection of the various rooms assured her that there was no immediate danger, and she sheathed her lightsaber. It seemed as if most of the damage had been confined to the foyer and the sitting room just off the mansion's entrance. If there were answers to be had, she'd most likely find them there.

When she returned to the front of the manse, she wasn't surprised to see that Set had disobeyed her orders. He was sitting on a chair that had survived relatively unscathed, his legs crossed and a glass of wine in his hand, casually waiting for her to arrive. A freshly opened bottle stood beside him on the floor.

"Your Master has excellent taste," he said, raising the glass and drinking a toast to the absent host.

It was clear from the evidence that someone had attacked Bane in the mansion, and it was only logical to assume they must have been on the drop ship. Who they were and why they had come, however, were still mysteries she couldn't solve.

"I told you to wait in the speeder," she said, descending the stairs and closing the mansion door.

"I was bored," he answered with a shrug, taking another sip of wine before changing topics. "Looks like that confrontation you were expecting isn't going to happen after all. I guess you're the new Sith Master by default."

"It doesn't work that way," Zannah muttered. "Besides, Darth Bane's still alive. If he was dead I would have felt it."

"Somehow I was afraid you'd say that," he said, bending forward to grab the wine bottle and refill his empty glass. "Any idea who might have done this?"

"None of our enemies even knows the Sith still exist," Zannah reminded him.

"I get the feeling there's something you're not telling me," Set noted. A second later he added, "Master."

"Bane just arrived back on Ciutric tonight." She saw no reason not to tell him what she had learned. "And Chet told me an unidentified drop ship touched down near the estate a short time before he arrived."

"You think the two are related?"

"I don't believe in coincidence," she replied. After a moment she decided to come clean with Set. "I think Bane might have sent me to Doan just to get me out of the way for a while. I think he was actually interested in something completely unrelated."

"Don't be so sure," Set replied, holding up what appeared to be a small blue button.

"Where did you find that?"

"Wedged into the wreckage of what used to be a couch over there in the corner," he replied, tossing it to her.

She reached out with one hand, easily snatching it from the air. A splash of dried blood was smeared across the surface, partially obscuring the gold insignia.

"That's the symbol of the Doan Royal House," Set told her as she studied the button.

"Doan?" Zannah was more confused than ever. "Why would someone from Doan come here? How would they even find us?"

Set shrugged. "You're the Master. You tell me."

Zannah didn't answer right away. Chewing on her lower lip, she analyzed the situation carefully, examining it from every angle. There were still too many unknowns for her to come up with a perfect plan, but she knew what had to be done.

"We need to go to Doan."

"Hold on a second," Set protested, holding up his hands. "Are you sure you want to do that? I mean, even if your Master's still alive it looks to me like he's probably a prisoner."

"Yes . . . a prisoner on Doan."

"So, what? We're going to rescue him just so you can try and kill him yourself?"

That would be in accordance with the Rule of Two, Zannah thought. But there were other, more practical, reasons to go.

"My Master is smart, powerful, and cunning. He's too dangerous to ignore. If they're holding him prisoner, he might find a way to escape. If he does, he will come after me . . . but it will be at a time and place of his choosing, not mine.

"Even if he never escapes, it's likely whoever took him will interrogate him for information. He may reveal something that exposes my existence to the Jedi . . . or some other enemy. I'm not willing to take that chance.

"Plus, I want to know who attacked him, and why. And if they did capture him, I want to know how they did it. What tactics did they use to bring down such a formidable opponent, and how can I make sure it never happens to me?"

"So this is all about you tying up loose ends?"

She heard reluctance in his voice—the same reluctance she'd sensed when she'd first offered to take him on as her apprentice. Set had spent much of his life running from problems rather than solving them. She knew he'd rather avoid his enemies than seek a way to destroy them. In time, she would cure him of this. As his Master, she would teach him the ways of the Sith.

For now, however, she simply needed his help.

"I have to go meet with someone," she said, remembering that Chet had told her Bane had met with Argel Tenn only a few days before all this had begun. It was possible the collector had found some interesting Sith manuscript that had prompted Bane to leave Ciutric.

"Am I coming with you?"

Zannah shook her head. "You need to find out everything you can about Doan. If the royal family was involved, where would they take my Master? And how can we find him?"

Set gave a dissatisfied snort. "So now I'm a glorified librarian?"

"Meet me back here in two days," Zannah said, ignoring his complaint. "By then I'll have figured out what to do next."

———

When Zannah returned to the mansion after meeting with Argel Tenn, she was mildly surprised to find Set there waiting for her. She had half expected him not to show up. The mission she had sent him on had been important, but it had also been a test of his commitment. If he was having second thoughts about becoming her apprentice, sending him away would have given him the perfect opportunity to try to disappear. The fact that he had come back was a sign that maybe he was a suitable choice after all.

She was relieved to see that things seemed to be improving with Set, because her meeting with Argel Tenn had not gone well. At first he had refused to discuss his business with Bane, claiming discretion was the cornerstone of his business. Zannah had done her best to persuade him to make an exception through nonviolent means; she knew Argel had access to rare Sith manuscripts, and she didn't want to throw away a potentially valuable resource.

However, much to her dismay, he had shown a surprising integrity when it came to protecting his clients' confidentiality. In the end she'd had to turn to less pleasant methods to make him talk. Of course, by resorting to brutal interrogation she had revealed herself as something more than just an interested collector, and after that she couldn't leave him alive.

The risk of Argel telling someone about her was too great; the information might make it back to the Jedi and cause them to investigate. Above all else it was critical that the Sith remained hidden, so Zannah was left with no choice but to eliminate Argel.

The real tragedy was that she never did manage to get anything more than a single name out of him: Darth Andeddu. Argel hadn't known why Bane was interested in this particular Sith Lord, and without more to go on Zannah was stuck.

"Welcome back, Master," Set said by way of greeting. "You'll be happy to hear that I've learned everything one could possibly ever want to know about a miserable little pit of a world like Doan."

"Too bad I didn't send you to find out about Darth Andeddu," she muttered, letting her frustrations boil up to the surface.

"Did you say Andeddu?" Set asked, obviously startled. "The immortal God-King of Prakith?"

Zannah's jaw nearly hit the floor. "You've heard of him?"

"Ah, so now I have something to teach you," Set said with a grin, recovering from his initial surprise. "Does that make me the Master?"

Zannah was in no mood for his jokes. "Tell me what you know about Andeddu."

To his credit, Set picked up on her tone and took on a more serious demeanor.

"My last few years with the Jedi were spent serving under an Ithorian Master named Obba," he explained.

"I've heard of him. He's on the Council of First Knowledge."

Ever since their battle against the Jedi on Tython, Bane had insisted they both know the name and reputation of every Master in the Order.

Set raised one eyebrow. "Impressive."

"Consider that your first lesson. Know your enemy as well as you know yourself."

"Noted. May I continue?"

Zannah nodded.

"While under Master Obba's insufferable tutelage, much of my time was spent researching the histories of the ancient Sith. The hammerheaded old fool had this grand idea he could best serve the light by making a catalog of every known Sith Holocron, then sending out his agents to round them up and bring them back to the Jedi Temple for safekeeping.

"In my research, I happened on several references to a man named Darth Andeddu. The Jedi had worked hard to remove all mention of him from the galactic record, but as a member of the Order I had access to the original confiscated materials."

"Get to the point," Zannah warned him.

"Of course. Andeddu ruled over the world of Prakith as a god. At least, he did until the hyperlanes into the Deep Core collapsed, effectively cutting the planet off from the rest of the galaxy.

"There was, however, some evidence to support the theory that

Andeddu created a Holocron during his reign. Master Obba believed it was still on Prakith, though he felt a journey into the Deep Core to retrieve it was too dangerous. To be honest, I kind of agreed with him."

"What's so special about Andeddu's Holocron?" Zannah demanded. "You nearly swallowed your tongue when I mentioned his name."

"If the legends are to be believed, Andeddu's Holocron contains the secret of eternal life."

Zannah cursed under her breath as all the pieces tumbled into place. Somehow Bane must have learned of Andeddu's Holocron and gone to Prakith to claim it. He was trying to become immortal!

That's why he had sent her off to Doan: so she wouldn't find out what he was up to. Despite everything he had taught her about the Rule of Two, he wasn't willing to accept the idea that his apprentice would one day surpass him. He actually thought that if he could find a way to stop the ravages of time and age, he could rule the Sith forever.

This is a betrayal of everything you taught me. You said you were teaching me all your secrets; you said the legacy of the Sith would one day be mine to carry on. You lied to me!

"Do you think it's possible your Master actually went to Prakith and found Andeddu's Holocron?" Set asked, making no effort to conceal the naked hunger in his voice.

"Bane's journeyed into the Deep Core before," she admitted, remembering his trip to Tython.

"So you finally decided to tell me your Master's name."

Zannah uttered another silent swear. She had meant to keep that information to herself as long as Bane was alive. But the realization of what he had done, of how he had betrayed the Rule of Two, had her rattled.

"I still don't understand how this ties in with Doan," Set wondered aloud.

That was one piece of the puzzle Zannah hadn't figured out yet, either, though she had a feeling it was all connected somehow.

"Whoever attacked him must have come for the Holocron," she guessed. "Whoever took Bane would have taken the artifact as well."

"So you think it's on Doan?"

It was obvious Set was more interested in claiming the Holocron than in finding and dealing with Bane. But Zannah had no idea who or what she would face when she went back to the mining world, and she suspected she'd need all the help she could get.

"You may not have been willing to risk a trip into the Deep Core to claim Andeddu's Holocron, but are you willing to travel back to Doan one more time?"

Set graced her with another of his extravagant bows.

"Lead the way, Master."

16

Serra sat alone in the small, windowless office, trying to gather her courage. The only furnishings were a simple desk and the chair she currently occupied. The unadorned walls were a depressing shade of brown, their stone surface rough and unfinished. A small safe had been built into the rock wall, and a single door led out into the hall beyond.

The princess wasn't naïve. She understood that the room reflected the opinion most offworlders had of Doan; they saw it as an ugly, grimy pit. She knew that those who lived in the strip mines on the planet's surface felt the same. But she had seen the planet's true beauty.

Built on the plateaus atop the rock columns towering high above the choking clouds of dust and pollution, the cities of the nobility were blessed with bright blue skies nearly every day of the year. Each morning the rising sun reflected off the burnished spires of castles built on plateaus hundreds of kilometers to the east, lighting them up like candles in the gray of the early dawn. In the evening the sandstorms rolling across the desert seemed to dance on the horizon, alive with flickering bursts of color as the setting sun flashed off quartz chips caught up in their swirling embrace.

Even after all these years, it could still take her breath away . . . just as it had when she first came to Doan. After leaving her father's camp on Ambria she had traveled the worlds of the Outer Rim, using what he had taught her to help the less fortunate and establishing her reputation as a skilled healer. When the crown prince contracted a mysterious illness, the king had hired her to tend to his son.

She had instantly recognized the symptoms of Idolian fever, a deadly but treatable infection. For three months she nursed him slowly back to health, and by the time Gerran recovered the two of them were in love.

You saved his life then. But you didn't have the power to save him from the terrorists. If you were stronger, he might still be alive.

Serra shook her head in momentary confusion. The thought had been in her own voice, but it had somehow seemed alien . . . as if someone else was speaking inside her head.

Except for herself, the office was clearly empty. The door was closed, and with the sparse furnishing there was no place for someone to hide. She cast a wary glance at the small, four-sided pyramid sitting on the edge of the desk.

It had been stashed away almost carelessly in a small duffel bag the mercenaries had brought back to her. Serra's connection to the Force was strong enough for her to feel the power inside the artifact, trapped beneath the surface, just waiting to be released.

Why didn't the Iktotchi claim this for herself? She should have sensed its power, too—even hidden inside the bag. Something else must have drawn her attention.

Picking up the pyramid and holding it at arm's length, she crossed the room to the wall safe. Punching in the combination, she unlocked it and placed the pyramid inside then closed the door, sealing it safely away. The man in the dungeon was a Sith Lord; anything he possessed was an instrument of the dark side. Serra wasn't interested in exploring its power; she was only interested in him.

He had arrived three days ago, yet she still had not gone to speak with him. As per her instructions, he had been kept drugged and helpless the entire time. Now she knew she couldn't put it off any longer; it was time to go face her demons. Her face set in grim determination, she left the office and marched through the twisting halls of Doan's infamous Stone Prison, heading for the interrogation cells.

When she had first learned about the vast dungeon complex built into the rock several kilometers below the castle, Serra had been horrified. Historically, the nobility had used the Stone Prison to make political opponents vanish. Trapped at the heart of a rock column several kilometers high and hundreds of meters in diameter, any prisoners inside would be shielded from detection by scanners. A person could disappear forever in the underground labyrinth, spending the rest of their years in shackles, tortured for information or simple sadistic pleasure without any hope of salvation.

In the event a rescue was somehow attempted, the entire complex was rigged so it could be collapsed with a series of explosions that would kill not only the prisoners but their would-be saviors as well. The carefully engineered detonator charges would activate in a precisely timed sequence, destroying the dungeon room by room while allowing the guards time to escape. The Royal Manse and other buildings on the surface thousands of meters above would suffer only a few mild—though unmistakable—tremors as the entire complex below was reduced to rubble.

Gerran had still been alive when Serra learned all this. He had explained that the Stone Prison hadn't been used in over forty years; it was a relic of a more brutal and repressive era. In response to public pressure brought to bear by the Senate, it had been closed down. It wasn't even staffed any longer. Yet at the urging of his betrothed, he swore that once he was king he would have the infamous dungeon permanently sealed: a gesture to symbolize the new relationships he wished to forge between the nobles and the miners.

But Gerran was dead now, just like her father. And she was the one who had hired mercenaries to capture her enemy and bury him forever inside the Stone Prison's cold, dark cells. She couldn't help but wonder what they would think of what she had done. What would they say if they were here right now?

Serra pushed the thought from her mind. They weren't here. Her father and her husband were both gone, forever taken from her. And she was left to deal with the Sith Lord alone.

It took her nearly ten minutes to make her way from the office through the maze of passages and rooms to where the prisoner was being held. Although the corridors she traveled were illuminated by pale lights in the ceiling, many of the halls led off into darkness—her mercenaries had only reopened one small section of the complex. The rest of it was still deserted.

The man she was going to see was being held in one of the maximum-security cells, accessible only by a single staircase guarded by locked durasteel doors at the top and bottom. The mercenaries standing guard on the other side of the door at the top unlocked it at her approach, and she quickly made her way down the steep stairs.

The door at the bottom similarly opened for her, revealing a small ten-meter-by-ten-meter guard station. Another locked durasteel door on the far wall led into the prisoner's cell; a small viewing window had been built into the door. There were two tables in the room. The larger stood off to the side of the door Serra had just entered. The smaller was on wheels; measuring only a meter by half a meter, it had been pushed against the wall beside the cell door.

Six of the soldiers she had sent to apprehend the prisoner were here, along with Lucia and the Huntress. The guards were seated in chairs around the larger table, playing cards. The two women were on opposite ends of the room, distancing themselves from those at the table and each other. Lucia was leaning against the wall for support, while the Huntress sat on the stone floor, her legs crossed, hands in her lap and her eyes closed. It looked as if she might have been meditating.

As Serra entered, the guards jumped up to stand at attention, as did Lucia. The Huntress opened her eyes and looked up at the princess, but otherwise made no move. Serra wasn't even sure what the assassin was still doing here; she had already been paid for her services. But for some reason she had chosen to stay, as if she had some vested interest in the outcome of events.

The princess shook her head. She had more important things she needed to worry about than the assassin.

"The prisoner is still sedated?" she asked.

"Yes, ma'am," one of the guards replied. "He was given another dose an hour ago."

She nodded and made her way over to the wheeled table in the corner. Atop the table were nearly three dozen hypodermic needles, color-coded by label according to their contents. Serra had prepared each of the needles herself. The ones marked with a green sticker contained senflax; they needed to keep the prisoner drugged at all times to prevent him from escaping. The others—red, black, and yellow—were filled with various compounds she would need during her interrogation.

From the corner of her eye she saw Lucia making her way from the wall toward her. Once at her side, her friend spoke in a whisper soft enough that only she would be able to hear.

"This isn't like you. Why are you doing this?"

"You wouldn't understand," she replied just as quietly.

"Hiring this assassin was one thing," Lucia continued, her voice rising only slightly with carefully held-in-check emotion. "But hiring mercenaries to secretly reopen the Stone Prison? What if the king finds out?"

"He won't," Lucia assured him. "This has nothing to do with Gerran, or Doan."

The dark-skinned woman refused to let it go.

"Holding someone for torture and interrogation? It's not right. You know that."

"He's a Sith. Not a soldier like you were. A Dark Lord. He doesn't deserve your pity. Or mine."

Lucia shook her head and turned away, but not before Serra clearly saw the frustration and disappointment in her face.

"Open the door," the princess called out to the guards. "I want to speak with the prisoner. Alone."

At her words the Huntress sprang to her feet, causing Lucia to step forward protectively.

"I want to come with you," the Iktotchi explained.

"Why?" Serra demanded, suddenly suspicious.

"Who else could have captured him for you?" she replied, avoiding the question. "Have I not earned the right?"

"If she goes, I go, too," Lucia insisted, crossing her arms.

Serra could have refused them. But deep inside she still didn't want to face the monster from her past alone. And what harm was there now if they learned her secrets? She had concealed her true identity all these years only because her father feared retribution from this man. With him as her prisoner, she had no reason left to hide.

"The three of us, then," she conceded, grabbing the little table and wheeling it into position to bring it inside with them. "Lock the door behind us," she instructed the guards.

———

Lucia was worried about the princess. Ever since their visit to the Jedi Temple she had sensed something different about her, but she had never suspected she was capable of going to such extreme lengths. She hadn't known mercenaries had been hired to reopen the Stone Prison; if she had, she would have tried to talk Serra out of such a foolish and dangerous plan. The princess must have known she would object, however, and so she hadn't told Lucia what was happening until after the prisoner was safely secured in his cell.

She had known about the dungeons, of course. As part of the princess's official security detail, she needed to memorize every possible entrance and exit to the castle. Up until three days ago, however, she had only ever seen blueprints. Coming face-to-face with the Stone Prison was an entirely different experience.

As soon as she stepped off the long turbolift ride down from the surface she had sensed the evil of this place. The stale air had an underlying stench of death. Too many dark and unspeakable things had happened here over the centuries.

Since then Lucia had kept a careful eye on her friend. She could see something eating away at her, and she feared the unholy gloom of the Stone Prison would only make things worse. The princess was obsessed with the man in the dungeon, yet at the same time she was unable to face him. Lucia knew it had something to do with her past, but when she had tried to broach the subject the princess had refused to discuss it.

Left with no other options, she had been forced to wait for Serra to make the next move. Now that she was about to face the prisoner for the first time, Lucia was determined to be at her side. She might not understand what her friend was going through, and she might not agree with what she was doing, but she was still going to be there in case the princess needed her.

As the three women entered the cell, Lucia was surprised at how much smaller it was than the room on the other side of the door: just three meters square. The cell was dimly lit, the only illumination coming from a single sputtering light overhead. The prisoner was restrained against the far wall. His arms were extended out to either side above, his hands shackled by chains dangling from iron rings set into the ceiling. His legs were similarly splayed, his ankles cuffed to the wall behind him.

Because of the drug he was unable to stand erect; his weight sagged forward, pulling the chains supporting him tight and putting incredible strain on his wrists and shoulders. The pain in his joints would have been excruciating, were it not for the numbing effects of the senflax coursing through his system. His head was slumped down, his paralyzed muscles making it impossible for him to look up as they entered.

Serra selected a needle with a red label from the table and injected it directly into the carotid artery running up the side of his thick neck. An instant later his head snapped up and back in reaction to the powerful stimulant.

Seeing his face, Lucia gasped in surprise. The other two glanced at her momentarily, but when she shook her head they dismissed her reaction as unimportant and returned their attention to the man in chains.

It had been more than twenty years, but Lucia had recognized him instantly. Des had been her commanding officer—her leader, her hero. Without him none of the Gloom Walkers would have survived the war. He had saved their lives on Kashyyyk. He saved them again on Trandosha. Time after time he had brought them through impossible situations against overwhelming odds, right up until their final mission together on Phaseera. And then Lieutenant Ulabore had ordered the enforcers—the Sith military police—to arrest him.

She had never heard from Des again; like the rest of the unit she assumed he had been executed for disobeying orders and striking a superior officer. And even though she had believed him to be dead, she had vowed she would never forget the face of the man who had once meant everything to her.

When she saw him hanging from the shackles in the cell, she hadn't been able to contain her gasp of surprise. Fortunately neither the princess nor the Huntress had realized why she had gasped, and Lucia recovered enough to avoid another outburst. But though she managed to keep her emotions from showing on the surface, inside her world had exploded.

She doubted whether Des had recognized her. He was drugged, for one thing. And she was only one face among many in the unit. He was the leader they all looked up to; he was the one they idolized. In the Gloom Walkers, she was just a low-ranking sniper, one of a dozen junior troopers in the squad. Did she really expect he'd remember her after all this time?

Not that it mattered; she didn't dare say anything with Serra and the Huntress standing right there. The princess was obsessed with the prisoner; she was gripped by some madness that had driven her to previously unthinkable acts. If she discovered that Lucia and Des knew each other, there was no telling what she would do. Or what she might order the Iktotchi to do.

And so Lucia was forced to just stand there, helpless to do anything to help Des. Just like the day the enforcers had dragged him away.

Serra instantly recognized the face from her nightmares. He was older, but his features were unmistakable: the bald head; the thick, heavy brow; the cruel set of his eyes and jaw.

Beside her Lucia gasped loudly as the prisoner fixed the three women with his cold, merciless gaze. Serra glanced over and saw a strange expression on the ex-soldier's face; something had obviously upset her.

Lucia was the bravest person the princess had ever met, yet she was clearly distraught. Was it possible she was actually afraid of this man, even while he was chained? Or did she feel sympathy for him? She knew Lucia disapproved of what she was doing. Did her friend think she was a monster now? Or was it something else?

Her friend's unexpected reaction unsettled Serra, and she fought the instinct to turn and flee from the man in the cell. She had nothing to fear from her prisoner this time. This time he was the victim, not her.

No matter what Lucia thinks, I have to do this.

"Do you know who I am?" she demanded.

His answer came slowly. The stimulant she had given him only countered the physical effect of the senflax; the toxin still clouded his mind, dulling his focus and concentration.

"An enemy from my past."

The words were slightly slurred, and it was impossible to read anything into the flat, emotionless tone. She couldn't tell if he actually recognized her, or if he was just making a generalization based on the fact that she had taken him prisoner.

"My name is Serra. Caleb was my father," she told him. She wanted him to know. She wanted him to understand who had done this to him.

"Is this revenge for him," he asked after a long moment, the senflax making his mind lethargic, "or for what I did to you?"

"Both," she replied, picking up a needle marked with a black sticker. Again, she injected it into his neck. This time, however, the effects were markedly different.

His eyes rolled back in his head and his teeth slammed shut, narrowly missing his tongue. Then his body began to convulse, causing his chains to rattle madly.

Lucia turned away in disgust, unable to watch. The Huntress leaned in closer, enthralled by his chemical-induced torment. Serra let the seizure continue for a full ten seconds before injecting him with one of the yellow needles to counter the effects.

"Do you see the kind of punishment I can inflict on you?" she asked. "Now do you understand what it is like to be at the helpless mercy of another?"

He didn't answer right away. His breathing was ragged, his face and bare scalp covered in sweat from the pain he had just endured. A spastic tremble had seized his left hand, causing it to twitch and flex madly in its iron cuff.

"You have no lessons to teach me," he gasped. "I understand suffering in ways you will never comprehend."

"Why did you kill my father?" Serra asked, picking up another black needle and holding it up for him to see.

"Caleb did not die by my hand."

She stabbed the needle into his neck, inducing another seizure. She let this one continue nearly twice as long before administering the antidote. She expected him to pass out from the pain, but somehow he managed to stay conscious.

"Lies will be punished," she warned him.

"I did not kill your father," he insisted, though his voice was so weak she could barely hear him.

"I told you that I saw another in my visions," the Huntress reminded her. "A young woman with blond hair. Perhaps she was the killer."

Serra glared at the Iktotchi before turning her attention back to the man in chains.

"Is this true?"

He didn't answer, though a cunning smile played at the corner of his lips.

"Tell me what happened to my father!" Serra shouted, slapping him across the face. Her nails raked his cheek, slicing the flesh with four long, deep furrows. Blood welled up quickly into the wounds and began to run down toward his chin.

Bane didn't answer, however. Jaw clenched, Serra reached down to grab another of the black needles, but Lucia seized her wrist.

"He didn't kill your father!" the bodyguard shouted. "Why are you still doing this?"

Serra yanked her wrist free angrily. "He may not have done the deed, but he's the reason my father is dead," she insisted. She turned back to the prisoner. "Do you deny that?"

"Caleb was weak," the man muttered. "When he ceased to be of use, he was destroyed. This is the way of the dark side."

Serra picked the needle up from the table.

"This won't bring your father back," Lucia pleaded.

"I want him to see what it's like to be helpless and afraid," Serra hissed. "I want him to know what it's like to be a victim. I want him to understand that what he did to my father—to me—was wrong!"

"The weak will always be victims," the prisoner said, his voice growing stronger. "That is the way of the universe. The strong take what they want, and the weak suffer at their hands. That is their fate; it is inevitable. Only the strong survive, because only the strong deserve to."

"You only believe that because you don't know what it's like to suffer!" the princess shot back at him.

"I know what it means to suffer," he replied, his words no longer thick and slurred. "I used to be a victim. But I refused to accept my lot in life. I made myself strong."

As he spoke, drops of blood from the gashes on his cheek fell from his chin and splashed to the floor.

"Those who are victims have no one to blame but themselves. They do not deserve pity; they are victims because of their own failures and weaknesses."

"But it didn't matter how strong you were!" Lucia said, suddenly jumping into the discussion. "Don't you see that? You still ended up as a prisoner!"

"Had I been stronger I would not have been captured," he countered, a fierce light burning in his eyes. "If I am not strong enough to escape, I will continue to suffer until I die. But if I *am* strong enough to escape . . ."

Serra slammed the black needle down and grabbed one of the green, injecting him with another dose of senflax.

"You will never leave this dungeon alive," she promised as her victim slipped back under the influence of the drug, his eyes glazing over as his head lolled forward again.

Even drugged and chained, he's still cunning enough to be dangerous.

Caught up in arguing with him, she had almost missed the signs of the senflax wearing off. She had thought it would be hours before he needed another shot, but she had underestimated the effects of the other drugs she had been pumping into his system. She'd have to be more careful in the future.

"Right now I am weak," the man mumbled with his head staring down at the floor, refusing to give up. "Powerless. You inflict suffering on me because you are strong enough to do so. Your actions prove the truth of what I believe."

Serra shook her head angrily. "No. My father taught me to help those in need. The strong should raise the weak up, not trample them down. He believed in that, and so do I!"

Somehow the prisoner managed to lift his head, fixing her with his bleary-eyed stare.

"Your father's beliefs got him killed."

The princess raised her hand to slap him again, then froze, struggling to control the flood of grief and rage that threatened to overwhelm her.

"You're not thinking straight," Lucia said softly, placing a hand on her shoulder. "You need to calm down."

Her friend was right. He was inside her head. She needed to get out of the room and regroup. The last shot she'd given him would keep him helpless for at least another hour. Time enough for her to collect her thoughts before facing him again.

Lowering her hand, she turned her back on him without saying a word, leaving the Huntress and Lucia alone with him in the cell.

17

As the princess stormed out of the cell, Lucia resisted the urge to go after her. She knew Des's words had hurt; normally she would have gone to comfort her friend. But everything had changed when she'd walked into the cell and recognized the man chained to the wall.

The Huntress was staring at her, smiling. The Iktotchi was evil. Twisted. She had enjoyed watching Serra torture the victim; she had relished in his suffering. Lucia suspected she took pleasure in Serra's emotional torment, as well.

She returned the assassin's gaze but refused to speak. For a moment their eyes locked, and then the Iktotchi turned away with an air of indifference, as if Lucia was beneath her notice. The bodyguard continued to stare at her back as the Huntress followed in the princess's wake, leaving her alone with the prisoner.

At first a part of her had actually wondered if Des deserved what was being done to him. After all, he was a Sith Lord now. She had fought on the side of the Sith during the war, but she was only a soldier. Like Lucia herself, most of her comrades-in-arms had enlisted because they saw no other way to escape the suffering and hopelessness of their lives. They had turned against the Republic out of desperation, but they were still decent men and women.

The Sith Lords, however, were monsters. Ruthless and cruel, they cared nothing for the soldiers who followed them. Sometimes it even seemed they enjoyed the death and suffering inflicted on the enlisted personnel under their command. Their mere presence inspired terror in the ranks, and at night the troops would share stories of the horrors they inflicted on their enemies . . . or their allies who had failed them.

Lucia never thought she could feel pity for a Sith Lord. But she also never imagined Des would become one of them.

If Des really had murdered Caleb, Lucia reasoned, then he had brought this on himself. But when questioned, he insisted he wasn't the one who had killed the healer, and Lucia was convinced he was telling the truth. Even the Iktotchi assassin had seemed to believe him. But despite all the evidence—the accounts of the Jedi, the Huntress's mention of a mysterious blond woman at the scene, and the refusals of Des himself—Serra had not been swayed from her course. The princess had refused to listen to facts or reason. Her hatred blinded her to everything else.

She had stormed off in anger, but Lucia knew it was only a matter of time until she returned to subject Des to another round of torture. She had seen the madness in Serra's eyes. The princess hungered for revenge.

Lucia recognized that look; she had seen it in the eyes of her fellow soldiers when the enforcers had dragged Des away in cuffs. Whether he was guilty of the crime didn't matter: Serra was going to make her prisoner suffer for the death of her father. And there was nothing anyone could say or do to make her change her mind.

And even if he didn't kill Caleb, he's still a monster. He probably deserves to die.

During the interrogation, she had listened with growing horror to the words coming from the prisoner's mouth. It was clear Des had embraced the teachings of the dark side in ways she could never have imagined. He was not the man she remembered; the camaraderie of the Gloom Walkers meant nothing to the creature he had become.

But it means something to me.

Lucia still believed in the ideals of the Gloom Walkers. They looked out for one another; they counted on one another to survive. There was honor in their code of unity, symbolized in the secret greeting reserved only for other members of the unit: a closed fist rapped firmly on the breastbone, just above the heart.

Whatever Des was now, she still owed him her life. He had saved her—the entire unit—too many times to count. Yet when the enforcers had taken him away she had been powerless to help him. Now fate was giving her another chance to repay her debt.

A small pool of blood was forming on the floor, dripping from where Serra had sliced open his cheek.

You're not just doing it for Des, Lucia told herself, turning her attention to the color-coded needles resting on the cart.

Serra's hatred would only fester and grow. She'd become more and more twisted each time she returned to inflict pain on her helpless victim. The loss of her husband had pushed her to the edge of madness, and this would take her over the brink.

She had watched as the princess had administered the various drugs, pumping them directly into Des's system through the thick artery in his neck. She didn't fully understand what the compounds were or what they did, but she had seen enough to gain some understanding of each one's effects.

The black needle induced the spasms Serra had used to torture her victim; the yellow caused the convulsions to end. The green seemed to force Des back into his stupor. But the red needle—the one her mistress had given him at the start of the interrogation—had

seemed to wake him up. It had to be some kind of stimulant or antidote, something to offset the drugs that kept him helpless and non-
responsive.

Glancing over her shoulder to make sure nobody in the guard
room just outside was watching, she picked up one of the red hypo-
dermics.

There were too many mercs for her to fight her way out—trying
to win Des his freedom that way would only get them both killed. But
she didn't have to break Des out to save him. He had always been capable of looking after himself, even before he gained the mystical
powers of a Sith Lord. She knew he was more than capable of escaping on his own if she just gave him a little help.

She gently pushed the tip of the needle into his thigh, hoping the
drugs would enter his system more slowly and less violently than
when Serra had plunged them into his neck. She knew it was possible
she might accidentally overdose him, but even if Des died it was better than leaving him alive to be tortured over and over again.

Placing the needle back on the cart, she turned and quickly left the
room. She didn't have time to wait around and watch the effects. She
needed to find the princess. If the drug worked as she suspected, he'd
quickly regain his faculties. And once he was able to call upon the terrible power of the dark side, no cell in the galaxy would be capable of
holding him.

She made her way back into the guard room. The mercenaries had
returned to their card game, oblivious of what she had done. Serra
and the Huntress were nowhere in sight.

"Where did the princess go?" she demanded.

There was a long silence before one of the mercenaries grudgingly
looked up from the hand and answered, "She didn't say. She just left."

"And you let her go off alone?" Lucia demanded angrily.

"That Iktotchi was with her so we just . . . ," the man answered, his
voice trailing off under her withering glare.

She realized they were mere hired guns. They didn't care for anything but the credits they'd been promised.

"Lock the cell door," Lucia spat out. "If anything goes wrong, hit the alarm." *That should give me enough of a warning to get the princess out of here in time.*

Two of the soldiers reluctantly got up and moved to obey her orders as Lucia climbed the staircase to the hall above.

She didn't care that when Des broke free he'd slaughter the guards. These men and women weren't her friends or colleagues. She knew they'd kill her without a second thought if the price was right. They were mercenaries; their lives meant nothing to her.

But she still cared about Serra. Despite what she had done, she was still loyal to her mistress. She was still sworn to protect her life. When Des broke free, she knew he'd come looking for the princess. When the alarms went off warning of the prisoner's escape, Lucia wanted to be there to help Serra get away to safety.

And if he catches us before we get away, she silently tried to reassure herself, *maybe he'll remember me. Maybe I can convince him to let Serra live.*

First, however, she had to find her.

18

Doan's scarred and ugly terrain rolled beneath them as the *Victory* sped low across the planet's surface.

In the cockpit Zannah braced herself as the sensors picked up a fierce sandstorm several hundred kilometers in the distance. Beside her Set was seated in his customary position: chair leaning back, feet up on the dash.

Making a slight change in her approach vector brought her on a collision course with the storm. She didn't bother to give Set any warning as the *Victory* was engulfed by the whirling vortex.

The stabilizers kept the ship from suffering any real harm, but the cabin bucked violently as the vessel was buffeted by the howling winds. Set was sent tumbling from his chair, but he managed to roll with the momentum as he hit the ground and came up on his feet.

"You did that on purpose," he accused, using the back of his chair to steady himself in the turbulence.

"You need to be alert and aware of your surroundings at all times," she instructed him. "Always be on your guard."

"I thought the information I gave you might have earned me a break from any more lessons today," he grumbled as he sat back into his copilot's chair and buckled the restraints.

"You were wrong."

Despite her words, Set had proved himself to be quite valuable. In addition to telling her about Darth Andeddu and his Holocron, he had actually come up with the most likely place Bane was being held.

"They probably took your Master to the Stone Prison," he had declared shortly after they had begun their journey.

"The Stone Prison?"

"A dungeon built centuries ago by the nobility on Doan to house political prisoners," he'd explained. "I found all sorts of references to it in the historical archives."

"What kind of defenses do they have?" she'd asked.

"Pretty standard. Anti-aircraft cannons. Armed guards inside. And they can set off a series of explosion to bring the whole place down as a last resort."

Zannah had scowled. "We'll have to avoid detection when we go in."

"That might be easier than you think," Set had answered with a smile. "The Stone Prison hasn't been used for almost two generations."

It all made sense to Zannah. A small team of elite guards or mercenaries could keep a single prisoner secured in the abandoned facility without attracting unwanted attention. All the infrastructure they needed—holding cells, interrogation rooms—would still be there. If they stayed deep inside the heart of the complex, nobody would even know they were there. Secrecy, as she well understood, was often the best protection from your enemies. But when your secrets were exposed, it could leave you vulnerable.

"They won't be expecting anyone to assault the prison, so I doubt they'll even activate the external defenses," Set had continued, speaking aloud the very thoughts running through Zannah's mind. "A small team couldn't spare the bodies to operate the stations, and powering the systems up would be like sending off a flare to alert everyone they were there."

It was at that point that Zannah realized Set, for all his seeming overconfidence and carefree attitude, actually liked to be prepared. He wasn't afraid to improvise and adapt, but he had the sense to know what he was heading into . . . at least in the short term. The trick would be teaching him to apply the same kind of diligence to long-term plans, then have the patience to bear them out.

The *Victory* passed through the eye of the sandstorm and out the other side, continuing on toward the tall stone column looming far in the distance. Even though they were enjoying a smooth ride once more, Zannah was pleased to see that Set didn't lean back and put his feet up again.

He was learning, and he'd shown several flashes of real potential during their time together. Maybe there was hope for him yet . . . or maybe, Zannah had to admit, she was just so desperate to find an apprentice she was willing to overlook his flaws.

"There. That column up ahead. That's the one we want."

Dusk had fallen and Zannah could just make out the silhouette of the massive stone pillar in the distance. From here it looked like an enormous candle: tall and straight, the top aglow with hundreds of lights from the royal family's estate that had been built on the wide, flat plateau at its apex.

Zannah brought the shuttle in low, skimming less than twenty meters above the ground to stay below the radar of the royal estate perched nearly five kilometers above them.

The *Victory* was picking up hundreds of life-forms when she scanned the column, but they were all concentrated in the buildings of the plateau. There was no evidence of life inside the pillar, but that was to be expected. The scanners wouldn't be able to penetrate the mountain of stone.

Reaching out with the Force, however, presented Zannah with a very different picture. She could feel something dark and powerful pulsing at the heart of the column. She recognized the presence of her Master, though from this distance it was impossible to get anything more than a vague sense that he was hidden somewhere inside.

"There should be hidden landing ports for the prison about halfway up the column," Set assured her. "They'll probably look like small caves. Easy to miss."

The *Victory* was less than a hundred meters from the pillar when Zannah angled its nose sharply upward. The ship reacted instantly, arching into a steep ascent, the g-forces pinning the two passengers back in their seats. The shuttle steadied in a perfectly vertical climb less than ten meters from the rock wall, running parallel to its contours as Zannah looked for a place to land.

It was too dark for a visual, but the ship's sensors provided her with a digital topography of the pillar's surface racing beneath the hull. What from a distance had looked smooth and sheer was, in fact, rough and irregular. Wind and erosion had sculpted grooves and channels in the rock, and the face was pockmarked with thousands of small, irregularly shaped openings. Most were nooks or fissures that went less than ten meters deep. Others were actual tunnels that extended deeper into the rock. Only a handful were large enough to accommodate a shuttle, however.

"Hold on," Zannah warned an instant before pulling hard back on the stick.

The *Victory* peeled away from the column into a backward loop. At the same time Zannah sent them into a half-barrel roll so that they finished right-side up, with the nose of the vessel pointed toward the opening she'd chosen. The landing thrusters fired at full force as the shuttle's momentum sent them rocketing into the mouth of the cavern, braking hard before settling into a perfect three-point landing.

Set didn't say anything, but Zannah saw him raise a brow in appreciation. She could have chosen a less dramatic maneuver to reach her destination, but she knew her would-be apprentice preferred doing things with a certain stylistic flair. Impressing him with her piloting skills was just one more small way to secure his respect and loyalty.

Through the cockpit window Zannah could see only darkness. She flicked on the *Victory*'s external lights, illuminating the cavern. The rock walls surrounding them were sharp and jagged, but the floor was smooth and even. A single passage led off to one side, the tunnel too perfectly straight to have been shaped by nature.

"There are probably about a dozen other landing bays like this one," Set informed her as they exited the shuttle. "Each one with a passage leading into the lower levels of the complex."

"It's too bad you weren't able to find any holomaps of the layout," she commented, not wanting him to get too cocky.

"Maybe we should split up," Set suggested. "With two of us searching we'll have a better chance of finding him."

"I'm going in alone," Zannah informed him. "You're going to stay here and guard the ship."

"Guard the ship? From whom?"

"Whoever took Bane might have someone patrolling the entrances. If they find our ship undefended they can disable it, cutting off our only method of escape."

"Fine," Set replied curtly after a moment's consideration. "I'll sit here and watch the shuttle like your personal Cyborrean battle dog."

"I assume you'll be able to handle anyone who stumbles across this landing bay without too much trouble."

"Everyone except your Master," he assured her.

Even I'm not sure I can handle him.

Satisfied with Set's answer, Zannah cracked a glow stick. Guided by its pale illumination, she made her way down the tunnel and into the Stone Prison.

———

Set watched his new Master's back, following her progress until she turned around a corner and disappeared, leaving him alone in the small landing bay.

He leaned casually against the *Victory*'s hull, thinking back on their arrival. He considered himself a pretty good pilot, but he would never have attempted a move like the backward barrel roll Zannah had used to bring them in to land. He knew she was just showing off for his benefit. Still, it had been impressive.

After a few minutes he began to pace restlessly back and forth, kicking at small stones in the dirt. Set didn't like taking orders, and he didn't like sitting around doing nothing.

Don't do anything stupid now. She was talking earlier about how important patience is. This is probably another test.

Obba, his Master before he had left the Jedi, had often encouraged his students to meditate when they had no other tasks or duties. He claimed it centered the mind and spirit. But Set had never been a fan of meditation. He preferred to be doing something—anything—to sitting around in a trance lost inside his own thoughts.

He squatted down and rummaged around on the ground until he had collected five fist-sized stones. He brushed the dust off as best he could, inspecting them for sharp edges that might cut his palms or fingers. Then, satisfied with his finds, he began to juggle, hoping it would help pass the time.

He started with simple tosses, getting a feel for the weight and balance of each stone. Then he shifted into a cascade, the rocks dancing in a circular, looping pattern as they leapt from hand to hand. Next he added in catches behind his back, alternating every other toss front-to-back without ever breaking his rhythm.

Peering around the cavern, he spotted another suitably sized rock on the floor a few meters away. Still juggling, he moved toward it with shuffling steps until he was close enough to slip the toe of his boot under the stone's edge. A quick flick of the foot sent it high into the air, where it joined the others in his pattern.

He repeated this trick several more times, moving around the cavern in search of more rocks, adding both numbers and complexity to the trick until, upon reaching ten objects being juggled simultaneously, he let them all drop to the ground in disgust.

You didn't come here to play games.

Zannah had been gone less than ten minutes, and already he was unbearably bored.

She could be gone for hours. You're not going to make it.

Closing his eyes to help him focus, Set reached out with the Force, probing the area around him. At first he didn't feel anything; Zannah had disappeared deep into the complex.

Concentrating intently, he pushed his awareness out even farther. Beads of sweat began to form on his brow, but after nearly a minute he began to detect faint signs of life. All living beings were attuned to the Force on some level, and the Jedi had trained him to sense their presence through it. Ordinary people were barely noticeable, as easy to miss as a dim light on a sunny afternoon. Those with power—men and women like Zannah or other Jedi—burned with a much greater intensity.

To his surprise, Set felt several strong, distinct flares as he extended his awareness out. He had expected to sense Zannah and her Master, but they were not alone. It was difficult to say exactly how many others there were, or their precise location; sensing others through the Force was a rather inexact science. But they were definitely there.

And they're not Jedi.

Those who served the light side had a certain unmistakable aura about them . . . as did those who called upon the dark side.

Maybe Bane's already found himself another apprentice. Zannah could be in for a little surprise.

In normal circumstances Zannah would have certainly felt the other presences just as he had, but Set knew she was focused on one thing—finding Bane. With her mind concentrating so intently on pinpointing the exact location of her Master, it was possible she might not notice anyone else. Not until she was virtually right on top of them.

Set hesitated, uncertain what he should do. Did Zannah need his help? If she did, would he bother?

If you want to bail, this is your best chance. Just jump into that shuttle and fly on out of here.

If he left and Zannah died, it was unlikely anyone else would ever know he had been here. He wouldn't have to worry about her Master coming after him; he could pretend none of this had ever happened. If Zannah survived, however, he had no doubt that she'd come looking for revenge. And since he wouldn't be around to see the final outcome of her confrontation with Bane, he'd have to spend the rest of his days looking over his shoulder just in case.

Not much different from what you do now. You've managed to stay one step ahead of the Jedi all these years; how much harder can it be to stay one step ahead of the Sith at the same time?

But there were other considerations. If he left, he was throwing away the chance to learn from Zannah. She was stronger than he was, much stronger. She could teach him things he'd never learn from anyone else. It wasn't easy to turn his back on that kind of power.

Torn between the two options, Set tried to extend his awareness out even farther in the hope of learning more. He was already approaching the limits of his abilities, but he knew this was the most important decision of his life. He couldn't afford to get it wrong.

A sharp pain was building in his forehead; it felt like someone was sticking a long needle into his skull right between his eyes. He wasn't used to this kind of prolonged effort; when he called on the Force it was for quick bursts of action. But he ignored the pain, gritted his teeth, and made one final push.

And then he felt it. Living creatures were not the only things with an affinity for the Force. Most of Set's adult life had been spent seeking out objects imbued with its power: initially on behalf of the Council of First Knowledge, then later on his own. He had become highly adept at recognizing the unique energy signatures projected by the talismans of the dark side; they called out to him more strongly than they did to most others.

That was why, despite the fact it was on the very fringes of his awareness, he was able to sense it. It was like nothing he had ever felt before; something so strong and powerful it caused him to gasp with yearning.

Andeddu's Holocron. It has to be.

Zannah had said her Master had gone to Prakith to find it. Whoever had captured Bane must have taken the Holocron for themselves.

Set opened his eyes and shook his head, collapsing his awareness back to his immediate surroundings. His looming headache was gone, replaced by an aching desire to claim the Holocron for himself.

He had only a vague idea of where to find it. Once he was inside the Stone Prison, though, he was confident he'd be able to zero in on it quickly. For him, tracking a Holocron was much easier than locating a person.

Zannah had commanded him to guard the ship, but he wasn't worried about anyone accidentally discovering it. He hadn't sensed anyone even remotely close to the landing bay.

The question is, can you get the Holocron and get back here before Zannah finishes with Bane?

It was risky. If she returned to discover he was gone, she might decide to end his apprenticeship . . . and his life. Even if she didn't, she might just take the Holocron for herself, and Set knew he wouldn't be strong enough to stop her.

But if you find the Holocron, who says you have to bring it back here?

Whoever had brought Bane to the Stone Prison had to be using one of the other landing bays for their own vessels. How hard could it be to steal one of those instead?

The secret of eternal life versus the undying hatred of a Sith Lord. Is it worth it?

That was one question Set had no trouble answering. Taking a glow lamp, he entered the Stone Prison through the same passage Zannah had gone down less than fifteen minutes earlier.

19

Bane could feel the hard iron of his shackles cutting into his wrists, and a grim smile played across his lips. The pain indicated that the sedative was wearing off. The dull gray fog that had clouded his thoughts was clearing, leaving his mind sharp and focused.

Once again he could feel the power of the dark side. It was strong in this place; the misery and suffering of centuries hung in the air here. Bane could almost hear the screams of all the countless victims still echoing off the walls.

The memories of the last hour were hazy and confused, but he knew enough. His capture had been orchestrated by Caleb's daughter and the mysterious Iktotchi who had stood at her side during the interrogation. And he owed his release to their other companion.

He didn't know why the dark-skinned woman had injected him after the others had left. Despite his drugged state at the time, he was certain it wasn't an accident or mistake. She had known what she was doing. Who she was and why she had done it, however, were beyond him.

Not that her identity or her reasons mattered in the immediate future. She had given Bane all the help he needed, and soon he would be ready to make his move.

The pain had spread beyond his wrists. His shoulders felt like they were being ripped from his sockets from bearing the brunt of his weight. The deep gashes on his cheek burned, and he could feel the small rivulets of blood creeping along his face and down along the line of his jaw before dripping to the floor.

It's time.

He lifted his head to make sure the door to his cell was still closed; he wanted to catch his captors by surprise. Then he began to gather the power of the Force. An instant later the cuffs on his wrists and ankles shattered, exploding into a million pieces at a mere thought from Bane.

He fell to the floor, his weary muscles unprepared to support his weight. It took him a moment to gather himself, and then a rush of adrenaline surged through his body and he was back on his feet.

Bane felt naked without his lightsaber, but he wasn't exactly helpless without it. There were plenty of other ways to dispatch his enemies.

Three quick strides brought him to the durasteel door of his cell. He reached out and placed his left palm flat against the surface, then used the Force to blow it outward. It flew across the room, striking and killing one of the guards sitting at a table playing cards.

The remaining five guards scrambled to their feet, grabbing for their weapons. Bane lashed out with the Force. The fury of his attack was muted by the last lingering effects of the drugs in his system, but it was still strong enough to knock them all to the floor and send the table flying into the wall, where it cracked in half.

Bane fell on the guards like an enraged animal, moving so quickly he was nothing but a blur. He brought his boot down on the throat of his nearest opponent, crushing his windpipe. He wrapped his muscular forearm around the next man's neck from behind in a choke hold, braced his other palm against his chin, and wrenched his head to the side, breaking his neck.

The last three opponents were back on their feet, blasters drawn. Bane yanked a short vibroblade from the belt of the man with the broken neck and plunged it into the belly of a woman before she could bring her pistol to bear. She doubled over from the fatal blow, releasing her grip on her weapon.

Bane dropped to the floor and caught it before it hit the ground, ducking under the bolts fired from the remaining two enemies as he rolled onto his back and fired a pair of perfectly placed shots. The guards both toppled over backward, their faces erased by the impact of a blaster bolt at point-blank range.

Another locked durasteel door blocked the only exit. Bane tossed the blaster aside and tore the door off its hinges. Up above, someone triggered the alarm, and a deafening klaxon began to blare.

Beyond the door was a narrow staircase, similarly barricaded at the top. The Dark Lord charged up the steps and threw himself shoulder-first into the door at the top. It burst open from the impact, sending him tumbling into the room beyond.

The four guards up here had been alerted by the blaster shots being fired down below; unlike the first wave they weren't caught off guard by his violent entrance. Weapons already drawn, they opened fire.

But Bane's visceral, primal assault on the squad in the room below had fueled the cycle of rising emotion and mounting dark side power. He met their assault with an explosion of crackling energy that rippled out in a violet wave from his body at the center.

The incoming bolts were absorbed harmlessly into the ionic storm, the blasters themselves melted in the hands of their owners. The stench of burned flesh mingled with their screams of agony and the relentless, hammering song of the alarms, further feeding Bane's power.

Crouched on one knee, he clenched both fists then threw his arms out to either side, fingers splayed wide. The resulting Force wave pummeled the guards, sending them hurtling backward so they bounced off the walls hard enough to leave cracks in the stone.

Bane rose to his feet in the center of the carnage. Half a dozen bodies lay strewn about him, bones shattered, internal organs crushed into pulp. One choked out a pink, frothing spray with his final breath; all the others were still.

To his dismay, he saw neither Caleb's daughter nor the Iktotchi among the dead. He had sensed a few guards fleeing the room as he had charged up the staircase, but he hadn't felt either of those two women among them. He also didn't recognize any of the corpses as the dark-skinned woman who had saved him, though he was—for the moment—less interested in her.

He had found Serra once before. During his first meeting with Caleb, the healer had tried to trick him with a simple illusion to hide his daughter. But Bane had sensed the little girl cowering behind the façade; he had tasted her fear. Yet it was more than that. Like her father, the girl had power that could be sensed through the Force.

You can't hide from me. I will find you.

Calling up the long-buried memory, he reached out with his mind, concentrating on picking out her unmistakable presence.

She's here. Still in the facility. But she's not alone.

His awareness had spread through the halls of the dungeon, whispering over the minds of all who walked the halls. He had sensed Serra, along with several other powerful individuals. Yet there was one in particular that had drawn his attention.

Zannah. What is she doing here?

Was his apprentice somehow involved in his capture? Had she come here to rescue him? Or maybe to stop him from escaping?

Whatever the explanation, Bane knew one thing for certain: He didn't want to face Zannah right now. Not while he was still recovering from the toxins Serra had used to render him helpless, and certainly not without his lightsaber.

She was searching for him; he could feel her reaching out, drawing ever closer. Still, there were ways to counter her efforts: subtle manipulations of the Force could confuse and misdirect her.

Fooling Zannah while tracking Caleb's daughter at the same time was possible in theory, though few individuals had the discipline to maintain the balance between two such mentally intensive tasks. But Bane's will was as strong as his body.

If he was quick, cunning, and careful he had a chance to find his quarry while still getting out of the prison alive.

———

Tears of anger, shame, and frustration were streaming down the princess's face. She had held them in check as she had passed the guards, but with nobody around to see her she had finally let them go.

Her plan to avenge her father's death and free herself from the traumatic memories of her childhood had so far failed miserably. She had wanted the Sith Lord to admit he was wrong. She had wanted him to apologize and ask forgiveness for Caleb's death. She had wanted him to beg her for mercy.

She had convinced herself that if this happened it would help her deal with the senseless death of not just her father, but also her husband. She had thought it would help restore some type of meaning to a cruel and random universe. She had hoped it would bring her peace.

But nothing had gone the way she had planned. The prisoner was completely unrepentant. He had twisted everything she had done and said into some perverse justification for what he believed in. He almost made it seem that Caleb's death was *right*.

And he turned your best friend against you.

As much as the words of the Sith disturbed her, the actions of Lucia had upset her even more. The bodyguard had been the one who hired the Huntress to avenge Gerran's death. But now she seemed determined to oppose Serra's quest to avenge Caleb.

It made no sense to the princess. She had expected Lucia to stand by her during the confrontation, to support her as she faced the demon of her past. To shore up her strength so she could conquer her fears and triumph over his evil. Instead she had defended him.

How could you turn your back on me like that? When I needed you the most?

Serra had fled the interrogation cell to escape the madness, not even paying attention to where she was going. Moving with long, quick strides, she had rushed heedlessly down the maze of halls without any purpose or direction.

She didn't know where she was going or what she was trying to do. She just needed to think. To try to make sense of it all. To be alone.

Only she wasn't alone.

The physical exertion had helped bring her swirling emotions back under control, and after several minutes she began to regain some semblance of composure. The tears stopped and her pace slowed. It was only then she heard the footsteps of someone following a few meters behind her.

She stopped short, bringing up a hand to wipe at her eyes before turning around. She was hoping to see Lucia. Instead, she found herself face-to-face with the Iktotchi assassin.

"Why are you sneaking along behind me?" she demanded.

"If I was sneaking, you wouldn't have heard me," the Huntress replied with her implacable calm. "I was following you, but I made no effort to mask my presence."

"Then why were you following me?"

"I wanted to see what you would do. I'm curious to learn how you will react to your failure."

Serra's lip twitched, but she managed to keep the rest of her face expressionless, mirroring the other woman's emotionless demeanor.

There was no point in denying what had happened; the Iktotchi had witnessed the entire exchange. But the princess wasn't willing to admit defeat.

"I will pick myself up from failure and try again," she declared. "Next time I speak with him I'll be ready for his tricks."

"There won't be a next time," the Huntress replied. "You had him in your power. His very life was in your hands. But you chose to let him live, and now it is too late. His fate and his future have slipped through your grasp. You are powerless once again."

The words were spoken without spite or malice, which made them sting all the more. Serra realized there was something evil about this woman. She wasn't just a hired assassin. She used her ability to sense the future so she could spread suffering and death.

"I don't want you here anymore," Serra told her, her voice firm. "Your job is done and you've already been paid. So go."

"The future is muddied right now," the Iktotchi admitted. "Events teeter on a knife-edge, and I cannot foresee which way they will fall. I want to stay and see what happens when the prisoner breaks free."

"He will never break free!" Serra snapped. "I won't let that happen!"

"You can't stop it. It's already too late," the Huntress replied. "Lucia has betrayed you. I saw it in her eyes when you left. She wants to save the man you want to destroy."

Serra shook her head, but though she wanted to deny it she couldn't speak the words.

She was defending him during the interrogation. Trying to protect him.

"Why didn't you say something earlier?" she asked, perplexed. "Why didn't you warn me?"

"As you said, I have already been paid. My job was to deliver him to you. Nothing more."

"So why are you telling me now?"

The Iktotchi didn't answer, but the first hint of emotion played across her face as the corners of her lips curled up into the hint of a cruel smile.

She feeds on the misery of others.

Serra started to say, *Lucia would never betray me,* but her words were cut off by the sudden clanging of the Stone Prison's alarms.

In that instant she knew everything the Huntress had told her was true. The prisoner had broken free, and Lucia had helped him.

"No!" Serra shouted, clasping her head in her hands as for the second time today her world came crashing down around her. "No!"

The Iktotchi was grinning now, transforming the tattoos on her lower lip into fangs.

"No!" the princess shouted again, her voice rising up over the alarms.

He can't escape. Not now. Not after everything that's happened.

"No!"

Serra turned and fled down one of the nearby corridors, a last, desperate plan forming in her mind.

20

As soon as Lucia was out of sight of the guards watching Des, she broke into a brisk jog. She knew she didn't have much time before he escaped, and she needed to find the princess before that happened. But figuring out where Serra had gone was no easy matter.

Dozens of passages branched off from the main corridor on either side, leading to other cell blocks in the wing, or to completely new areas of the dungeon complex. Fortunately only a small section of the Stone Prison had been reopened. Most of the halls Lucia passed were still dark and deserted: she didn't think the princess would have gone down any of these.

Even so, there was a lot of area to cover. She had started with the administrative office for the maximum-security wing, only to find it empty. After that she had backtracked, moving quickly up and down the halls that were illuminated, occasionally calling out Serra's name in what she hoped came across as a calm, normal voice.

She needed to find her, but she also didn't want to make her suspicious. Lucia had no intention of revealing what she had done. She had helped Des because she felt it was right, but she doubted Serra would understand.

Her hope was that she would be at the princess's side under the guise of a supportive friend when the alarms went off. As her body-guard, it would make perfect sense for her to whisk Serra away to safety at that time, and her friend would never have to know the truth about how Des escaped.

Unfortunately, the first part of her plan fell apart when she heard the alarms ring out a few minutes later.

She cursed under her breath and broke into a full run. Her plan could still work: if she found Serra she could still convince her to leave without exposing her betrayal. But now she was in a race against Des to see which one of them could find the princess first.

Where could she be?

The clanging alarms made it hard to think. Lucia skidded to a stop, taking a moment to collect her thoughts.

From the corridor off to her right she heard the princess scream out "No!"—her voice carrying even over the cacophony of the alarms.

She had to be close! Turning, Lucia ran down the hall in the direction of the sound. She came to another intersection: the corridor branched right, left, and continued straight ahead. Pausing, she listened for another clue, but heard nothing.

Thinking back to the blueprints she had memorized when she had first joined the Royal Guard, she remembered that the corridor on the left led deeper into the dungeon, toward an area that was still closed. That left only two options.

She continued on straight ahead, knowing the hall carried on for about twenty meters before turning sharply and ending in an old guard barracks. The room was on the same power grid as the maximum-security wing, so it would be illuminated. But it wasn't being used: the hired mercenaries had been given lodging in the bar-racks on the other side of the wing.

Lucia was guessing the princess had gone there to find some privacy as she struggled to deal with her emotions. She guessed wrong. Finding the barracks empty, she was forced to double back and take the other branch, knowing precious seconds had been lost.

Running at a full sprint, she dashed down the hall and around the corner, nearly barreling into the Huntress. The Iktotchi stepped quickly to the side to avoid the collision. At the same time Lucia pulled up short, throwing herself off balance so that she stumbled and fell. Her knee smacked hard into the floor and skidded across the rough stone, tearing a hole in her trousers and scraping away a layer of skin.

"Have you seen the princess?" she asked as she got back to her feet, ignoring the warm blood already welling up from the deep scrapes on her injured knee.

"She knows what you did," the assassin said. "She knows you betrayed her."

The unexpected accusation caught Lucia off guard; she didn't even try to deny it.

"How?"

"I told her."

Lucia was stunned, unable to fathom how her secret had been exposed. And then she remembered the rumors that claimed the Iktotchi could see the future and read minds. She was on the verge of asking why the Huntress would let this happen only to tell Serra of her betrayal after the fact, but then she remembered whom she was dealing with.

She did it to hurt her. She's as much a monster as any Sith.

For a moment she thought about going for her blaster. She wanted to kill the Huntress. She'd be doing the galaxy a favor. But despite her outrage, she knew she had no chance of killing the assassin. Attacking her would result only in Lucia's own death, and it would do nothing to help the princess.

You can still find Serra. Even if she knows what you did, maybe you can still convince her to get away before Des finds her. You can still save her.

"Which way did she go?" she asked, wondering if the Iktotchi would even bother to tell her.

"She ran off that way," the assassin replied, tilting her horned head to indicate the direction.

Lucia's mind flashed back to the blueprints of the complex, and she knew where Serra was heading. The princess was still determined to kill Bane. She was going to the control room to detonate the Stone Prison's self-destruct sequence.

Not bothering to waste another second on the Huntress she turned and ran off down the corridor in pursuit, her gait clumsy and uneven because of her bloody and rapidly swelling knee.

———

The Huntress watched the princess's bodyguard rush off down the hall. She knew what lay at the end; in her visions she had seen the walls of this prison come crashing down in a series of explosions.

For an instant she had thought the bodyguard was going to try to kill her. She was somewhat disappointed when it didn't happen. Yet she knew Lucia's end was inevitable: she had seen it.

She turned and made her way with purposeful strides in the other direction, heading for the main hangar bay: a large cavern where she and the mercenaries had landed their shuttles. There was no point in sticking around, not when she knew the self-destruct sequence was going to be activated in a few minutes. Yet when she reached the hangar, she hesitated.

The prisoner's escape hadn't surprised her. She knew he was not destined to die chained like an animal. She had seen him too many times in her dreams, locked in battle with the blond woman from her visions on Ambria. Her subconscious mind was obsessed with them, and the Huntress suspected she finally knew why.

Her life had become stagnant, hollow. She moved from job to job, but she had no real purpose, no greater goal. Despite her ability to see visions of the future, she had never sought to shape it. She had always felt a greater destiny awaited her, yet she had made no effort to pursue it.

From her pocket, she drew out the lightsaber hilt and the small pyramid she had taken on Ciutric. These were instruments of power; she could feel the importance of them. They had significance and meaning. They had purpose.

She knew the Jedi claimed the light side had triumphed over the dark. They claimed the Sith were extinct. Yet the Huntress also knew this was a lie. The Sith still lived; she had tasted their power. And she had found it intoxicating.

Securing the lightsaber and the pyramid back under her robe, she made her way over to lean against the guardrail of the large metal balcony overlooking the landing pads. From her vantage point she could look out across the tops of the four vessels parked below, giving her a clear view of Doan's night sky through the wide entrance on the cavern's far side.

Two of the ships were unremarkable: shuttles owned by the mercenaries the princess had hired to staff the station. The third was the princess's personal vessel: newer than the others, it bore the blue-and-yellow symbol of House Doan on either side. And then there was her own vessel, the *Stalker*. Smaller than any of the other ships, its shining black hull and blood-red trim still made it stand out.

After a moment she made her way slowly down the stairs, but when she reached the ground below she didn't board her ship. Instead, she began to wander slowly up and down the aisles between the vessels, idly running her hand across their hulls.

She felt compelled to wait a little while longer. Something important was about to happen, something more than the spectacular implosion of the Stone Prison. She could feel it coming on the currents of the Force. She couldn't quite grasp what the event was—sometimes the future could be as slippery as a fleek eel. But she knew it had something to do with her visions, and she intended to wait around long enough to see this through.

Her destiny depended on it.

———

Zannah knew she was getting close. The part of her journey through the Stone Prison's maze of rooms and halls had been conducted in near total darkness. Only the pale green light of her glow stick had guided her—that, and the Force.

She could feel her Master's presence deep inside the complex, drawing her forward. Even so, she made several wrong turns and came across a number of dead ends as she moved silently through the darkness. The layout of the dungeon was intentionally confusing to thwart any efforts to rescue those held captive within its walls.

Yet Zannah had persevered, never giving in to frustration or anger even when she was forced to turn around and go back the way she had come. Eventually, she knew, she would reach her destination.

Up ahead she saw a faint glimmer of light spilling from around a corner, and she knew her patience had been rewarded. Moving forward, she found herself traveling through an illuminated corridor. She had reached the section of the facility that had been reopened; Bane had to be nearby.

Tossing her glow lamp aside, she proceeded forward cautiously, keeping her awareness open to warn her before she ran across any guards even as she continued to home in on the cell where they were holding her Master.

She had gone less than a hundred meters when she felt a sudden and powerful disturbance in the Force. An instant later alarm bells rang out, and Zannah knew what had happened—Bane had escaped!

Her lightsaber ignited with a buzzing hum, and she picked up her

pace. She was no longer trying to sense any guards who might be
ahead: with Bane on the loose she needed to focus on him. Her Master would be on the move, and she had come too far to lose him now.

The alarms continued to ring out. Zannah ignored them, focusing
instead on the flashes of power she felt through the Force, each one a
beacon bringing her ever closer to Bane.

She darted down a hall and around a corner. Up ahead she saw a
door swinging freely on its hinges.

He's there. In that room or one just beyond it. She could sense his
presence, his unmistakable power.

Creeping along the wall she approached the edge of the door, then
ducked into a roll and somersaulted through into the room beyond.

The scene inside gave testament to the fact that Bane had been
here. The mangled bodies of guards littered the room. A durasteel
door hung askew on its hinges, revealing a steep staircase leading down
to another room below.

The dark side had been unleashed here only a few minutes ago.
She could still feel its lingering power.

She approached the staircase carefully, probing with her mind
into the room below. Again, she felt the unmistakable power of her
Master.

He's trapped.

She broke off her efforts to track Bane and instead concentrated
on using Sith sorcery to mask her own presence as she raced down
the stairs. There was no need for her to be silent; with the alarms
echoing throughout the prison, there was little chance he would hear
her footsteps.

She burst into the lower chamber only to be disappointed yet
again. Another pile of dead guards were gathered around the remains
of a table, but Bane was nowhere to be found. She had been tracking
an echo of his power, and somehow she had missed the real thing.

That's impossible. Unless . . .

Bane knew she was here! He had tricked her, leaving his imprint on this room to lure her here while he made his escape. But she knew he couldn't have gone far.

She turned to head back up the stairs, then paused for a moment to examine the bodies. One looked as if he had been killed by Bane's bare hands. One was stabbed with a vibroblade. Two others had been shot with a blaster at close range.

Curious, Zannah made her way back to the room above. The bodies here were, quite simply, broken. Limbs twisted at grotesque angles, the bones beneath the skin shattered and splintered.

There was nothing remarkable about how they had died; she had seen Bane use similar tactics many times in the past. Zannah was interested, however, in what was missing. There were no lightsaber wounds.

Bane had been unarmed when he took on these foes. It was possible he had found and reclaimed his lightsaber since then. But if he hadn't—if he was wandering the halls of the prison without it—he was vulnerable. As powerful as Bane was, Zannah believed she was his equal. And without his lightsaber he had virtually no hope of defeating her.

Closing her eyes and blocking out the earsplitting sound of the alarms, she reached out with the Force once more. This time she ignored the powerful dark side imprint Bane had left on the guard rooms. It only took a few seconds for her to pick up his trail again. As she suspected, he was still inside the prison.

I'm coming, Master. And only one of us will leave here alive.

———

Set knew he was close. He had left the darkness of the unlit tunnels behind as he had gone deeper and deeper into the Stone Prison, drawn forward by the call of Darth Andeddu's Holocron.

The section of the complex he was in now was lit, though it still seemed deserted. He had expected to run into somebody: a patrol, a guard wandering the halls. Whoever had taken Zannah's Master must have done it with a small team: twenty, maybe thirty people at most.

Despite this, he was bracing for an encounter soon. He had reached a long hall with a closed wooden door at the end. He was certain the Holocron was inside the room beyond, and he fully expected it to be guarded by at least half a dozen armed soldiers.

Gathering himself, he drew his lightsaber and raced down the hallway, leaping toward the door. He hit it square with both feet, knocking the door open as he flew into the room.

Much to Set's surprise, there were no guards waiting for him. The only witnesses to his grand entrance were an old wooden desk and chair. He felt a second of panic when he didn't see the Holocron anywhere in the small office; then he noticed the safe built into the wall.

There was a combination pad, but Set ignored it. Using his lightsaber, he simply cut several long horizontal and vertical slices in the door. The glowing blade carved through the thick metal with ease, reducing the front of the safe to several heavy chunks that fell to the floor.

The Holocron was the only thing inside. Set reached out slowly, trembling slightly as he wrapped his fingers around the obsidian pyramid. He drew it reverently from the safe, cradling it with both hands.

He nearly dropped his prize when alarm bells began to ring throughout the prison.

Whirling to the door he whipped out his lightsaber, his left hand still clutching the Holocron. He dropped into a fighting stance, bracing himself to meet the reinforcements he expected to burst into the room.

For several seconds he didn't move, listening for the sound of running feet or the shouts of soldiers. Hearing nothing, he carefully reached out with the Force—only to find he was still alone.

The alarms were still blaring away, and it took a minute for Set to realize they had nothing to do with him.

They spotted Zannah. Or her Master's escaped.

Extinguishing his lightsaber, he tucked it back into his belt.

Nobody's going to be worrying about you. Not with a couple of Sith Lords wreaking havoc in one of the other wings.

He had what he had come for; it was time to leave Doan. Hopefully he would never have to come back again.

Set still intended to stick with his original plan of stealing one of the other ships, rather than risk running into Zannah by going back to where they had landed her shuttle. He just needed to look around until he found the hangars where the other vessels were being stored.

Shouldn't be too hard. Just stick to the lit halls and keep out of everyone else's way. Let them fight it out while you sneak off with the real prize.

Fortunately, that was something Set was very good at.

———

The echoing alarms chased Serra as she ran down the long hall toward the Stone Prison's emergency control room. She punched in the code to the access panel, her fingers stabbing frantically at the keys as she kept glancing over her shoulder, fearing her enemy would appear in the hall behind her at any second.

The panel beeped sharply, and an ACCESS DENIED message popped up on the readout.

"No," she whispered to herself. "No."

When she had married Gerran, he had shared his personal access code with her. As the crown prince, his code was supposed to override every electronic security system in the royal family's estate.

Maybe the king didn't trust you. Maybe he disabled it when Gerran died.

No, that couldn't be it. The code had worked on all the other locks here in the Stone Prison. Without it, she would never have been able to reactivate the generators that powered this section of the complex.

She tried to punch the code in again, her fingers trembling with desperate urgency. The alarms overhead were an inescapable reminder that every second she lost made it more and more likely that her prisoner would find a way to escape the dungeon before she destroyed it.

Once again, the harsh beep and ACCESS DENIED message were the only results.

Maybe Gerran's code doesn't work on this door. Maybe only the king is authorized to use the self-destruct sequence.

Slamming her palm against the door in frustration, Serra was unable to hold back the tears any longer. Beaten, she sank slowly to her knees, her face pressed up against the cold metal door.

For several seconds her body was racked by ragged, hitching sobs. Everything had gone wrong. Lucia had betrayed her; the dark man of her dreams was going to escape. Everything she had worked to accomplish had fallen apart.

This isn't like you.

Although she hadn't heard it in more than a decade, she instantly recognized the voice.

"Father?" she said aloud, though of course Caleb was nowhere to be found but inside her own head.

You're stronger than this.

She nodded, not even caring if the voice she was listening to was nothing but a figment of her own imagination. Blocking out the alarms, she took a long, deep breath and carefully analyzed the situation.

It didn't make any sense for the king to be the only one with access to this room. He couldn't be expected to come here in person if there was ever a prison break or a riot. The warden would have access.

Probably the guard captain, as well. And if the king trusted any of his servants with the code, he would also have trusted his son.

You're rushing. Making mistakes. Try again. Slowly.

She rose to her feet and began to punch in the code for a third attempt. This time when she felt the panic threatening to possess her fingers, she fought back by calling up the image of her father's face, calm and certain. Taking slow, deep breaths, she took extra care to hit the buttons in the correct sequence. For a second nothing happened; then there was a soft chime and the door swung slowly open.

Relief flooded over her, and Serra tried to laugh at her own foolishness in entering the number wrong twice before getting it right. What came out was a strangled croak that bordered on the hysterical, startling her back into silence.

The room inside was small, with a single control panel and another door on the other side. Beyond the second door was a small tunnel that led to a small emergency pod, allowing whoever entered the self-destruct sequence to escape before the prison came crashing down.

She approached the console and examined the controls. It was simple enough: There was a button to initiate the self-destruct sequence, a number pad for her to enter her access code, and another button to confirm the command. There was a CANCEL key on the number pad, but no ABORT button; once the self-destruct was confirmed there was no way to stop it. After that, anybody inside would have less than five minutes to escape before charges wired into the ceiling, walls, and floors detonated in rapid succession, collapsing the entire prison.

This was it: Her last chance to stop the man who had terrorized her as a child. Her last chance to rid the galaxy of a Dark Lord of the Sith. She pressed the INITIATE button down, and the console lit up in response. Next, she punched in her access code, slowly, to make sure there were no mistakes. But when the CODE ACCEPTED—CONFIRM

SELF-DESTRUCT SEQUENCE warning popped up on the screen, Serra hesitated.

If she did this, her life on Doan was over. The king had no idea she was using the Stone Prison for her personal vendetta; if she did this her secret would be exposed. The explosions that would destroy the complex would send tremors through the floors of the Royal Manse on the plateau thousands of meters above; everyone would know what had happened.

He would know she had put her personal wants and desires above those of the royal family. Her actions would almost certainly be considered high treason: the best she could hope for would be permanent banishment from the planet.

And what about Lucia? She would probably be killed in the explosions. Although her bodyguard had betrayed her by helping the prisoner to escape, was Serra willing to condemn her friend to death without even giving her a chance to explain her actions?

Unable to make a decision, Serra stood frozen, her finger hovering above the button marked CONFIRM as the alarms continued to ring out.

21

Set had always prided himself on being able to extricate himself from virtually any predicament. He had a knack for working himself free from a bind, and a natural talent for finding the outs in any situation. So he wasn't surprised when, after less than ten minutes, he managed to stumble across the prison's main landing bay.

It was much larger than the secondary entrance he and Zannah had arrived at. The alarms that had been all but deafening inside the cramped corridors were merely thunderous here in the massive chamber.

Set was perched atop a large metal balcony overlooking the room. Below he could see four vessels, spaced about ten meters apart. All of them appeared to be unguarded. Pleased with himself, he tapped the Holocron he had tucked away inside his vest pocket as he studied his options.

Just like a buffet: plenty to choose from.

Two of the ships were standard, run-of-the-mill passenger shuttles, their hulls weathered and dented. He quickly dismissed them as unworthy of stealing. The third was the largest of the group, and appeared to be in mint condition. It was also marked with the crest of the royal family.

Set smiled. There was something appealing about the idea of escaping Doan in a shuttle owned by the ruler of the planet. It definitely had a certain flair. And then he saw the fourth vessel.

We have a winner.

The smallest of the lot, the ship was sleek and stylish, with red trim and a black hull. The perfect vehicle for a man of Set's discriminating taste.

Eager to escape, the Dark Jedi made his way down the staircase and across the hangar, his lightsaber clutched in his right hand. When he reached his chosen shuttle, he let out a low whistle of appreciation and reached up to stroke the smooth, dark hull.

"Look but don't touch," a soft female voice whispered in his ear.

Set snapped his hand back and whirled around, his lightsaber springing to life as he slashed at the empty air behind him.

Just out of range of his attack stood an Iktotchi in a black cloak. Her hood was thrown back to reveal the long curved horns that curled down along her neck and under her chin. Black tattoos marked her lower lip, and her small, pointed teeth were bared in an eager grin.

Set wasn't normally one to shy away from a fight, not if he thought he could win. But there was something unsettling about this red-skinned opponent. It was practically impossible to sneak up on a Jedi, yet Set hadn't felt her presence until she'd spoken.

Careful. That probably isn't the only trick up her sleeve.

"Nice ship," he said, extinguishing his lightsaber and letting his hand fall casually to his side. "How many credits did that set you back?"

As soon as the words were out of his mouth he pounced toward her, his reignited lightsaber carving a deadly figure-eight pattern meant to disembowel his unsuspecting foe even as she answered his question.

The Iktotchi wasn't fooled. Instead of replying to his query, she took a quick step back and to the side, nimbly avoiding his attack.

"Too slow," she admonished.

The two adversaries turned to face each other again, and Set paused to consider the situation. He had Andeddu's Holocron; all he needed now was a ship and he was home free. But standing between him and escape was an unknown, though obviously skilled, opponent. She didn't appear to be armed, but she could easily have blades, blasters, or any number of other weapons hidden in the folds of her cloak. He decided it might be a good idea to try to talk his way out of the situation.

"My name is Medd Tandar," he lied, trying to project an air of noble self-importance into his voice. "I'm here on behalf of the Council of First Knowledge. Step aside in the name of the Jedi Order."

"You're no Jedi," she replied.

"Not anymore," Set confessed. "But I used to be."

He sliced the air half a dozen times with his lightsaber. He spun around, the humming blade dancing and twirling, before ending the demonstration with a backflip.

The Iktotchi was obviously unimpressed by his display of martial prowess, and Set realized he wasn't going to intimidate her into backing down.

"The Jedi teach you any useful tricks?"

"A few," Set replied, thrusting out with the Force.

A wave of raw energy rippled out toward his enemy, but Set knew instantly something was very wrong. Instead of the exhilarating rush of power he normally felt, there was a cramping ache in the pit of his stomach that caused him to double over.

The concussive wave that should have sent the Iktotchi flying twenty meters was reduced to a nothing more than a hard shove. It hit her full in the chest, but she simply absorbed the impact by falling into a backward roll that ended with her still on her feet.

A pair of short vibroblades appeared in her hands while Set staggered backward, clutching at his stomach and trying not to throw up.

With horror, he realized she was disrupting his ability to draw on the Force. He'd seen this talent mentioned in a number of ancient texts, but he'd never encountered it himself . . . and he didn't know how to counter it. His only option was to try to fight through.

Gritting his teeth, he stood up straight. Feeding on the pain and his mounting anger, he tried once more to summon up the power of the dark side. He felt a small surge in response to his efforts, but it was a thin trickle rather than the flood he had been hoping for. Still, it was better than nothing.

The Iktotchi lunged in with her twin blades, and Set staggered awkwardly out of the way, barely avoiding her attack. She moved faster than any opponent he had ever faced. Or maybe her ability to interfere with the Force was just making him slower than he'd ever been. In either case, the outcome was the same . . . and it wasn't good for Set.

He ducked his head and darted under the nose of the black-and-red shuttle to the far side, knowing his best chance of survival would be to keep ten tons of metal between the two of them.

He couldn't see her anymore, but by concentrating he was just barely able to sense her position. The effort made his head spin; it was like trying to see with mud in his eyes.

She was stalking him slowly, cautiously creeping around the tail end of the ship. And in that moment Set realized his opponent had no formal training in the ways of the Force. She was operating on instinct. She had never been taught the most basic skills—like how to sense the location of opponents even when they were out of sight.

Set turned and made a dash for one of the other vessels, reaching his new hiding place just before she emerged from behind the black shuttle's thrusters. Crouching down to peer beneath the belly of the ship he was using for cover, he could see her turning her head from side to side, trying to figure out where he had gone.

"I love a good chase," she called out, her lips curling into a feral smile. "That's why the call me the Huntress."

This isn't going to end well.

————

Bane could still feel the lingering effects of the drugs in his system. He'd done what he could to burn them away with the fire of the dark side, but the Sith were not as adept as the Jedi at cleansing their systems of impurities. The last dregs of the chemicals would simply have to break down naturally over time.

Until then he would be at less than full strength. A fraction slower in thoughts and actions, less adept at wielding the power of the Force. And he was still without his lightsaber.

Despite all this, he was confident victory was only minutes away. The alarms were still ringing throughout the dungeon, but he knew there would be no guards rushing in to answer their call. The few mercenaries who had survived his attack were in full retreat, leaving Caleb's daughter defenseless.

Sometimes vengeance needed to be cold and calculating. There were times when it was better to be careful, patient. But sometimes retribution could not be deferred. Sometimes action needed to be fueled by anger and hate; it needed to burn with the heat of animal emotion.

Peace is a lie; there is only passion. Through passion I gain strength. Through strength I gain power.

He could sense he was closing in on Serra's location. His stride quickened as he marched purposefully down the empty corridors toward his revenge.

Through power I gain victory. Through victory my chains are broken.

He had been careless, weak. He had allowed himself to be captured. He had let himself become a victim. For that he had suffered. But now he was strong again. Now it was someone else's turn to suffer.

"Des!" a voice from behind him shouted out over the alarms.

The mention of the name he had left behind twenty years ago caused the Sith Lord to stop dead in his tracks. He turned slowly, and found himself face-to-face with the dark-skinned woman who had aided his escape.

She was breathing hard, as if she had been running. Her pants were torn over the left knee; the edges of the rip were bloody. Her face was a mixture of conflicting emotions: fear, desperation, and hope.

"Do you remember me, Des? It's Lucia."

For a second Bane simply stared in confusion at the woman standing before him. Then he began to think back to his youth. To a time when he was not Darth Bane, Lord of the Sith, but rather Des, a simple miner from Apatros.

The memories were buried deep, but they were still there. The weekly beatings from Hurst, his father. Long, grueling shifts digging cortosis from the rock while choking on clouds of dust stirred up by his hydraulic jack. His escape from the misery of Apatros, and his assignment to the Gloom Walkers.

It was like trying to recall a dream upon waking. These were scenes from someone else's life; they didn't feel real to him. But as he cast his mind back, other memories began to surface: long nights sitting watch on Trandosha, forced marches through the forests of Kashyyyk.

Stirring up the ghosts of the past brought back the face of Ulabore, the cruel and incompetent commanding officer who had inadvertently turned Des over to the Sith and set him on the path of his true destiny. But there were other faces, too—the men and women of his unit, his brothers- and sisters-in-arms. He remembered the blue eyes and cocksure grin of Adanar, his best friend. And he remembered a wide-eyed junior trooper, a young sniper named Lucia.

Bane had intelligence and foresight. He had the wisdom and vision to redefine the Sith Order so that it could begin its long, slow ascent to galactic domination. He had schemed and planned for nearly every conceivable situation he might one day find himself in. Yet he had never prepared himself for this.

He knew many of the former soldiers who served in Kaan's armies had become mercenaries and bodyguards, but he had never considered the possibility of ever running into someone who had known him before his transformation through the dark side. After joining the Sith, he hadn't allowed himself to wonder or care about what had happened to the people from his past. He had needed to learn to survive alone, to rely on nobody but himself. Attachment to family and friends was a weakness, a chain to bind and drag you down.

Now someone from the life he had worked so hard to forget was standing between him and his revenge. She was an obstacle in his way, one to be easily overcome. He knew he could cast her aside as easily as he had disposed of the guards outside his cell.

Instead, he asked, "Why did you help me?"

"We served together in the Gloom Walkers," she answered, as if that explained everything.

"I know who you are," he told her.

She hesitated, as if she expected him to say more. When he didn't, she continued to speak.

"You saved my life on Phaseera. You saved all our lives. And not just then. You were there in every battle we fought, watching over us. Protecting us."

"I was a fool back then."

"No! You were a hero. I owe you my life a dozen times over. How could I not help you?"

At first he thought she was a sentimental idiot, blinded by irrational nobility and spouting foolish drivel. But then he realized what was really going on, and it all began to make sense. She had released him hoping to win his favor. She was after something. That was why she had betrayed Caleb's daughter—for her own personal gain.

"What do you want?" he demanded, the alarms a constant reminder that time was running short.

"I want . . . please . . . I'm begging you . . . let Serra live."

Her request made no sense. Lucia's actions were the only reason Serra's life was in danger.

"Why? What use is her life to me?"

The woman didn't answer right away. She was searching for something to offer, but in the end she had nothing.

"Look into your heart, Des. Think back on the man you used to be. I know you turned to the dark side to survive. Becoming a Sith was the only way you could survive. Please, Des; I know part of what you used to be still lives inside you."

"My name is not Des," he said, his voice rising as he stood up to his full height so that he towered over Lucia. "I am Darth Bane, Dark Lord of the Sith. I feel neither pity nor gratitude nor remorse. And Caleb's daughter must pay for what she did to me."

"I won't let you do this," she declared, spreading her stance wide and bracing herself before him.

"You can't stop me," he warned her. "You can't save her by sacrificing yourself. Are you willing to throw your life away for no purpose?"

Lucia didn't budge. "I already said I owe you my life. If you want to take it now, that is your right."

Bane's mind flashed back to his first encounter with Caleb on Ambria. The healer had stood before him as Lucia did now, utterly defiant despite the knowledge he was no match for a Sith Lord. Yet

Caleb had known he had something Bane needed; Lucia could make no such claim. There was nothing to stop him from extinguishing her life in a single instant.

He began to gather the dark side, the power slowly building. But before he could unleash it he was hit by a wall of thunderous force rolling out from a corridor to his left. Instinctively he threw up a defensive shield, absorbing the blow. Despite this, he was slammed against the opposite wall, knocking the breath from his lungs.

Lucia was not so fortunate. Unable to call upon the Force to protect herself, she was sent careering down the corridor, flipping and twisting. Her skull smashed against the stone half a dozen times as her body ricocheted off the walls and ceiling, reducing it to a bloody, misshapen mess. Her corpse finally tumbled to a stop thirty meters away where the hall made an abrupt ninety-degree turn.

Bane was back on his feet in an instant, turning to face his foe.

"You couldn't bring yourself to kill her," Zannah said, her voice filled with contempt. "You've become weak. No wonder you tried to violate the Rule of Two."

She was standing with her double-bladed lightsaber drawn, the hilt grasped firmly in her hand. Her arm was extended, holding the weapon out in front of her, the twin blades horizontal to the floor. It was a defensive posture, one meant to guard against a sudden attack from an armed opponent. He realized Zannah didn't know that he hadn't found his lightsaber yet.

"I have lived by the principles of the Rule of Two ever since I created it," Bane replied. "Everything I have done has been in accordance with its teachings."

Zannah shook her head.

"I know you went to Prakith. I know you went after Andeddu's Holocron. I know you were searching for the secret of eternal life."

"I did that out of necessity. I taught you everything I knew about the dark side. I waited years for you to challenge me. But you were content to toil in my shadow, to remain an apprentice until the ravages of age robbed me of my power."

All thoughts of Lucia were gone, swept away along with the memories of his past life. The only thing he cared about was this confrontation, for he knew the fate of the Sith hinged on the outcome.

"You are unworthy of becoming the Master, Zannah. That was why I went to Prakith."

"No," Zannah said, her voice calm and cold. "You won't turn this back on me. You said you were training me so that I would one day succeed you. You said it was my destiny to become the Master.

"Now you want to live forever. You want to cling to the mantle of Dark Lord of the Sith and deny me what is mine!"

"That mantle must be earned," Bane countered. "You wanted to wait, to take it by default."

"You taught me patience," she reminded him. "You taught me to bide my time."

"Not in this!" Bane shouted. "Only the strongest has the right to rule the Sith! The title of Dark Lord must be seized, wrenched from the all-powerful grasp of the Master!"

"That is why I am here," Zannah said with a grim smile. "I have found an apprentice of my own. I am ready to embrace my destiny."

"Do you really believe you can defeat me?"

Bane let his right hand drop to his hip, feinting as if he was preparing to draw his lightsaber. His only chance to survive was to somehow trick her into backing down.

Zannah's eyes flickered, drawn by the subtle motion. He kept his hand open, his massive palm completely covering the place where she would normally be able to see the hilt of his lightsaber clipped to his belt. With his mind he tried to project an image of his hook-handled weapon resting just beneath his empty fingers.

His apprentice didn't move. She stayed in her defensive stance, her brow furrowing as she weighed her chances. Then her gaze fell on

Bane's left hand, quivering ever so slightly with one of the uncontrollable tremors.

"You allowed yourself to be captured by mercenaries," she said, slowly twirling her weapon and taking a confident step forward.

Bane held his ground, clenching the fingers of his left hand so that they dug into the palm, stilling the tremor.

"You couldn't bring yourself to kill the woman who stood in your way."

She took another step toward him, casually tossing her lightsaber from one hand to the other. Had Bane been armed, it would have been the perfect opening to launch a sudden attack.

When he failed to do so, she tilted her head back and laughed.

"You even let yourself get trapped in these halls without your lightsaber."

She took another step forward and Bane responded by taking several steps back.

The double-bladed lightsaber began to pick up speed, slicing the air in quick, circular patterns.

She had one final thing to say before she launched herself at him.

"Your time is over, Bane."

22

Serra stood as if she was paralyzed, her finger hovering just above the button that would confirm the Stone Prison's self-destruct sequence and initiate the destruction of the facility and everyone in it. She had been standing in this exact position for several minutes, unable to push the button.

Do it! Who cares about Lucia? She betrayed you! Do it!

The princess took a deep breath, then let her hand fall. But instead of hitting CONFIRM, she pressed the key marked CANCEL. There was a soft beep, and the glowing keyboard became dark as it powered down.

She couldn't do it. As much as she didn't want the prisoner to escape, she simply couldn't bring herself to condemn Lucia to death. The older woman had been more than her bodyguard; she had been Serra's confidante and closest friend. Whatever she did, there must have been a reason. And she owed it to her friend to find out what that reason was.

Leaving the small confines of the emergency control room behind her, Serra headed back out into the hall. With the alarms ringing, there was no need to worry about the sound of her footsteps giving away her position. She set off in a brisk jog, making her way back up the long hall toward the cells where the prisoner had been held in search of her friend.

He's looking for you, and he won't need to hear your footsteps to hunt you down. Do you really think you can find Lucia before he finds you?

The princess understood the risk. But she had had already lost her husband and her father; she wasn't about to lose her best friend, too. Even if that meant confronting the monster from her nightmares one more time.

Winding her way through the corridors of the complex, she headed back to where the Iktotchi had first told her of Lucia's betrayal. Before she got there, however, she saw a body lying up ahead, crumpled against the wall where the passage bent around a sharp corner.

"No," she whispered under her breath as she broke into a run. "No!"

She recognized Lucia's body long before she crouched down before her. Her arms and legs jutted out at bizarre angles, the bones snapped clean through. These injuries were nothing compared with the trauma that had been inflicted to her face and skull.

As Serra knelt over her friend's corpse she didn't cry any tears, however. Instead of grief, she felt only a strange numbness fall across her mind.

This is your fault. If you hadn't been so set on seeking revenge, if you hadn't brought the prisoner here, none of this would have happened. Lucia would still be alive.

The voice inside her head spoke the truth, but Serra still felt nothing. It was as if her emotions, so damaged by the deaths of Gerran and Caleb, had finally shut down completely.

Then she became aware of a strange high-pitched hum behind the clang of the alarms—not the sound of any lightsaber she had ever heard, and not a sound her ears found comfortable. She rose and walked farther down the hall toward the source of the noise, leaving Lucia's broken body behind her.

As she drew nearer, she began to hear other sounds: grunts of exertion, short exclamations of anger and pain, the heavy thump of feet on the stone floor. She recognized them as the sounds of battle.

No blasters, though.

Reaching the intersection of another corridor, she saw a flicker of movement from the corner of her eye. Turning to the left she saw two figures at the far end of the passage, less than twenty meters away from where she stood. She recognized the prisoner instantly. The second figure she had never seen before, yet she knew who this was.

The blond woman the Huntress spoke of.

They were facing each other, clearly locked in an intense struggle. The prisoner was nearly twice the size of his opponent, but she was clearly the aggressor. The woman was armed with a double-bladed lightsaber, but the prisoner had no weapon as far as Serra could tell. He was backing up warily, his eyes locked on the woman as she approached. She was closing in on him slowly, trying to back him into a corner and cut off his retreat.

Just before she had him pinned, however, a bolt of violet lightning shot forth from his palm. The woman countered by catching the bolt with one of her lightsaber blades. It absorbed the energy, emitting the strange, high-pitched hum Serra had heard earlier.

The two combatants were so focused on each other that neither had noticed Serra. She should have been terrified. She should have turned and fled, running back the way she had come. Yet she felt only the empty calm that had settled over her on discovering Lucia's body.

Without any real sense of urgency, she turned and walked back down the hall to where her friend lay on the floor. Crouching down, she seized the muscular woman by her wrists and began to drag her down the hall, groaning under the strain as she walked backward.

Burdened by the weight, she made her way slowly back to the control room. The muscles in her neck, shoulders, and lower back began to throb almost immediately, but Serra didn't stop. The sensation was muted, as numb and distant as her feelings of grief.

Eventually she reached the control room, but she didn't pause at the self-destruct console. Instead, she dragged Lucia through the door at the back and, with some difficulty, hoisted her into the hold of the small escape shuttle. Then she returned to the keypad and punched in the self-destruct code. This time there was no hesitation before she pushed the CONFIRM button.

The sound of the alarms changed. Instead of the relentless *clang-clang-clang* warning of an escaped prisoner, it became a long, whooping wail.

Serra knew she had only a few minutes before the first series of explosions would begin, but she couldn't bring herself to leave. Not yet.

Time seemed to stand still as she stood by the console, waiting expectantly. Hours seemed to pass, though in truth it was only a matter of minutes. And then she felt a small tremor beneath her feet . . . the shock wave from the first detonation in the deepest level of the facility. A few seconds later it was followed by another tremor, and then another after that.

Satisfied, she turned and headed out to the escape shuttle. The destruction of the Stone Prison had begun.

———

The Huntress had never faced a more frustrating opponent. Despite the lightsaber in his hand, the man refused to stand and fight. He ducked and ran back and forth between the hulls of the ships, moving from one hiding place to another, always a step ahead of her.

She could have sheathed her vibroblades and drawn the twin

blasters tucked inside the folds of her cloak, but she knew it wouldn't do any good. Her adversary was too quick for her to ever get a clear shot, and even if she did he'd probably just slap the bolt away with his lightsaber.

She caught a glimpse of him darting across the aisle between her shuttle and the one parked beside it. She didn't chase him, though: she turned and ran behind her own shuttle, taking a path parallel to his in the hope of cutting him off.

Chewing the ground up with long, effortless strides she raced around the side of the ship, hoping to flank her unsuspecting opponent. Instead she came within a centimeter of being decapitated as his lightsaber came hurtling through the air toward her.

She let herself collapse to the ground, falling awkwardly back and to the side as her legs shot out from under her. The maneuver was ungainly, but it saved her life. The deadly energy blade whistled by her ear, slicing a thumb-sized chunk out of one of her horns before circling back on a tight arc and returning to her opponent's hand.

Ignoring the stinging pain from her horn she scrambled back to her feet, vibroblades ready. But her opponent didn't press his advantage; he disappeared again, vanishing around the nose of the ship.

Her injury wasn't serious; Iktotchi horns contained no vital organs or major arteries. Even if completely severed the wound would not be life threatening, though it would be agonizingly painful. In time the missing chunk would even grow back, leaving no evidence of how close she had come to dying in the hangar.

But she *had* nearly died. She realized her opponent was cunning; he had wanted her to see him, knowing she'd double around to try and cut him off.

She had underestimated him and he had manipulated her, goading her into a careless mistake. He had set a trap and she had walked right into it. She wouldn't make the same mistake twice.

Set crouched down behind one of the ships, gasping for breath. To some extent he had been able to resist the Iktotchi's strange ability. He was able to fight through her ability to draw on the Force, but the effort had left him exhausted.

And it still messed you up enough so that she was able to dodge your lightsaber.

The Dark Jedi frowned at the memory of how close he had come to ending this battle, even as he forced himself to get up and get moving again. He couldn't stay in one place for more than a few seconds, not unless he wanted to end up dead. He knew she'd be more careful now; he'd missed his best chance.

The Iktotchi was too quick for him to beat in a straight-up fight . . . not with her disrupting his connection to the Force and slowing him down. So far he'd managed to avoid a direct confrontation, but he couldn't keep running for much longer. He had a stitch in his side, and his lungs felt like they were going to burst. Unless something happened to change the situation, the outcome was inevitable.

As if in answer to his prayers, there was a sudden change in the sound of the alarms. It only took Set a moment to figure out what had happened, and a new escape plan began to form in his mind.

————

The Huntress heard the change in the sound of the alarms, and she knew that they had maybe five minutes before the detonations began, and maybe ten before the entire complex was reduced to rubble.

Her opponent noticed the change as well.

"Hear that?" he called out from somewhere on the other side of the hangar. "This whole place is going to come crashing down around our ears. Why don't we each just hop on one of these shuttles and get out of here before that happens?"

"I still have enough time to find you," she shouted back, slowly heading in the direction of his voice. It sounded like he was near one of the shuttles on the far side of the room. "You're getting tired. Wearing down. You won't last much longer."

"I was afraid you'd say that," he answered as she stepped from behind one of the ships, giving her a clear view of the man she had been chasing.

He was leaning casually against the side of one of the shuttles, near the thrusters at the rear. He glanced toward her but made no attempt to hide. Instead he just stood there, holding his lightsaber casually at his side.

Wary of walking into another trap, the Huntress began a cautious approach. As she took her first step, the silver-haired man pulled his arm back and brought his lightsaber down hard against the shuttle's hull. There was a shower of sparks, and the blade bit a full centimeter into the ship's reinforced exterior plating.

The man pulled his arm back and struck again, hitting precisely the same spot, the glowing blade carving even deeper this time. It was only on the third blow that the Huntress realized what he was doing.

The third chop brought the lightsaber deep enough to sever one of the shuttle's fuel lines. Her opponent flung himself backward and she threw herself to the floor as a stray spark ignited the flammable liquid. Hundreds of tiny metal shards that had once been a fuel cell were sent hurtling through the air. The shuttle bucked once, its tail leaping a full meter off the ground from the force of the blast. A thick cloud of greasy black smoke curled up from the gash the lightsaber had left in the hull.

"Amazing weapons, aren't they?" the man noted as she picked herself up from the ground. "Cut through almost anything."

His face was cut and scraped from flying debris, but somehow—probably through shielding himself with the Force—he had managed to avoid the worst of the explosion. Before she could reply, he had ducked around the corner of the shuttle, disappearing from sight once again.

A few seconds later she heard the unmistakable sound of the lightsaber shearing through metal yet again from the far side of the hangar.

She broke into a run, heading in the direction of the noise. She was only halfway there when another explosion knocked her to the ground. When she got back to her feet she saw that a second shuttle had been disabled.

Knowing his next target, she turned and ran toward the *Stalker*. She pulled up short when she came around a corner and saw her opponent standing beside her shuttle, his hand gently along the hull.

"What are you doing?" the Huntress shouted.

"All I want is to get out of here alive," he explained. "But for some reason you seem intent on killing me."

"You took the first swing at me," she reminded him. "When I caught you about to steal my ship."

"A simple misunderstanding," he said, waving his hand to dismiss her accusations. "There are two shuttles left. You take yours and leave the other one for me, and we never have to see each other again."

"What if I say no?"

"Then I destroy your shuttle and we see if you can stop me before I get to the last one. My guess is you can't, and then we're both stuck here when these walls come crashing down."

"You're a coward," the assassin shot back. "You wouldn't even stand and fight me. Now you expect me to believe you'd sacrifice yourself to trap us both here?"

"I'm a realist," the man explained. "If we fight, I'm dead. If I trap us here, I'm dead. Either way the outcome is the same . . . but if I destroy the shuttles, then at least I take you with me."

She didn't answer right away. It was possible he was telling the truth: people did desperate things when cornered.

Her thoughts seized on the hooked handle in her belt; he wasn't the only one armed with a lightsaber. She briefly considered trying to use the weapon she'd taken from the Sith Lord's mansion to block the attack if he tried to damage her shuttle, then dismissed the idea. She had no training or experience; she'd never even held a lightsaber until a few days ago. Even if she did, by the time she crossed the distance between them the damage could have been done.

Next, she tried to calculate her odds of getting to the last remaining shuttle before her enemy could disable it. She might be able to beat him there, but as soon as she climbed inside the cockpit he'd be able to run up and wreak havoc on the engines.

Finally, she weighed the possibility that he wouldn't actually go through with his threat. Even when faced with a hopeless situation, few people would have the strength of will to destroy their only chance of escape. There was a very good chance he was bluffing.

But even if he was, what did she gain by calling his bluff?

She didn't know anything about this man: who he was, how he got here, or why he had shown up in the first place. What did she really accomplish by killing him? And what did she lose by letting him go?

The only reason she hadn't left yet was the belief that this was where she would find her destiny. Whether this man lived or died was of no consequence compared with that.

A deep thrumming boom rolled through the cavern. The silver-haired man swayed slightly on his feet.

"We're running out of time," he warned, cocking his arm back and taking aim.

"We have a deal," she shouted.

"Stay where I can see you," the man warned, backing away from her carefully.

Keeping his eye on her, he scooted over to the other shuttle. He disappeared around the far side of the vessel. She heard him fumbling with the access panel as he sliced the security systems, followed by the unmistakable *whoosh* of the boarding ramp descending. A few seconds later he reappeared, visible in the cockpit viewport.

The Huntress simply watched, knowing there was nothing she could do. Unlike a lightsaber, neither her vibroblades nor her blasters were capable of inflicting any serious damage on the hull of a shuttle. She momentarily considered drawing the lightsaber and mimicking the trick he had used against her, but even if she was able to damage his vessel, it just meant he would still be here, and she'd have to find some way to get to her own ship before he returned the favor.

The shuttle engines roared to life as it rose up and turned to face the exit, hovering for an instant just below the chamber's high ceiling. She could clearly see the Doan royal crest on the side, as well as the silver-haired man inside the cockpit. He waved to her and flashed a self-satisfied smile, and then the thrusters kicked in and the ship swooped away, flying out of the hangar and disappearing into the night sky.

For the first time in the Huntress's life, someone she had wanted to kill had gotten away. Yet it would be a small price to pay if she managed to find what she was truly looking for.

23

Zannah wasn't used to being the aggressor. In all the times she and Bane had sparred he had been the one pressing the action. Her lightsaber style was built on a foundation of parries and counter-strikes, hiding behind her virtually impenetrable defense while waiting for her opponent to make a mistake.

This confrontation was completely different. Yet even though Bane had no lightsaber, that didn't mean he was helpless. Zannah knew she couldn't simply rush in: despite his bulk, Bane was incredibly quick and agile. He had also learned close-quarters pit-fighting tactics during his days as a miner and soldier. She had to be wary of letting him get close enough to grapple her; she couldn't let him get the opportunity to use his size and strength against her.

There was also his incredible command of the Force to contend with. Simple tactics like pushing an opponent from across the room were impractical against any foe with proper training. Both she and Bane knew how to surround themselves with an invisible field of energy that absorbed or repelled the most basic tricks taught to any Jedi or Sith. But Bane could unleash devastating bolts of dark side lightning from his hands almost at will.

As long as she was careful, she was able to avoid them or intercept them with her lightsaber. This caution, however, allowed her Master to keep her off balance just enough to stay alive.

The pair were entwined in an intricate dance. She swept in low, spinning and twirling her lightsaber. He leapt up high, planting his feet on the wall at his side and pushing off hard, sending himself into a tumbling roll just beyond the reach of her blade's arc.

Back on his feet, he sprang backward as Zannah stabbed her blade straight forward, keeping just out of range. She pursued him down the length of the hall, jabbing and thrusting her weapon and sending the Dark Lord into a full retreat. Bane fought back with short, concentrated bursts of lightning, aiming at her boots to disrupt her footwork and keep her off balance.

Zannah took quick stuttering steps to avoid the attack and keep him from gaining a reprieve. Bane feinted as if he was going to fall back to the right, then lunged forward, flipping over her head and reaching down with a huge hand to seize her wrist.

She ducked out of the way, lashing out with a kick as he landed behind her. Bane spun, grabbed her ankle, and wrenched the boot to the side, trying to snap the bone. Zannah rolled with the violent motion, her entire body spinning along a horizontal plane. At the same time she brought her lightsaber back up over her shoulder to slice Bane's arm off at the elbow, but caught only air as he released his hold and fell back once more.

She had him cornered against the wall with nowhere to go. As she moved in for the kill another burst of lightning came toward her. She caught it with her lightsaber, but the impact drove her backward a step, giving Bane just enough room to duck down beneath her coup de grâce and scramble clear of the wall.

They had switched positions, each facing the opposite way as they began the dance yet again. The ebb and flow of their battle fell into a rhythm of feints and counters, their dance keeping time to the clanging alarms as she forced him back up the hall she had chased him down only moments before.

Zannah suspected if their positions were reversed, Bane might have ended the confrontation already. Yet she knew her victory was inevitable. Her Master was in an impossible situation. He needed to do everything exactly right just to keep her at bay for another pass. He had no margin for error, and even the Dark Lord of the Sith couldn't sustain perfection forever. The only way she could lose would be to make a careless mistake.

The best Bane could hope for was to try to frustrate her with his elusiveness. But Zannah understood patience. She had waited twenty years for this moment, and she was content to play their battle out as long as necessary.

They reached the end of the hall, and Zannah thought she had Bane trapped. This time she used her lightsaber to slap aside the violet bolts of lightning rather than trying to absorb them and stumbling back. Bane still had one more trick up his sleeve, however.

She was less than a meter away, her blade already slashing in for the killing blow, when she felt all the hair on the back of her neck rise. A shimmering purple cocoon of dark side energy enveloped Bane, a fragile shell holding back a storm of pure power.

She tried to pull back but it was too late. As her blade bit into the cocoon the energy was released in a sudden burst that sent both of them flying backward. Bane slammed hard into the wall against his back and crumpled to the ground. Zannah was tossed ten meters farther, landing hard on the stone floor.

They rose to their feet at the same time, neither seriously injured. But yet again Bane had managed to thwart her attack and work himself out of a corner.

Zannah merely shrugged and began another slow, relentless advance. She paused for a moment when the sound of the alarms changed.

She knew almost instantly what had happened. They had only a few minutes to escape before the explosions buried them alive.

There were two options: break off the battle and run for the ship, or throw caution to the wind and take one last reckless charge at her Master. She couldn't let Bane get away. She had to end this now!

As she gathered herself to charge, Bane fired off another bolt of lightning. She ducked to the side and it whizzed past her ear, striking the wall and sending up a shower of dust and stone flecks.

Despite missing her the first time, Bane followed it up with another blast on the exact same trajectory. Turning her head to follow the course of the misguided bolt, Zannah saw where the first had hit the wall. The stone had been disintegrated in a fist-sized hole, revealing something that looked like bright red plastic beneath it.

She recognized it as the casing of a demolition charge just in time to throw herself backward, using the Force to shield herself from the worst of the explosion. She was thrown clear as the entire wall blew out, sending huge chunks of stone spewing into the passage. The ceiling was shredded, tearing loose massive blocks that tumbled to the ground.

Choking on the cloud of dust and smoke, Zannah picked herself up. The passage in front of her was completely blocked by rubble and debris from the blast. She could feel Bane on the other side of the rocks; he had survived the blast, just as she had. But now they were separated by tons of impassable stone.

She walked slowly over to the collapsed section of the hallway and placed a hand on the edge of one of the massive stones blocking her way. Even using the Force, it would take hours to clear a path. There was no way to deny the truth: she had him, and she had let him get away.

The vibrations of another explosion, this one far away in some deep chamber of the dungeon, rumbled up through the floor, re-minding her she was out of time. Cursing her missed opportunity, she turned and ran back the way she had come, racing for her ship.

Overhead, the evacuation alarms continued to wail.

————————

Bane had hoped his apprentice would be caught off guard by his un-expected tactic. There was a small chance she would actually be killed by the explosion, buried under the collapsing rock. But as he picked himself up in the aftermath, he could sense she was still alive. Despite the fact she had been trying to kill him, the knowledge brought him a small measure of satisfaction. He had trained her well.

The primary goal of the explosion hadn't been to kill her, anyway. The desperate ploy was actually Bane's last chance to escape a battle he knew he couldn't win. In that he had been successful . . . though if he wanted to survive he still had to find a way out of the prison be-fore the whole place came crashing down.

He had no real sense of where he was in the labyrinthine dun-geon. Before Zannah found him, he had been following Caleb's daughter, letting the Force guide him with no real conscious thought as to the path he was taking.

Reaching out with his mind, he sensed that the princess was gone now. But Bane had slaughtered more than a dozen guards during his escape; they had to have shuttles somewhere in the facility. And even if he didn't know where to find them, he knew he could trust in the Force.

He broke into a run, darting left and right down passages as they opened up without any thought or hesitation, doing his best to ig-nore the incessant howls of the evacuation alarms.

Throughout his life, even before he had known who and what he was, he had been guided by the Force. During his military career he had led a charmed life, somehow leading the Gloom Walkers virtually unscathed through some of the war's bloodiest campaigns. He had simply considered himself lucky, or blessed with good instincts.

He skidded around a corner, his boots losing traction for a second. At the same time, he felt the shock wave of a massive explosion rippling up from chambers somewhere far below. He fought for his balance and managed to keep his feet, accelerating down the next hall.

It was impossible to tell if he was going in the right direction; the unadorned stone walls looked the same in every passage. He felt the reverberations of a second distant explosion, reminding him that he was running out of time. Yet the slope of the corridor was leading him upward, which encouraged him.

It was only after he had began his training at the Sith Academy on Korriban that he realized his incredible run of fortune had actually been a manifestation of the Force. Even before he was aware of its power it had acted through him, shaping the events of his life by guiding and directing his choices and actions.

Learning to harness that power—to take control of his destiny, rather than to let it keep controlling him—had allowed him to ascend to his current position. The Force had become a tool; its power was his to command and bend to his will.

But here, only minutes away from complete annihilation, Bane allowed himself to revert to the ways of his youth. Focusing on trying to find a way out would require effort and concentration that would only slow him down. He couldn't think and plan; he had to react and hope.

He wheeled around another corner, sprinted down a short hall, and charged out onto a steel balcony overlooking a massive, high-roofed chamber. He arrived just in time to see a shuttle with the Doan royal crest rising up and flying away. For an instant he thought the princess might be on board. However, when he reached out he felt a very different presence piloting the craft . . . someone with a powerful connection to the dark side. Bane couldn't allow his attention to be drawn by the mysterious individual escaping in the shuttle, however: he had a far more pressing problem.

From his vantage point atop the balcony he could clearly see the Iktotchi who had led the ambush against him back at his mansion. She was dressed in the same black cloak, and she was standing beside a black-and-red shuttle.

She had been looking at the escaping vehicle, but as it sped away she turned to face Bane. Seeing him, an expression of satisfaction flickered across her features.

"I have been waiting for you," she called out to him.

The last time they had fought she had bested him; this time he was unarmed and drained from his battle with Zannah. Yet he was still confident he could defeat her. Without the advantage of surprise and twenty mercenaries backing her up, she was no match for him one-on-one. And if she cut him with her poisoned blades again, he'd be ready to burn away the toxin before it overwhelmed his system.

Bane grabbed the railing of the balcony and pulled himself over, ignoring the tremor caused by another explosion from inside the facility.

His feet were already moving as he hit the floor below, driving him toward his foe. To his surprise, the Iktotchi didn't retreat as he bore down on her. She didn't even draw her weapons. Instead, she dropped to one knee and bowed her head, holding her hands out palms up as if presenting him with an offering.

The unexpected reaction caused him to pull up short a few meters from her. At this distance he could clearly see she was holding the hooked handle of his missing lightsaber and what appeared to be his own Holocron in her hands.

"A gift, my lord," she said, tilting her head to look up at him.

"You tried to kill me," Bane said warily, not taking his eyes off her.

"I was hired to capture you," she corrected. "It was just a job. Now that job is finished."

Reaching out, Bane took the hilt from her hand. His fingers slipped around the familiar curved grip, and he ignited the blade.

The Iktotchi rose to her feet but showed no fear.

"Why are you still here?" Bane asked.

"I knew you had broken free," she explained. "I hoped you might come here during your escape."

"You had a premonition I would find you?" Bane was aware the Iktotchi were supposed to have precognitive abilities, but he had only the vaguest idea of how powerful or accurate their visions might be.

"Night after night I have seen you in my visions," she answered. "Our destinies are intertwined."

"What if your destiny is to die at my hand?" he asked, raising up his blade.

"Neither of us is fated to die in this place, my lord."

As if in opposition to her words, another explosion from inside the facility rocked the chamber.

"What do you want from me?"

"Let me study under you," she implored, seemingly oblivious to the rapidly mounting danger from the collapsing prison. "Instruct me in the dark side. Teach me the ways of the Sith."

"Do you realize what you are asking?" Bane demanded.

"My existence has no meaning," the Iktotchi explained. "You can give my life purpose. You can guide me to my destiny."

"What can you offer me in return?"

"Loyalty. Devotion. A shuttle to escape this prison before it collapses. And Caleb's daughter."

The next explosion was close enough that they could actually hear it echoing from down the hall.

"I accept," Bane said, extinguishing his lightsaber after a moment's consideration.

Less than a minute later they were aboard the Iktotchi's shuttle, leaving the Stone Prison and the final, violent throes of its destruction behind them.

————————

Zannah was retracing her steps, following the long route back through the dungeon and up to the small hangar where she hoped Set and her shuttle would still be waiting for her. Her entire body was infused with the Force, her legs propelling her along so fast the wind caused her hair to stream out behind her.

As she ran she could feel the tremors rising up from deep within the dungeon, each blast a little nearer than the one before it. The explosion Bane had caused had been a single charge set off by his crackling bolt of lightning. These explosions were far more powerful: eight or ten charges in close proximity all detonating at the same time, collapsing not a small stretch of corridor but rather an entire section of the facility.

By the time she crossed from the lit halls of the reopened areas of the dungeon into the darkened passages of the unused wing where she had first come in, the explosions were close enough for her to hear them as well as feel the vibrations through the floor. They were coming more frequently now, too. Instead of every ten seconds, they pounded out in a steady rhythm.

She plunged into the blackness, not even bothering with a glow stick. Her breath was ragged and irregular, but her stride never faltered. Every muscle and nerve in her body was tingling with the power of the Force, her senses heightened to supernatural levels. She didn't need to see to find her way: like a bat she could hear the alarms echoing off the walls, floor, and ceiling, painting a sonar image of her surroundings. The rumbling *boom-boom-boom* of the charges rang out in counterpoint to the wail of the alarms.

When she burst into the hangar where her shuttle waited, she was surprised by two things. The first was how bright the lights from her shuttle seemed after the total darkness of the subterranean passages she had been racing through. The second was that Set Harth was missing.

She'd always suspected he might cut and run, but she couldn't think of a reason Set would disappear but still leave her shuttle behind. She didn't have time to worry about it now, however. She heard the roar of another explosion, this one so close it actually made the walls of the hangar shake.

Jumping into the shuttle she fired it up as another detonation caused the entire vessel to rock back and forth on its struts. Fighting not to be thrown from the pilot's chair, Zannah pulled back on the stick and the ship rose up off the ground. Banking sharply, she turned it toward the entrance and jammed her fist down on the thrusters.

The *Victory* sprang forward, hurtling through the cavern's mouth as the final explosion set off the charges built into the hangar walls, collapsing the entire structure behind her.

Safely away, Zannah punched in a trajectory and activated the autopilot, letting the ship skim across Doan's surface as she tried to catch her breath. The mad dash to freedom had left her both mentally and physically exhausted. Her body was covered in sweat, and the muscles of her thighs and calves were quivering as she slumped in her seat, threatening to cramp up at any second.

She had survived, but she could hardly call the mission a success. She had let Bane slip through her fingers, and she had no doubt her Master had found a way to escape the Stone Prison's destruction just as she had. On top of that, she had lost her apprentice.

She didn't know if Set had escaped or if he had perished in the blast, and she had no easy way to find out. The connection she had forged with Bane over twenty years was strong enough to stretch across the breadth of the galaxy: she would feel his death no matter where or when it happened. Set had only been her apprentice for a few days. She would sense him if he was in close proximity, as she would any individual who possessed a powerful affinity for the Force, but there was no special bond between them.

But Set was the least of her problems. Bane was still out there, and as soon as he found another lightsaber he'd come looking for her . . . unless she found him first.

The problem was, Zannah had no idea where to begin her search.

24

The Stone Prison's escape shuttle was small in size and lacked the luxuries of the princess's personal ship, but it had been fitted with a Class Five hyperdrive and was well provisioned for interstellar travel. Theoretically, if there was ever a need to activate the dungeon's self-destruct sequence, there was also a strong possibility that key members of the royal family or their staff might be forced to flee Doan.

In Serra's case this was actually true. She could only imagine the political fallout she had caused. The king's father had decommissioned the Stone Prison; officially it was still inactive. Its destruction would lead to a host of questions as to what exactly was going on in the complex beneath the royal family's estate. Any investigations would turn up nothing, of course: the demolition charges had been carefully engineered to inflict maximum structural damage. Any proposed recovery operation would prove too expensive and impractical. Whatever secrets the Stone Prison held would be buried forever.

That wouldn't stop the rumors and speculation, though. The

miners already mistrusted the nobility; discovering the infamous dungeons had been reopened—even temporarily—would stir up bad blood and reopen old wounds. Sympathy and recruitment for the rebels would increase.

Her own disappearance would add to the confusion, but in the long run it would be better if she just disappeared. She had sworn loyalty to House Doan and she had betrayed them, bringing trouble and misfortune down on Gerran's kin. If the king and everyone else believed she was dead, sealed away forever beneath ten thousand tons of rock, it would be easier for them to clean up the mess she had left behind.

Unable to return to her home on Doan, she had charted a course for the only other place in the galaxy she had ever known happiness. However, as she brought the shuttle in to land on the edge of her father's camp on Ambria, it wasn't joy she was feeling.

In the space of only a few short months it seemed as if she had lost everything. Alone, confused, and racked by guilt, she had come here in the hope of finding peace . . . for herself, and for her friend.

It was early evening; the last light of day was just fading over the horizon as she unloaded Lucia's body. Laying her friend gently on the ground, she returned to the shuttle and found a small shovel tucked away in the supplies at the back.

The sandy ground was soft, making her chore far easier than it would have been on most other worlds. Even so, it took her more than an hour of steady digging before the grave was complete. As best she could, she lowered Lucia's body into the hole she had dug, then picked up the shovel and buried her friend.

The desert heat had faded quickly with the setting of the sun, and once her exertions were over, the chill made Serra shiver. But the physical activity had been cathartic. The numbness that had clouded her thoughts and emotions had faded.

A light breeze kicked up, and she shivered. Instead of going to the

shuttle, however, she crossed the camp and sought shelter in her father's old, abandoned shack.

Inside, she huddled in a corner and closed her eyes. She could still
feel her father's presence here. Even though he was gone, being in this
place made it easy to call up memories: his face, his voice. She was
able to draw solace from them, as if her father's quiet strength and
wisdom were somehow being passed from the place he had lived
nearly all of his adult life into her.

It was only now that she realized how wrong she had been. Caleb
had always warned her about the evils of the dark side, yet when the
time came she had ignored his words. And everything that had gone
wrong—all the blood that now stained her hands—could be traced
back to her own hatred and desire for revenge.

It had begun with Gerran's death. Instead of grieving and moving
on, she had clung to her sorrow until it transformed into bitter anger
that consumed her every waking moment. In desperation, Lucia had
hired an assassin to seek revenge on her behalf in the hopes it could
somehow save her friend from the darkness that had enveloped her.
Instead, she had unwittingly set in motion the wheels of Serra's
downfall.

The Huntress had slain the Jedi Medd Tandar. This led to the in-
volvement of the Council and the king. When Lucia confessed her actions to Serra, she should have been horrified. Her father would have
been. She should have told the king about the assassin, leaving Lucia's
name out of it to protect her friend. She could have averted all the
suffering that was to come with one simple act of honesty. Instead,
she chose to deceive him, hoarding the secret and reveling in the terrible crime committed on her behalf.

That lie had resulted in her trip to Coruscant, where she had
learned about her father's fate. Looking back, she had no doubt Caleb
had given his life rather than submit to the will of the dark side. But
instead of honoring his memory and following his example, she let

her grief twist and pervert her sense of justice. Yet again she let anger and hate rule her actions, and Lucia was sent out to hire the Huntress for a second job.

When the dark man of her dreams was captured, Serra was given yet another chance to turn away from the abyss. She could have turned him over to the authorities. Instead she chose to imprison and torture him.

By this point she had sunk so far into the pit of darkness that even Lucia had sensed her corruption. Her friend had tried to warn her. She had recognized what Serra was turning into. But now Lucia was dead, as well.

Anger, revenge, deception, cruelty, hate: these were the ways of the dark side. Ever since Gerran's death Serra had allowed them to dominate her life, drawing her farther and farther down the path. And it was only now, cowering alone in the corner of a hut in the middle of the desert, that she understood the true price.

The dark side destroys. It can't bring peace or closure; it only brings misery and death.

Caleb had understood this. He had tried to teach her. But she had failed him, and it had cost her everything.

"I'm sorry, Father," she whispered, reaching up to wipe a tear from her eye. "Now I understand."

What was done could not be undone. She would have to live with the burden of her crimes. But going forward she would not allow herself to be seduced by the dark side again. Whatever fate awaited her, whatever consequence or punishment befell her, she would accept it with stoic calm and quiet strength.

I am still my father's daughter.

————

Bane was well aware how close he had come to dying at Zannah's hand in the Stone Prison. Yet he was still alive, proof of his enduring strength and power. He had gone in a prisoner, but he had emerged more powerful than when he had entered. Andeddu's Holocron may have been lost, most likely buried forever in the dungeon's collapse, but he had already claimed its most precious knowledge: the secret of essence transfer. And though his apprentice was still alive, he might just have found her replacement.

He studied the Iktotchi carefully as she worked the shuttle's controls, making subtle adjustments to keep them on course as they left the calm vacuum of space and descended into the turbulence of Ambria's atmosphere.

She had told him her name was the Huntress, and that she had spent the past five years as a freelance assassin, honing her ability to identify and exploit weakness in her targets. It was hard to argue with the results; in her brief encounters with Bane she had already demonstrated both notable ambition and incredible potential. Her achievements were even more impressive when one considered that she had never been given any formal training in the ways of the Force. Everything she did came from natural ability. Pure instinct. Raw power.

Her ability to disrupt the Force in others only gave further testament to her strength. She had never been trained in this rare and difficult technique; she simply unleashed it against her enemies through sheer force of will: crude but effective.

However, it was her other talent that truly intrigued the Dark Lord.

"How did you track me to Ciutric?" he asked as the shuttle dropped down toward the planet's desert surface.

"My visions," the Huntress explained. "If I concentrate, they allow me to see images: people, places. Sometimes I catch glimpses of the future, though they do not always come true."

"The future is never static," Bane told her. "It is constantly shaped by the Force . . . and those with the power to control the Force."

"Sometimes I also see visions of the past. Memories of what was. I saw you here on Ambria. With a young blond woman."

"My apprentice."

"She still lives?"

"For now."

On the horizon they could see the first light of Ambria's sun stretching out toward them. As the bright yellow beams fell across the nose of the shuttle, Bane couldn't help but wonder how far the Iktotchi's abilities could extend if she was given proper instruction and guidance.

He had the wisdom to interpret events and foresee their most likely outcome, but he rarely experienced true visions of the future. He was able to manipulate the galaxy around him, driving it inexorably toward a time in which all bowed down to the Sith, but it was a struggle to keep everything on course. His long-term plans to wipe out the Jedi and rule the galaxy were in a constant state of flux, reacting to unexpected and completely unforeseeable events that altered the social and political landscape.

Each time this happened, Bane had to retreat and regroup until he was able to evaluate and properly react to the changes. But if the Huntress could learn to properly harness her power, the Sith would no longer be limited only to reacting. They could anticipate and predict these random changes, preparing for them long before they happened.

And there was an even greater possibility. Bane knew fate was not preordained. There were many possible futures, and the Force allowed her to see only examples of what might be. If she could learn to sort through her visions, separating out the various divergent time lines, was it possible she could actually control them, too? Could she one day have the power to alter the future simply by thinking about it? Could she use the power of the Force to shape the very fabric of existence and make her chosen visions become reality?

"In the hangar you said you were waiting for me," Bane noted, anxious to get a better understanding of her talent. "Your visions told you I was coming?"

"Not exactly. I had a sense of . . . something. I could feel the significance of the moment, though I didn't know what would happen. My instincts told me it would be to my benefit to wait."

Bane nodded. "Are your instincts ever wrong?"

"Rarely."

"Is that why we're here on Ambria? Your visions—your instincts—told you Caleb's daughter would come here?"

"The princess met me here when she hired me to find you," the assassin replied. "This place haunts her. I didn't need a vision to know this was where she would run."

The Dark Lord smiled. She was smart as well as powerful.

A few minutes later the ship touched down on the edge of Caleb's camp, landing beside a small escape shuttle.

Disembarking from the craft, Bane was reminded of the power trapped within Ambria's surface. The Force had once devastated this world before its power was trapped by an ancient Jedi Master in the depths of Lake Natth. Now the planet was a nexus of both dark and light-side power.

He noticed a freshly dug grave a few meters off to one side, but he didn't give it a second glance. The dead were of no consequence to him.

With long, purposeful steps he made his way across the camp toward the dilapidated shack. The Huntress followed at his side, matching him stride for stride.

Before he reached his destination, however, the princess emerged from the hut to confront him. She was unarmed and alone, but unlike their last meeting in the prison cell, he didn't sense any fear in her this time. There was a sense of serenity about her, a tranquillity that reminded Bane of his first meeting with her father.

Bane's own mood had changed as well. He was no longer driven by an unquenchable desire for bloody vengeance. In the Stone Prison he had needed to draw strength from his anger to survive and defeat his enemies. Here, however, he was in no danger. Afforded the luxury of careful consideration, he had realized that there was no need to kill her . . . not if he could make use of her skills.

They stood face-to-face, staring at each other, neither speaking. In the end, it was Serra who broke the silence.

"Did you see the grave when you landed? I buried Lucia there last night."

When Bane didn't respond, she slowly reached up and wiped a single tear away from her eye before continuing.

"She saved your life. Don't you even care that she's dead?"

"The dead have no value to the living," he told her.

"She was your friend."

"Whatever she was is gone. Now she is nothing but decaying flesh and bone."

"She didn't deserve this. Her death was . . . pointless."

"Your father's death was pointless," Bane said. "He had a valuable skill; twice he saved my life when no other could have healed me. Had it been my choice I would have left him alive in case I ever needed his services a third time."

"He would have never helped you by choice," Serra countered. There was no anger in her voice, though her words had the steely ring of truth.

"But he did help me," Bane reminded her. "He was useful. I could have a use for you as well, if you share his talent."

"My father taught me everything he knew," she admitted. "But, like him, I will never help a monster like you."

She turned to address the Iktotchi standing silently by Bane's side.

"If you follow this man he will destroy you," she warned. "I've seen the rewards given to those who walk the path of the dark side."

"The dark side will give me power," the Huntress replied confidently. "It will guide me to my destiny."

"Only a fool believes that," the princess replied. "Look at me. I gave in to my hate. I let it consume me. My desire for revenge cost me everything and everyone I care about."

"The dark side will devour those who lack the power to control it," Bane agreed. "It's a fierce storm of emotion that annihilates anything in its path. It lays waste to the weak and unworthy.

"But those who are strong," he added, "can ride the storm winds to unfathomable heights. They can unlock their true potential; they can sever the chains that bind them; they can dominate the world around them. Only those with the power to control the dark side can ever truly be free."

"No," Serra replied, gently shaking her head. "I don't believe that. The dark side is evil. You are evil. And I will never serve you."

There was a quiet defiance in her words, and Bane sensed nothing he could say or do would ever persuade her. For a brief moment he considered attempting the ritual of essence transfer, then quickly dismissed the idea. The ritual would consume his physical form, and if he failed to possess her body his spirit would be trapped forever in the void. Her will was as strong as her father's, and he didn't know if he was powerful enough to overcome it.

He didn't need to do this now. He still had several years before his current body failed completely. It was better to wait and try to find a technician to create a clone body. That, or find someone younger and more innocent.

"She is of no use to us, Master," the Iktotchi noted, an eager gleam in her eye. "May I kill her for you?"

He nodded, and the Huntress stepped forward, advancing slowly on the other woman. Bane sensed the assassin liked to savor the kill, reveling in the fear and pain of her victims. But Serra made no move to defend herself. She didn't try to run, or beg for mercy. Instead, she stood perfectly still, willing to meet her fate with mute acceptance.

Recognizing she would get no satisfaction from Caleb's daughter, the assassin ended Serra's life.

25

Zannah's fingers hesitated over the *Victory*'s nav panel as she pondered her next destination. Ever since escaping the Stone Prison, she had kept the shuttle in a low-level orbit around Doan.

She didn't want to go back to Ciutric. Bane was still alive and she needed to find him, but she didn't think he'd be returning to their home anytime soon.

For a time she had considered heading to Set's estate on Nar Shaddaa. If he was dead, he certainly couldn't object if she used his place as a temporary base while she set out to hunt down her Master. And if he happened to be there when she arrived—if he had somehow escaped the dungeon's collapse—then Zannah had plenty of questions for him.

However, the more she thought about confronting the man she had chosen as her apprentice, the less the idea appealed to her. Looking back, it was clear to her that Set had been a mistake. Overeager to assume the role of Dark Lord, she had convinced herself that he was an acceptable choice. Desperate to find an apprentice of her own, she had ignored his obvious flaws.

Set was a dangerous man—one she suspected she might have to deal with later on if she discovered he was still alive—but he wasn't fit to be a Sith. His affinity for the Force was strong, and he willingly embraced many of the dark side's more self-serving aspects. But he lacked discipline. He was consumed by worldly wants and desires that clouded his greater vision. Worst of all, he clearly lacked ambition.

Zannah had lured him into her service with a combination of threats to his life and promises of power. But she had been deceiving herself as much as Set. It was obvious he had no real desire to rule the galaxy. He was content with his lot in life, and was unwilling to make the sacrifices necessary to turn himself into something more. And for some reason, she had been unable to see it. Maybe she was afraid to look. Maybe Set reminded her too much of herself.

The words Bane had thrown at her when she accused him of violating the Rule of Two still rang in her mind.

I waited years for you to challenge me. But you were content to toil in my shadow.

Was he right? Was it possible that on some level she was afraid of taking on the responsibility of Sith Master? No. She had tried to kill him.

Tried and failed, even though Bane didn't have his lightsaber. Was it possible she hadn't really been trying to beat him? Had some small part of her subconscious mind held her back just enough so that Bane could survive until he saw his chance to escape?

No. That's what he wants me to think.

Bane's words had been a ploy. He was trying to undermine her confidence, looking for any edge that would let him survive. But he was wrong. Zannah had truly wanted to kill him in the halls of the dungeon. And yet somehow he still managed to live.

Zannah was forced to admit that there was another, even more disturbing, possibility. Was Bane simply stronger than her? If she couldn't defeat him when he was unarmed, what chance would she have once he reclaimed his lightsaber?

No. That didn't make sense, either. Bane may have escaped with his life, but her Master did not win that battle. Her lightsaber had given her a huge advantage; it had forced Bane to be on the defensive. So why hadn't she been able to finish him?

She had obviously made a tactical error. But what was it?

The question gnawed at her as she sat back in her seat and crossed her arms, the nav computer still awaiting its next destination. She bit down on her lip, concentrating. The answer was there; she just had to figure it out.

In her mind she replayed the scenario, analyzing it over and over again. She had been patient, careful. Because of this her Master had been able to keep her at bay despite her advantage. But if she had been more aggressive during the duel, she would have opened herself up to a potentially lethal counterattack.

Was that the answer? Did she have to risk defeat to claim victory?

Zannah shook her head. That wasn't it. Bane had taught her that risk should always be minimized. Gambles relied on luck. Take enough chances and sooner or later luck will turn against you, even with the Force on your side.

And then it came to her. She had tried to defeat him using brute force; she had fought the battle on his terms.

She would never be Bane's equal in physical strength. He would always be superior to her in martial skill. So why had she tried to defeat him in lightsaber combat, when her true talents lay elsewhere?

She had fallen into his trap. He had pretended to have a weapon, knowing she would see through his bluff. Bane had wanted her to focus on his missing lightsaber above all else. He was goading her into battle.

Using her lightsaber to defeat an unarmed opponent was the simplest, most obvious path to victory . . . one Bane had expertly led her down. But the most obvious path was rarely the best one.

Bane didn't fear her blades. There was only one thing she possessed that he was wary of: Sith sorcery. Zannah could do things with the Force that Bane couldn't even attempt. She could attack the minds of her opponents, turning their own thoughts and dreams against them.

During her apprenticeship, Bane had encouraged her in her studies of the magical arts. He had given her ancient texts filled with arcane rituals, urging her to expand her knowledge and push the boundaries of her talent. He had directed her training so that she could achieve her full potential. But he did not realize just how far she had come.

In addition to the tomes her Master had provided, Zannah had sought out her own sources of hidden Sith knowledge over the years. Practicing in secret, she had progressed far beyond Bane's expectations, learning new spells to unleash the dark side in ways he had never even imagined.

Next time we meet, Master, I will show you just how powerful I have become.

She had a feeling that meeting would be soon. Bane was out there, somewhere. Plotting and planning for their next encounter. If she didn't find him soon, Zannah knew, then he would find her.

———

Night was falling by the time the Huntress returned to the camp. Bane had ordered her to bury Serra's body—not out of a sense of respect or honor, but simply to keep away scavengers and remove the corpse before it began to decay. To her credit, the Iktotchi hadn't protested or questioned his command: she either understood the need or trusted his judgment.

While she was gone, Bane had collected kindling from a small woodpile at the back of the hut and started a fire to ward off the chill. The Iktotchi now stood before him, the glow of the flames transforming her red skin to a bright, sinister orange.

"You said you want me to teach you," he noted, crouching down to stir the fire with a stick. He held it in his left hand, his grip tight to keep the tremor from returning.

"I want to learn the ways of the Sith."

"If you are to become my apprentice, you must cast away the chains of your old life. You must sever all ties to family and friends."

"I have none."

"You will not be able to return to your home; you must be willing to leave behind all your worldly possessions."

"Wealth and material goods mean nothing to me," she replied. "I crave only power and purpose. With power, anything you want or need can simply be taken. With purpose, your life has meaning."

Bane nodded approvingly, stirring the fire once more before continuing.

"If you become my apprentice, who you were will cease to exist. You must be reborn in the ways of the dark side."

"I'm ready, my lord." There was no mistaking the eagerness in her voice.

"Then choose a new name for yourself, as a symbol of your new and greater existence."

"Cognus," she said after a moment's consideration.

Bane was impressed. She understood that power rested not in her blades or her bloodlust, but in her knowledge, wisdom, and ability to see the future.

"A good name," he said, setting the stick down and rising to his full height. As he did so, the Iktotchi dropped to one knee before him and bowed her head.

"From this day forward you are Darth Cognus of the Sith," he said.

"I am ready to begin my training," Cognus replied, still down on one knee before him.

"Not yet," he said, walking past her and heading to the shuttles on the far side of the camp. "There is still one important matter to take care of."

Cognus jumped up to follow him. "Your old apprentice," she guessed.

Or was it a guess?

Bane stopped and turned back toward her. "Have you seen what will happen between me and my apprentice?"

"Ever since I came to this world to meet the princess I have dreamed of you both," Cognus admitted. "But the meaning is unclear."

"Tell me what you've seen," Bane ordered.

"The details are always changing. Different locations, different worlds, different times of the day or night. At times I see her dead at your feet, other times she is the victor.

"I have tried to make sense of it, but there are too many contradictions."

"The future of the Sith is precariously balanced between Zannah and myself," Bane explained. "Whoever survives our confrontation will control the destiny of the Sith, but our strength is too evenly matched for you to foresee the outcome."

The Iktotchi didn't reply, pondering his words in silence.

Bane left her alone to think on her first lesson, continuing on to her vessel. He passed the twin graves without a second glance.

Climbing inside the shuttle, he set the commtransmitter to the frequency of Zannah's personal shuttle and sent out a coded distress signal.

————

Zannah had drifted off into a restless sleep, only to be awakened by a slow, steady beep from her control console. Examining the source, she saw it was a long-range distress call. Instead of being broadcast across multiple band lengths, however, this one was coming in on the

Victory's private channel. Only one person besides her knew that frequency.

Curious, she decoded the message. It comprised only four words: *Ambria. The healer's camp.*

Her first thought was that Bane was setting a trap for her, trying to lure her in. But the more she thought about it, the less likely that seemed. It was obvious who the message was from. If he was setting a trap, why reveal himself like this when it would only put her on her guard?

Maybe he just wanted this to end. Before drifting off to sleep, Zannah had been thinking about what he said to her before their confrontation in the halls of the Stone Prison.

Only the strongest has the right to rule the Sith! The title of Dark Lord must be seized, wrenched from the all-powerful grasp of the Master!

If Bane still believed in the Rule of Two—if he still believed it was the key to the survival and eventual dominance of the Sith—then this message was a challenge, an invitation to his apprentice to come to Ambria and end what they had begun in the Stone Prison.

She had to admit, it was better than wasting years chasing each other across the galaxy, setting traps and plotting each other's destruction. Bane had reinvented the Sith so that their resources and efforts would be focused against their enemies rather than each other. When the apprentice challenged the Master it was meant to be decided in a single confrontation: quick, clean, and final.

Now, however, the Order had been fractured. They were no longer Master and apprentice, but competing rivals for the mantle of Sith Lord. They were effectively at war, and as long as they both lived, the Sith would be divided. Was it so hard to believe that, for the sake of the Order, Bane wanted to end it with a duel on Ambria? If Bane still honored the Rule he had created, then the message could be taken at face value.

But what about Andeddu's Holocron?

She had initially thought he was seeking eternal life so that he could defy the Rule of Two by living forever. Now she wasn't so certain. Would immortality really be a violation of the Rule's underlying principles? The secrets inside the Holocron might keep Bane from aging, but she didn't think they could protect him from falling in battle. If she was strong enough to defeat him, she would still earn her place as Master, just as Bane had intended when he first found her as a young girl on Ruusan.

Now she wondered if the Holocron was just a safeguard to keep the Order strong. Perhaps Bane saw it as a way to protect against an unworthy candidate ascending to the Sith throne simply because the Master became weak and infirm with age.

Zannah leaned forward and plotted in a course for Ambria, wondering what had made Bane choose the healer's camp as the location of their final encounter.

The world was steeped in the energies of the dark side; for the first decade of her apprenticeship Bane and Zannah had dwelled there near the shores of Lake Natth. But he wasn't calling her back to their camp; he was waiting for her at Caleb's.

Two times the Dark Lord had nearly died there. Did that have anything to do with his choice of location? Or was there some other explanation?

It was still possible she was about to walk into a trap. Ambria was a sparsely inhabited world. It would be easy to make preparations there without drawing unwanted attention.

Yet her instincts told her that wasn't what Bane was plotting. And if her instincts were wrong about something as important as this, then she deserved whatever was waiting for her.

Either way, she reasoned as the ship made the jump into hyperspace, *this will all be over soon.*

———

Night had passed on Ambria, giving way to the scorching heat of day. With the rising of the sun, Bane and Cognus had retreated inside the shelter of the hut. There the Dark Lord had sat cross-legged on the floor, meditating and gathering his strength in preparation for Zannah's arrival.

"She'll probably show up with an army at her heels," the Iktotchi warned.

Bane shook his head.

"She knows she must face me alone."

"I don't understand."

"The Sith used to be as plentiful as the Jedi. Unlike the Jedi, however, those who served sought to tear their leaders down. Their ambition was natural; this is the way of the dark side. It is what drives us, gives us strength. Yet it can also destroy us if not properly controlled.

"Under the old ways, a powerful leader would be brought down by the combined strength of many lesser Sith working together. It was inevitable, a cycle that repeated over and over. And each time, the Order as a whole grew weaker.

"The strongest were killed, and the weak tore the Sith apart with their petty wars of succession. Meanwhile, the Jedi remained united, confident in the knowledge their enemies were too busy fighting one another to ever defeat them."

"You discovered a way to break this cycle," Cognus chimed in.

"Now everything we do is guided by the Rule of Two," Bane explained. "One Master, one apprentice. This assures that the Master will only fall to a worthy successor.

"Zannah knows that if she is to rule in my place, she must prove she is more powerful by defeating me herself."

Cognus nodded. "I understand, Master. I will not interfere when she arrives."

As if on cue, the sound of a shuttle's engines roared through the camp. The two of them rose to their feet and stepped out into the desert heat just as Zannah's ship touched down.

She emerged a few seconds later. As Bane had predicted, she was alone.

He marched forward to meet her, Cognus hanging back near the entrance to the hut. He stopped in the center of the camp. Zannah took her stand halfway between the shuttles and where Bane now stood, eyeing the Iktotchi in the background suspiciously.

"She will not interfere," Bane assured her.

"Who is she?"

"A new apprentice."

"She has sworn allegiance to you?"

"She is loyal to the Sith," Bane explained.

"I want to learn the ways of the dark side," Cognus called out to Zannah. "I want to serve under a true Sith Master. If you defeat Bane, I will swear my loyalty to you."

Zannah tilted her head to the side, studying the Iktotchi carefully before nodding her agreement to the offer.

"Who lies in the graves?" she asked, turning her attention back to Bane.

"Caleb's daughter and her bodyguard," he replied. "She was the one who imprisoned me. She fled here when the Stone Prison was destroyed."

He felt no need to explain in any further detail. Zannah didn't need to know who Lucia was, or her connection to Bane.

"I wondered why you chose this place to meet," Zannah muttered. "I thought it might have some symbolic meaning for you."

Bane shook his head.

"The last time we were here you were too weak to even stand," his apprentice reminded him. "You were helpless, and you thought I had betrayed you to the Jedi.

"You said you would rather die than be a prisoner for the rest of your life. You wanted me to take your life. But I refused."

"You knew I still had things to teach you," Bane recalled. "You swore you would not kill me until you had learned all my secrets."

"That day is here," Zannah informed him, igniting the twin blades of her lightsaber.

Bane drew out his own weapon in response, the shimmering blade rising up from the curved hilt with a low hum.

The two combatants dropped into fighting stances and began to circle slowly.

"I have surpassed you, Bane," Zannah warned him. "Now I am the Master."

"Then prove it."

He lunged toward her, and the battle began.

26

Zannah expected Bane to come at her aggressively, but even so she was caught off guard by the ferociousness of his attack.

He opened with a series of two-handed overhead chops, using his great height to bring his blade hacking down at her from above. She easily blocked each blow, but the momentum of the crushing impact caused her to stagger back, throwing her off balance.

She recovered quickly, however, spinning out of the way when he followed up with a low, looping swipe meant to hew her off at the knees. She retaliated with a quick jab with the tip of one of her blades toward Bane's face, but he ducked his head to the side and came back with a wide-arcing, single-handed slash at chest level.

Zannah intercepted his blade with one of her own, angling her weapon so that the momentum of Bane's attack was redirected downward, sending the tip of his lightsaber into the dirt. This should have exposed him to a counterthrust, but he was already reacting to her move, driving his entire body forward into Zannah's before she could bring her weapon up.

His weight slammed into her, knocking her back as Bane snapped his neck forward. Zannah threw her head back just in time, and the head-butt that would have smashed her face glanced off her chin instead.

Scrambling to stay on her feet, Zannah raised her weapon back up, spinning the handle so that the twirling blades formed a defensive wall that repelled Bane's next half a dozen blows.

During her years under Bane, they had sparred hundreds of times. During these sessions she had always known he was keeping something in reserve for the day they would inevitably fight for real. Only now did she realize just how much he had been holding back.

He was faster than she could ever have imagined, and he was using new sequences and unfamiliar moves he had never revealed during their practice sessions. But somehow she had survived the initial flurry, and now she knew what to expect.

The next exchange had a more familiar feel. Bane pressed the action with a devastating, complex combination of attacks, but Zannah was able to intercept, parry, or deflect each one. Her defensive style was simple, but performed correctly it was nearly impenetrable.

Recognizing this, Bane backed off and changed tactics. Instead of a savage, relentless pressure meant to overwhelm her, he settled into a pattern of feints and quick thrusts, probing and prodding her defenses in search of a weakness as the two of them settled in for a long battle of attrition.

Zannah had fought him once before, back when he was still encased in his orbalisk armor. She remembered it had been like battling a force of nature: the chitinous parasites covering his entire body had been impervious to lightsaber attacks, allowing him to attack with pure animal rage. She had survived that encounter only by convincing Bane she hadn't betrayed him, and in the end he had let her live.

His style back then had been brutish and simple, though undeniably effective. Now, however, his technique was more advanced. Unable to simply bully his way heedlessly forward, he had developed an unpredictable, seemingly random style. Each time she thought she could anticipate where the next attack was coming from, he changed tactics, disrupting the rhythm of the battle and causing her to give ground.

She was being driven back in a slow retreat, and she realized he was herding her toward the shuttles, hoping to pin her against the metal hull with no place to go. Zannah was content to play along, taking quick, careful steps backward over the soft, sandy terrain as she began to gather her power.

The key was subtlety. She couldn't let Bane sense what she was doing or he would launch into another wild flurry of attacks, forcing her to focus all her energy on keeping him at bay. She had to give him the illusion he was controlling the action, when in fact she was only a few seconds away from unleashing a burst of dark side sorcery that would rip his mind apart.

Bane circled wide trying to come in on her left flank. Zannah simply altered the angle of her retreat, taking several more steps backward to keep him at a safe distance as she swatted away a few token slashes and strikes.

With her attention split between the enemy in front of her and the Sith spell she was preparing to cast Zannah didn't notice how close she was to the freshly dug graves. Her heel caught on the uneven ground as she backed up, throwing her off balance as she fell awkwardly to the ground and landed on her back.

Bane was on her in an instant, his lightsaber slashing viciously, his heavy boots kicking and stomping at her prone body. Zannah thrashed and twisted on the ground, her lightsaber flailing desperately to parry Bane's blade. She felt a sharp crack as the toe of his boot caught her in the ribs, but she rolled with the impact and managed to end up back on her feet.

Her vision was blurred with stars, pain shooting through her left side with each gasp as she tried to catch her breath. Bane didn't let up, coming at her with a frenetic assault. The next few seconds were a blur as Zannah relied purely on instincts honed over twenty years to parry the wave of blows, miraculously keeping him from landing a lethal strike.

Zannah threw herself into a back handspring, flipping head over heels three times in quick succession just to put some space between her and Bane. Before the fourth one she suddenly stopped and went into a crouch, thrusting forward with her lightsaber like a spear to impale her opponent as he charged after her in pursuit . . . only Bane wasn't there.

Anticipating her move, he had stopped several meters away.

Gritting her teeth against the pain from her broken rib, Zannah rose to her feet. Bane hadn't killed her, but her survival had come with significant cost. She was tired now, the desperate scramble to escape after tripping on the grave had pushed her one step closer to physical exhaustion. She felt the broken rib with each ragged breath, and she sensed that the injury would make it harder for her to pivot and turn, limiting the effectiveness of her defensive maneuvers.

She couldn't wait any longer. She'd wanted to surprise Bane, slowly gather her strength before unleashing it so he wouldn't be able to properly defend against it. But she knew she wouldn't survive another clash of lightsabers.

Opening herself up to the power of the dark side, Zannah reached out and touched the mind of her Master.

———

Bane sensed the attack, bracing himself.

He had encouraged Zannah's training in Sith sorcery, knowing she might very well use it against him one day. If it turned out he wasn't strong enough to survive, then he wasn't worthy of being the Dark Lord of the Sith.

That didn't mean he was unprepared, however. Dark side sorcery was complex; it attacked the psyche in ways that were difficult to explain and even more difficult to defend against. Bane had no talent for it, yet he had done his best to study the techniques. What he learned was that the only real counter was the victim's strength of will.

Zannah's assault began as a sharp pain in his skull, like a hot knife stabbing directly into his brain before carving down to slice the two hemispheres in half. Then the knife exploded, sending a million burning shards in every direction. Each one burrowed into his subconscious, seeking out buried fears and nightmares only to rip them free and haul them to the surface.

Bane let out a scream and dropped to his knees. When he stood up the sky was thick with a swarm of flying horrors. Their wings were torn and ragged, leather flaps of skin hanging from exposed bone. Their bodies were small and malformed, their twisted legs ending in long, sharp talons. Their flesh was a sickly yellow: the same color as the faces of the miners who had died on Apatros after being trapped in a gas-filled chamber.

Their features were inhuman, but their burning eyes were unmistakable: each creature was staring at him with the hate-filled gaze of his abusive father. As one, they swooped down on him, their mouths screeching out a cry that sounded like his father's name: *hurst, hurst, hurst!*

Swinging his lightsaber wildly at the demon flock, Bane crouched low to the ground, his free hand coming up to cover his face and ward off the talons clawing at his eyes. As the swarm enveloped him, he caught a glimpse of Zannah standing a few meters away, her face frozen in a mask of intense concentration.

Bane knew it was a trick; the beasts weren't real. They were just figments of his imagination born from the repressed memories of his childhood, his greatest fears manifested in physical form. But he had conquered these fears long ago. He had turned his fear of his abusive father into anger and hate—the tools that had given him the strength to endure and eventually escape his life on Apatros.

He knew how to defeat these demons, and he struck back. Unleashing a primal scream, he channeled his terror into pure rage and lashed out with the dark side. It tore through the swarm in a burst of searing violet light, utterly obliterating them.

———

Zannah watched as Bane huddled against the ground, his lightsaber flailing wildly at invisible ghosts, but she didn't let her concentration falter. Bane's mind was strong; if she let up even for an instant he might break free of the spell.

For a second she thought she had won as Bane let out a shriek, but the burst of energy that followed sent her reeling backward.

Regaining her balance she saw that Bane was on his feet again, and she knew he had resisted the spell. But she still had one more surprise for her Master.

Again she opened herself up to the dark side. This time, however, she didn't attack Bane directly. Instead, she let it flow through her, drawing it from the soil and stone of Ambria itself. She called to power buried for centuries, summoning it up to the surface in wispy tendrils of dark smoke snaking up from the sand.

The thin tendrils crawled along the ground, reaching for one another, twining themselves together into writhing tentacles each several meters long.

Then, in response to her unspoken command, the tentacles rose up and lashed out at her foe.

———

Bane saw the strange black mist crawling across the dirt and knew this was no illusion. Somehow Zannah had given substance and corporeality to the dark side, transforming it into half a dozen shadowy, serpentlike minions rising up from the ground.

Suddenly the tendrils flew at him. He slashed out with his lightsaber to chop the closest one in half, but the blade simply passed through the black mist with no effect. Bane threw himself to the side, but the tip of the tentacle still brushed against his left shoulder.

The material of his clothes melted away as if it had been splashed with acid. A chunk of flesh beneath simply dissolved, and Bane screamed in agony.

Once, orbalisks had fused themselves to his body with a burning chemical compound so intense it had nearly driven him mad. Ten years ago they had been removed when Bane's flesh had been literally cooked by a concentrated blast of his own violet lightning. During her interrogation, Serra had pumped him full of a drug that had felt like it was eating him alive from the inside. But the excruciating pain he felt from the mere touch of the dark side tendril was unlike anything Bane had ever experienced before.

The damage was far from life threatening, but it nearly sent Bane into shock. He fell hard to the ground, his jaw slack and his eyes rolling back into his head. His mind was reeling from the brief contact. The pain radiated through every nerve in his body, but what he felt went far beyond any mere physical sensation. It was not the raw heat of the dark side but rather the empty chill of the void itself spreading through him. It touched every synapse in his mind, it clawed at the core of his spirit. In that instant he tasted utter annihilation, and felt the true horror of absolute nothingness.

Somehow he managed to stay conscious, and when the next tentacle coiled in he was able to scramble to his feet and roll out of the way.

His wounded shoulder was still throbbing, but the hollow darkness that had threatened to overwhelm him had faded, allowing him to ignore the pain.

The tendrils were massing for another assault, moving faster as Zannah fed them with a steady stream of power. Bane unleashed violet lightning from his fingers, but when the bolts struck the sinewy black forms they were absorbed with no apparent effect. They were made of pure dark side energy, and there was no way he could harm them.

That left him with only one option—kill Zannah before the tentacles killed him.

He unleashed another lightning blast at his apprentice. She caught the incoming bolts with her lightsaber, rendering them harmless. But her reactions were a fraction slower than normal, and Bane knew it was more than just her injured ribs. The effort to keep the tendrils animated was pushing Zannah's ability to draw on the Force to its limits, leaving her vulnerable in other areas.

Lightsaber in hand, Bane charged toward her. The tendrils flew to intercept him, but Bane ducked, jumped, and dodged, weaving his way under, over, and around them as he bore down on Zannah.

She brought her lightsaber up to defend against his attack, but without the full power of the Force behind them her movements were awkward and clumsy. She parried the blow, but didn't react fast enough as Bane dropped down and took her feet out from under her with a sweep of his leg. As she fell he twisted the handle of his lightsaber so that his blade caught one of hers, wrenching the hilt from her grasp and sending her weapon flying across the camp.

With his foe unarmed and helpless at his feet Bane brought his arm down for the coup de grâce, only to have it intercepted midswing by one of the dark side tendrils. It wrapped itself around the elbow. Skin, muscle, sinew and bone dissolved instantaneously, severing the limb.

His disembodied forearm and fist tumbled harmlessly to the ground, his lightsaber flicking off as the hilt slid from his suddenly nerveless fingers. The Dark Lord didn't scream this time; the pain was so intense it left him mute as he collapsed to the ground.

Everything went black. Blind and alone, he felt the void closing in. In desperation he reached out with his left hand, clutching Zannah's wrist as she lay on the ground beside him. With his last act, he summoned all his remaining power and invoked the ritual of essence transfer.

Working at the speed of thought, his mind tapped into the currents of the Force, seizing on the power of the dark side, spinning, shaping, and twisting it into the intricate patterns he had ripped from Andeddu's Holocron.

The cold darkness swallowing him up vanished, replaced by a searing burst of crimson light as the power of the ritual was unleashed. Bane was aware of his flesh being utterly consumed by the unimaginable heat, reduced to ashes in a thousandth of a second. But he was no longer a part of his own body. His spirit had discarded it like an old shell in favor of a new one.

Bane was suddenly fully aware of his physical surroundings. He could see with Zannah's eyes, he could hear with her ears. He could feel the intense heat of the ritual's crimson glow through her skin. But Zannah was still there, too. She sensed his assault; he could feel her terror and confusion as if they were his own. And when she screamed in horror he screamed with her.

The black tendrils vanished as her concentration was shattered, disappearing like smoke on the wind. Instinctively, she fought to repel the invader. Bane could feel her pushing him away, rejecting him, trying to drive him out even as he relentlessly tried to force his way in and snuff out her existence.

It became a battle of wills, their two identities locked together inside Zannah's mind, grappling for possession of her body. They teetered on the precipice of the void, Bane seeking to obliterate all trace of her identity while she sought to cast him down into the blackness.

For a moment they seemed to be evenly matched, neither gaining nor giving ground. And then suddenly it was over.

27

From a safe distance, the Iktotchi had watched the two figures from her dreams wage battle. She was an impartial observer, having no preference as to which one would emerge victorious. She only wanted to serve whoever proved the stronger.

The conflict had been brief but intense: she had marveled at the speed of their blades, their movements so fast she could barely follow the action. She had felt the awesome power of the Force unleashed through bursts of lightning and the sinister tendrils that crawled up from the ground. She shivered in anticipation with the knowledge that she, too, could one day learn to wield such power.

She had seen Bane knock the woman to the ground and slap her weapon away, only to have his arm hewn off by the touch of one of the black tentacles. And then there had been a flash so bright she had been forced to close her eyes and look away.

When she looked back Bane was gone, his body reduced to a pile of ash. The blond woman still lay on the ground, dazed but alive. The deadly tendrils were nowhere to be seen.

Cautiously she approached the scene. Bane's severed arm lay on the ground, but the rest of his body had been consumed by the crimson flare. In the instant before she had looked away, however, she had felt something.

Even from a distance, she had sensed an incredible burst of power—the same power she had sensed in Bane himself. She didn't know how it was possible, but it almost seemed as if the Dark Lord's life energy had burst free of his physical form in one glorious instant, releasing itself upon the material world. Then, as suddenly as she had sensed the presence, it was gone, vanishing like an animal gone to ground.

Crazy as it might seem, there was only one place she could imagine it could have gone.

The woman on the ground shifted, her eyes fluttering open as she rose slowly to her feet. She moved awkwardly and couldn't seem to stand up straight, as if she was unfamiliar with how her own limbs and muscles worked . . . though this could simply have been the result of exhaustion from the battle.

She shook her blond head from side to side, and the motion seemed to restore some sense of her equilibrium. Standing straight and tall, she turned and fixed the Iktotchi with a cold stare.

Knowing how insane her words would sound, Cognus hesitated before asking, "Lord Bane?"

"Bane is gone," the woman replied, her voice confident and strong. "I am Darth Zannah, Dark Lord of the Sith and your new Master."

The Iktotchi dropped to one knee, folding her hands in supplication and bowing her head.

"Forgive me, Master."

"What is your name?" Zannah demanded.

"I am . . . Darth Cognus." She had almost answered *the Huntress,* but she managed to catch her mistake just in time. "Bane had me take the name to symbolize my new life as a Sith apprentice."

"Then your training has already begun," Zannah replied. "Did he explain the Rule of Two that guides our Order?"

"He started to. But there was no time for any real lessons before you arrived," she admitted.

"I will teach you the Rule of Two and the ways of the Sith," Zannah promised. "In time, I will teach you everything.

"Rise, Cognus," she added, and the Iktotchi did as she was instructed.

Zannah turned away from her and walked over to pick up her lightsaber from where it had fallen to the ground.

"Eventually you will construct your own lightsaber," Zannah said, speaking but not turning to look back at her. "For now, take Darth Bane's."

Cognus scooped the curved hilt of Bane's lightsaber up from the ground, unfazed by the gruesome severed limb resting only a few centimeters away.

"Bane reinvented the Sith," Zannah explained, standing with her back to her new apprentice as she stared out across the vast, empty expanse of the Ambrian desert. "We are his legacy, and though he is gone his legacy will endure.

"Now I am the Master, and you are my chosen successor. One day you will face me just as I faced Bane, and only one of us will survive.

"This is the way of our Order. An individual may die, but the Sith are eternal."

"Yes, Master," Cognus answered.

She couldn't help but notice that, as she was speaking, Zannah was continually clenching and unclenching the fingers of her left hand.

EPILOGUE

Set Harth was too smart to go back to his estate on Nal Hutta. If Zannah had survived the destruction of the Stone Prison it was only a matter of time until she went there to look for him, and he had no desire to ever run into her again.

Luckily, Set had built his life on the underlying principle that he might have to go on the run at any time. He had other mansions on other worlds, from Nar Shaddaa all the way to Coruscant itself, and at least a dozen false identities he could assume if he didn't want to be found. He wasn't worried about Zannah, not when he had something far more interesting right in front of him.

He was sitting cross-legged on the floor of the shuttle he had stolen from the Stone Prison, Andeddu's Holocron resting on a small table a few meters away. All his attention was focused on the small holographic figure being projected from the black pyramid's top.

"It will take years for you to learn the lessons I must teach you," the gatekeeper warned him, its skeletal features serious and grim. "You must prove yourself worthy before I reveal the ritual of essence transfer to you."

"Of course, Master," he said, nodding eagerly. "I understand."

He had chafed under the tutelage of Master Obba and the Jedi. He had felt serious reservations about serving as an apprentice under Zannah. But Set was more than willing to do whatever the gatekeeper required of him.

For one thing, he knew he only had to answer to the gatekeeper when the Holocron was active. Unlike a living Master, Set was the one who would decide where and when he would begin each lesson.

More important, however, the Holocron was offering him something he actually wanted. Zannah had tried to tempt him with promises of power and the chance to destroy the Jedi and rule the galaxy. But Set already had more than enough power to get what he needed from life.

Plus, you're charming, smart, and handsome. What more could anyone ask for?

The last thing he wanted was to rule the galaxy. Let the Jedi and Sith wage their endless war. The outcome made no difference to him. He was a survivor; all he wanted was to live a long and prosperous life. And if he learned the secrets of essence transfer, his life would be very long indeed.

He would have to be careful, of course. Never draw too much attention to himself. Try not to cross paths with the Jedi or powerful people like Zannah.

No problem. Basically, just do what you're already doing.

That, and guard the Holocron as if his life—his long, long life—depended on it.

"Are you ready to begin your first lesson?" the gatekeeper asked.

"You have no idea, Master," Set replied with a wry grin. "You have absolutely no idea."

ABOUT THE AUTHOR

DREW KARPYSHYN is the *New York Times* bestselling author of *Star Wars: Darth Bane: Path of Destruction* and its sequel, *Star Wars: Darth Bane: Rule of Two*. He also wrote the acclaimed Mass Effect series of novels, and is an award-winning writer/designer of video games for BioWare. After spending most of his life in Canada he finally grew tired of the long, cold winters and headed south in search of a climate more conducive to year-round golf. He now lives in Texas with his wife, Jennifer, and their cat.

ABOUT THE TYPE

This book was set in Minion, a 1990 Adobe Originals typeface by Robert Slimbach. Minion is inspired by classical, old style typefaces of the late Renaissance, a period of elegant, beautiful, and highly readable type designs. Created primarily for text setting, Minion combines the aesthetic and functional qualities that make text type highly readable with the versatility of digital technology.